# THE LOST ONES

# THE LOST ONES

## SHEENA KAMAL

WILLIAM MORROW

*An Imprint of* HarperCollins*Publishers*

The term "red market" used on pages 240, 243, and 323 was coined
by Scott Carney in his book *The Red Market*, published in 2011 by
William Morrow & Co.

HarperCollins books may be purchased for educational, business, or
sales promotional use. For information, please email the Special Markets
Department at SPsales@harpercollins.com.

FIRST EDITION

*Designed by Bonni Leon-Berman*

Library of Congress Cataloging-in-Publication Data has been applied for.

ISBN 978-0-06-256590-7 (hardcover)
ISBN 978-0-06-266632-1 (international edition)

17 18 19 20 21   LSC   10 9 8 7 6 5 4 3 2 1

*For my mother*

# THE LOST ONES

# ONE

# 1

THE CALL COMES in just after five in the morning.

I am immediately on guard because everyone knows that nothing good ever happens this early. Not with a phone call, anyway. You never get word that a wealthy relative has passed and is leaving you his inheritance before 9 A.M. It's fortunate, then, that I'm already awake and on my second cup of coffee, so I'm at least moderately prepared.

I've just come back from my walk, where I leaned over the edge of the seawall and contemplated water that is calm and gray, just like the city itself at this time of year. As usual, I had tried to see the warm, dark current that flows from Japan and turns into the North Pacific, tempering the cold and spreading its tepid fingers to the coastline. And, as usual, it refused me the pleasure.

Vancouver. Some people say it's beautiful here, but they've never idled in the spaces that I call home. They've never been down to Hastings Street, filled with its needles and junkies. They've never considered the gray sky and the gray water for months on end as rain pours down in an unsuccessful attempt at cleansing. Then comes summer and it is so hot that you can roast marshmallows on the fires that burn through the forests in the province. Summer right on the coast is nice enough, but still several months away when my phone rings.

I stare at the unfamiliar number on my call display and, after a moment of hesitation, decline to take it. Several seconds later, it rings again. I'm intrigued. I answer, if only because I've always admired persistence in a caller.

"Hello?"

There's a long pause after the person on the other end explains in a hoarse voice why he is calling. The pause becomes awkward. I can tell the caller is fighting himself, wanting to say more but knowing this is a bad idea. No one wants to talk to a rambler over the phone. Especially one you've never met before. I imagine the caller sweating on the other end. Maybe his hands have gone clammy. The phone slips from his grasp and I hear it clatter on the ground. He swears for a full thirty seconds as he struggles to pick it back up and regain his composure.

"You still there? Did you hear what I said?" he asks.

"Yeah, I heard," I say, when the silence has become excruciating. "I'll be there." Then I hang up.

I've never heard the name Everett Walsh before, but according to him I may know something about a missing girl. He does not tell me what, though. I consider not meeting him but he sounds desperate and if there's one thing that draws me more than persistence, it's desperation.

Even though finding people is part of what I do for a living, what would I possibly know about a missing girl to warrant a call at this hour?

His desperation is so fresh and raw I can almost taste it.

# 2

IT'S A BRISK winter morning in Vancouver. I would have said wet, but that's implied when you're talking about the west coast at this time of year. In this city, when in doubt, err on the side of precipitation. I sit at a bus shelter across the street for an hour before the meeting, even though my ancient, beat-up Corolla is parked in the lot. People in cars tend to avert their eyes from those waiting at bus stops, unless the light is red and they have nowhere else to look. Since there is no traffic light here, I feel invisible. From my perch, I can see the café and the parking lot clearly. The café is brightly lit at the counter, but dim everywhere else. So this is to be a clandestine rendezvous. Fine with me. I can do clandestine with the best of them. But can this Everett Walsh?

The bus pulls up and I wave the driver away. He moves off with a grunt and the bus belches exhaust fumes into my face as it leaves.

Just off the busy Kingsway, the café is a cross between a coffee shop and a diner, surrounded by auto mechanic outfits and fast food joints. Out of all the dives he could choose from between his Kerrisdale home and the seedier side of Vancouver that I live in, he decided on one that has a pretty red canopy and fading yellow trim. Something in between. Maybe he is hoping to make both of us comfortable.

I can tell that the coffee here is terrible, but the muffins are not too bad. People exiting with takeout cups in their hands peel back the lid, gulp, and then grimace. Those with muffins never bat an eye. They shrug and move on, seeing the muffins as money well spent.

Twenty minutes before go time, a sporty dark Audi circles the parking lot. A well-groomed couple, both wearing sunglasses, peer into the shop. They don't see who they're looking for and start to bicker. The Audi tears away from the lot and returns five minutes later.

They park near the door and the man gets out, sans sunglasses, and makes his way into the shop. He is short and square with a thick neck. A baseball cap covers thinning brown hair. He wears a dark jacket and his shoulders beneath it are hunched with defeat. The woman gets out, flipping her long red hair over her shoulder, and follows him inside. She doesn't care who sees her. She's beautiful and used to being looked at. She does, however, keep her sunglasses on because it adds to her air of mystery and sex appeal. It's very effective. The middle-aged man at the counter ogles her casually as he pours her coffee. He doesn't look at the man beside her, except to take his money.

Then they wait. Both in their forties, nicely groomed, well dressed. They don't speak to each other, but the silence between them is not comfortable. If there was once chemistry between these two, years of marriage have completely eroded it. The man is still interested, but the woman ignores all of his attempts to catch her attention and stares out the window to the entrance of the parking lot. They both sip at the coffee with no outward reaction. Either they're not paying attention or their taste buds are in shock.

I study them for the remaining time left on the clock. They are obviously not a couple that goes for coffee together. They wouldn't be here if they didn't have to be, so the situation must be bad. I have a terrible feeling about this, but I have to admit that I'm curious, too. From a web search earlier this morning, I know that they are both architects but work for different firms. They seem innocent enough so I make my way around the back and through the side door. They were not expecting this and are surprised when I appear in front of their table, muffin in hand.

The woman stares at my worn jeans and oversize cardigan with the pulled threads exposed. The man, however, is arrested by my face. My skin that is not light or dark, just something muddy and in between. High cheekbones. Stubborn chin. What he seems most taken with are my eyes. This is not unusual for those who bother to look. I am unremarkable without them factored in. They are so dark that pupil and iris are virtually indistinguishable, fringed by long lashes that might make them pretty until you take a closer look, and then you will see that they absorb all the light around them and refuse to budge an inch. When looking into them, if you ever do, you will suddenly remember appointments that you should be making and previous engagements that you've forgotten to put in your calendar.

"Everett Walsh?" I pull up a chair next to their table and sit. I look only at the man. The woman needs a bit more time to get over my entrance.

"What? Oh, yes. I am. That's, um, me." He wipes a bead of sweat under his cap and then discards the cap entirely. The woman frowns at him in disgust. "This is my wife, Lynn."

"Pleasure," she says, her cool, clear voice indicating that it's anything but. They don't recognize me from the bus shelter and were probably not aware that there had been a bus shelter at all. These are not people accustomed to searching out public transportation. Lucky them. Public transportation in Vancouver is best described as a clusterfuck, to be avoided at all costs unless you're poor or your luxury vehicle is in the shop.

Seeing that Lynn has decided to be unhelpful, Everett takes over. "Thank you for coming. I mean, I know this is out of the blue and you don't know us, but . . ."

"Who referred you to me?" Somebody must have for them to have my phone number.

Everett blinks. "What? Nobody. We hired someone to find you."

Now it's my turn to be confused. It's usually the other way around. "What are you talking about?"

"Our daughter is missing," Lynn says.

Everett glances over at her. "I told her that on the phone, honey."

Lynn turns to him. Years of history pass between them in the look that they share now. "*Her* daughter is missing. Did you tell her that?"

I stare at her with my mouth hanging slightly open. This is the bomb that she expects it to be. For a brief moment, all of the air is sucked out of the room and an unexpected tension arises. Lynn gives me her full attention now and even though she doesn't smile, I can tell that behind the sunglasses, she's pleased with herself.

Everett clears his throat. Opens his mouth to speak, then closes it. We gawp at each other, him and me, until he musters up the courage to try again. "She means the baby you put up for adoption fifteen years ago." He's concerned about my reaction, which up until this point has been a blank expression. Now I'm tempted to check if there's a floor underneath me or if I have, as I suspect, fallen down some kind of nightmarish rabbit hole.

He pulls a photograph from his wallet and sets it in front of me.

A chubby teenage girl with golden skin stares back at me. Though the eyes in the photograph are deeper set and upturned at the edges, there is no denying that they are mine. Almost black, and fathomless. She has dark hair that falls to her shoulders, darker than mine, and an adorable dimple on her chin. I look past the cataloging of her features to get a sense of what's underneath. What she's hiding. After a moment, I see that she is smiling with her mouth, but the smile doesn't reach her eyes. She is lying to the camera, pretending that she's happy.

"This is Bonnie. Bronwyn, actually, but we just call her Bonnie." There is pride in Everett's voice. Love, too.

I glance at Lynn. She refuses to look at the picture. I munch on my muffin, gathering thoughts that have slipped through the creases in the wooden table and scattered on the floor.

Everett can't read my expression, but now that he has started he can't stop. "She went missing almost two weeks ago. We thought she'd gone camping with friends, but—"

"But she lied and stole all the money we keep in the house. She also stole my bank card and withdrew a thousand dollars before I realized it and deactivated the card." Lynn removes her sunglasses and I see shadows under her bloodshot eyes. I begin to understand what is happening here. Lynn is at the end of her rope. The child she'd jumped through hoops in order to adopt has turned into a teenager and she is looking for the receipt in order to return to sender. "She's done this twice before, but never for this long."

"The police have been no help at all," Everett interjects. "They've put out an alert but because she took the money, they assume she wanted to have stayed away this long. They've stopped looking. I don't know if they ever started. I think one of them talked to some of her teachers at school, but got nowhere. She's a good kid—"

Lynn scoffs. "They're calling her a chronic runaway or something like that, Everett. She stole from us."

"She is a good kid!" Everett insists. "But she's been a handful lately," he concedes. "New friends. Staying out late. Been hanging out with these hip-hop dance people. We think she's been drinking and doing drugs. Yes, she has run away before this, but she always came back! Just not . . . not this time. Why? Why wouldn't she have come back home by now?" Emotion overwhelms him. He covers his face with his hands. It's a sad thing to see a grown man cry, but I refuse to look away. It is in these moments that you can see whether someone is being genuine. Fake tears are easy to spot, so to go that route, it is best to be committed. He is. This is a man in pain.

Lynn stares at Everett for a few moments, then turns back to me. No hand on shoulder. No there, there, honey. "On her computer we found some search history. She knew that we were against it but she was looking for her biological parents online. Through those . . . what do you call them?"

She looks at me like I should have the answer ready. I shrug.

Lynn's expression does not waver. "Those sites that reunite adopted children with their biological parents. She's a minor so she can't sign up for the official ones, but we've heard there are other unsanctioned sites out there. Online communities of people looking for each other. We're hoping that she hasn't contacted you, for her own sake, but if she has . . ."

Everett collects himself long enough to send Lynn an annoyed glance. "Please excuse my wife. We just want to know where our daughter is."

It's easy to read between the lines. What they mean is that I'm a bad influence, even though I've only met the child once and she couldn't possibly remember making my acquaintance. I see now that they blame me for her dabbling in alcohol and drugs. That in their minds, she has somehow tossed away their nurture and made a beeline for my nature; she has run off to be with her true family and together we will live a wasteful, booze-soaked life. That we will laugh at them from over the tops of our forties.

There is nothing more demeaning than having decent people look down on you. I don't dare let this show, though, and take small comfort in the evidence that their lives seem to be unraveling quicker than mine. I see now why Everett was so desperate to meet with me.

I'm his last resort.

"A few years ago she was obsessed with finding her biological parents. She used to talk to her friends about it, then she stopped and we thought she was over it. But we realized that she found the adoption papers. Her birth certificate. You're a hard woman to find; we had to hire an investigator to help, but we thought maybe Bonnie was able to get in touch somehow."

I frown at him. "That doesn't make any sense. Legally you're supposed to get an amended birth certificate. My name isn't supposed to be anywhere near it."

"We know," Everett replies. "There was a mix-up and we were given the wrong one. We got the amended certificate after and were asked to destroy the original."

Lynn does not look at Everett, but her next words are directed at him. "But Everett kept it."

"I'm sorry," he says. "Okay? How many times do I have to say it? I'm so very sorry."

"I haven't heard from her," I tell them, after a minute. The muffin is almost gone and both the front and side doors are looking mighty inviting right about now. In the end, my curiosity gets the better of me. "What happened the day she went missing?"

Lynn shrugs. "She said she was going camping."

"Yes, I heard that. Where were you?"

An exchange of glances. They're not comfortable with their own parenting abilities put under scrutiny. "We were working," Lynn tells me. Her eyes narrow and her voice is several decibels louder than she intended. A few café patrons glance over at us before returning to their terrible coffee.

"Maybe she's been in touch with her biological father?" Everett says, attempting to resume control of the conversation. He smiles apologetically for Lynn. This is something he appears to be quite used to.

Fat chance of that. I shake my head. "Can't help you there." I get up and leave the table, my departure as abrupt as my arrival. It occurs to me to apologize, but I've never understood the Canadian impulse to say sorry when you've done nothing wrong.

As I head for the door, I hear Lynn hiss, "Great idea, Ev. Just brilliant."

There are footsteps behind me as I cross the parking lot. I tense as they close in. It's Everett. He shoves the photograph into my hands. "Nora? That didn't go the way I wanted it to. Lynn . . . She's under a lot of strain at work right now and things have been difficult between her and Bonnie for quite some time."

Again, his expression is apologetic. He expects me to say, There, there. It's all right. But, like Lynn, I ignore his blatant plea for comfort and understanding. He stiffens and a flush grows from his collar and spreads up his neck. I try to return the photo but he steps just out of reach.

"Keep it. But, please, if you hear from her call us. I wrote our contact information on the back of the picture. She's . . . she's a good kid. Despite everything. I just want her to come back home."

This is the second time he's said that. He is trying desperately to believe it. A good kid. I wonder what he means by that. She sounds wretched. "Why did you hire a PI to look for me and not her?" I ask. And then the answer occurs to me. "Because you thought she came to me, so I'm your starting point."

"Our end point, too," he says, turning away. "She's gotten pretty good at running away by now. She's left us with nothing else to go with."

As I walk to my rusty Corolla, I try to fight the panic rising inside me. Everett Walsh has gone out of his way to contact the biological mother of his missing daughter, even though there is no evidence that points to me being in touch with the child I gave up all those years ago. She has been looking for me, but so what? Many children look for their biological parents, with no luck. It's not uncommon. He gives me a photo, even though I haven't requested one. He tries to impress me with her worthiness. He's not lying, but his attempts at manipulation are becoming clear. Her history as a runaway has jeopardized any serious investigation into her disappearance and he is grasping at straws.

That he's managed to find me is not a stretch. My name is on her original birth papers, clear as day. But how the hell does he know that I help look for missing people for a living?

And does he know that his wife was lying about where she was the day their daughter went missing?

# 3

THE GIRL SITS on the rocks and contemplates her next steps. She thinks she has a concussion but does not know how to tell for sure. She is bleeding from her head, her arms, her wrists. There is a dull pain at the back of her hip, but she cannot remember ever being struck there. Her ears are full of the sound of waves crashing on the rocks, threatening to sweep her out into the ocean. She is so lightheaded that she knows she wouldn't be able to fight it. The water has a power of its own, a power that scares her.

She must get moving.

Soon they will think she is dead and stop searching for her. She holds on to this thought like a talisman and huddles deeper into herself. The salt in the air bites at her eyes. She flicks her tongue to catch a droplet of seawater on her face and realizes that it is a tear.

# 4

THE INTERSECTION OF Hastings and Columbia is located in the worst neighborhood in Vancouver, the downtown east side. The city is about to embark on a rejuvenation effort targeted at the area, but for the moment it remains what it has been for most of its existence: a shithole. Vancouver real estate prices being what they are, however, it's the only affordable option for a die-hard downtowner looking to open his own private investigation outfit alongside the love of his life, an award-winning journalist who rents out some office space to freelance, write his book, and work on his syndicated news blog.

I am the receptionist and research assistant for both. Neither can afford to pay me on his own, but in this new cost-sharing economy, they have found a way to make it work. So have I, for that matter. For the past three years, I've been living beneath the firm for free in order to save a down payment for a place of my own. But my bosses don't know that. They think it's just a basement with old records and a broom closet and they've never bothered to check. Sometimes they comment on my Corolla, always parked in the back lot, but they don't know that it's mine. They assume it belongs to the marketing services guy down the hall, and I've never bothered to correct them.

Just down the street, a street filled with junkies, dealers, pimps, and whores, is the hipster haven of Gastown. Gastown is the buffer between the rich and the poor, the people who can afford to live in the nice parts of the city and the others, like me, who squat for free and take whatever we can get. The boss men live in Kitsilano, which is close to the beach but far enough away from the stench of their office environs to make them happy. They are Sebastian Crow, a slope-shouldered divorce survivor, and Leo Krushnik, the most flamboyant homosexual I have ever met. The two are wildly in love, though less on the wild side for Seb—he's just in love. A brilliant foreign correspondent by all accounts, Seb reconciled himself with his homosexuality late in life, at age forty-three, after two ulcers due to post-traumatic stress of covering the war in Kosovo and during marriage to a lawyer. His passion for his wife's much younger private investigator and forensic accountant could not be tamed, however, so he left everything to help Leo open up his own investigation firm, which he now works out of. His own journalistic skills contribute every now and then, but it's mostly Leo's business.

Which brings me to a lesson I take to heart: do not ever open a business with your lover. Work and home are now inextricably linked and Seb's only respite is alone at his desk or alone in the bar across the street when Leo is otherwise engaged.

"Ah, there's our expert bullshit detector," Leo says as I come in.

I'm late today. This is unusual. I'm never late—living in the basement has its perks—but my meeting with the Walshes has thrown me off my game. Instead of a bringing in a new client, I've arrived thirty minutes past nine with nothing to show for it and no desire to offer up an explanation. On the other side of the reception area, Leo peers at me from behind his desk. With his designer spectacles and professionally tailored business casual wardrobe, he doesn't meet your average expectations of a private investigator, which is part of why he's so good at it. People usually underestimate him, which is a mistake.

Seb opens the door to his office and stares at me from the doorway. His own drugstore reading glasses are taped up on one side and perched midway down the bridge of his nose. "Everything okay, Nora?" Seb says quietly. My tardiness has upset his routine. He has had to make his own coffee this morning and is most likely wondering why.

"Yup." I sit behind my desk. The red light on the office phone is not blinking. We have not had any calls since yesterday. "Sorry I'm late."

"You can be late more often," Leo intercedes. "Seriously, Nora, you need to get a life. Go out a little. Invest in your wardrobe."

All of these three things are unlikely to occur and Leo knows it. He's had this one-sided conversation many times. My lack of exciting life stories to tell, along with my unfortunate office wardrobe consisting of two pairs of frayed jeans and three ancient oversize cardigans that cover the holes in my T-shirts, are points of contention for him.

Just as he is about to embark on yet another explanation about the importance of good quality basics and signature pieces, the front door to our suite flies open and hits the opposite wall with a bang. There is a collective wince in the room. A slim blond woman strides in and surveys the place like she owns it. She ignores both Seb and me. Her focus is on Leo. It's our most regular client. "I have work for you."

"Melissa—" Leo begins.

She narrows her eyes at him. "You're supporting the father of my child. How is he supposed to make child payments for Jonas if he's broke? God knows that book money of his is gone and his next one is past deadline while he fiddles with a god-damn blog. Who makes money off of blogs these days?" She announces this to the room, reminding everyone yet again of how well informed she is. Seb's ex-wife knows that she can't play the alimony card because she makes more money than him. So she uses their son, conceived as a last-ditch attempt to save their marriage, as leverage to come in here and find out if he really is happier with another man.

She drops the file on my desk. "We need to find this guy by next week."

Seb sighs from his office. "Really, I don't need your handouts. We've talked about this."

"Well, I do," says Leo. His smile has a false edge to it. "If your firm wants to hire me, by all means. I am the best private investigation operation in town. Here, take a pamphlet." He holds out a slickly designed foldout sheet that he invested close to two hundred dollars in last year as a rebranding effort. "Please, tell your friends."

Everyone in the room knows that Melissa, a prominent defense attorney, has no friends. She registers the dig and stares hard at Leo, hostile and bewildered. She doesn't see how this cheery, overweight Polish émigré could be more attractive than her. She doesn't understand how the private investigator her firm used from time to time, the one she hired to follow her husband when he grew distant, could end up seducing her husband instead of just investigating privately like he was supposed to do. She doesn't see how her husband turned gay right under her nose.

It all becomes too much for her. She goes to the door. "Next week," she says to the room.

And then she's gone. There is a collective sigh of relief as the door is shut with as much force as it was opened.

Seb glares at Leo and slams his door. Leo busies himself with some paperwork at his desk. Everyone pretends not to be humiliated that we need as many cases as we can get because it has been two years since Seb's moderately successful book on the genocide in Kosovo was published and the money, mostly spent on their townhouse and the divorce, is gone.

Still, a case is a case and we can't afford to be picky.

The folder, of course, is for me.

I locate the witnesses in this operation and I sit in on the interviews to discern whether or not they're lying. To see through the bullshit to what people are trying to hide. That is my specialty. Leo offered to pay for me to go to a special training program in lie detecting, just to make it official, but I know he doesn't have the money for it and I've never been one for having my knowledge on the radar, so to speak. Sometimes your greatest strength should be kept under wraps. I've learned that lesson the hard way.

I open the folder and stare at the glossy image of Harrison Baichwal smiling earnestly at the camera. My first impression is of heavy brows and neatly trimmed beard that covers most of his lined face. Behind him is the seawall and overhead the sky is a perfect blue with not a cloud in sight. The man in the photo has no idea what his future holds and how darkness can just seep into any sunny picture, casting shadows. Harrison Baichwal has witnessed a murder, has given a flimsy statement in which he claims not to have seen anything out of the ordinary leading up to the events in question, and has since then disappeared.

I push all thoughts of missing progeny from my head and get to work. But still. Still it nags at the back of my mind, creating horrific scenarios of what happens to young women who don't come home. I don't know this girl from Eve, but I can't lie to myself anymore. She still occupies a space in my consciousness. In all these years, I've never allowed myself to think about just how much real estate she actually owns there.

# 5

PEOPLE WILL LIE about anything, anytime. When you ask them pointed questions, they will lie then, too. The important thing about catching a liar, even the most seasoned, is to ask the right question. Be specific. "Where were you last night, baby?" is open ended. An amateur bullshitter can coast on dodging questions like these for years. Always better to say, "Were you fucking the cashier from the gas station yesterday between 9:37 P.M. and 10:18 P.M.?"

An amateur bullshitter will spill the beans almost immediately when presented with a question like that. A seasoned liar will realize that the game may not be over just yet. Perhaps your best friend Nancy saw someone who *looked* like him go into a motel room with someone who *looked* like the cashier from the gas station. It was night. Night is dark. There was no moon out the previous evening and he chose a room farthest from the streetlights. There may or may not be photographic evidence. The liar will always try to see the possibility of an out and rebut with questions of his own to discern how much you actually know. Also, can this be proven in court, if voiding a prenuptial agreement is at stake? A very good liar will turn it back on you and make you feel bad about your lack of trust and your jaded worldview.

There are still many outs to consider when a liar is confronted, but as these thoughts fly through the liar's head, his body will give evidence that he is thinking them. A flicker of the eye. A twitch at his lips. Tapping fingers or an involuntary clench of the jaw. An almost imperceptible shift in tone. That's how you know he's a dirtbag.

And he could easily be a she. Young, old, and everything in between. Lying is a perfectly normal part of the human experience. Everyone does it and most people do it well enough to fool those closest to them.

Well, everyone except for me. Lying doesn't come easily to me. Even the most mundane bullshitting is not an option. Generally I prefer to avoid the truth rather than seek to alter it.

I stare at the photo of Harrison Baichwal and wonder what it is about his statement that makes him so uncomfortable that he doesn't want to defend it in court.

Leo isn't stupid. He knows I'm unqualified for this work. That's why the most serious surveillance assignments in our operation go to Stevie Warsame, a young Somali ex-cop from Alberta. Stevie is a very committed freelance contractor and only takes one case at a time, for a substantial chunk of the fees. His thoroughness is astounding; his pace, not so much. You cannot rush what is unfolding, he is in the habit of reminding me whenever he deigns to stop by the office, usually to pick up a check. You can watch and listen and only after you have the full picture can you act.

Leo quickly realized that subsisting only on legal investigations, the boring stuff, the research, the assignments he did well, was not an option for a new firm. He needed a surveillance guy who had access to a team, if required, and Stevie fit the bill.

He is good and, more important, available. Because he knows how easy it is to monitor people, he is secretive to the point of obfuscation. His previous employers could not deal with him. He has no personality or people skills. When on assignment, you can't find him to save your life, or his, or the client's.

That's why the smaller jobs go to me. I don't have Stevie's resume, but I usually get the job done.

As the receptionist and shared research assistant, it's a lot to ask, but it was through these witness locations and taking notes at interviews that the bosses discovered the peculiar skill I have. It's unscientific, though there are plenty out there who claim a scientific knowledge in this field. It's neither Dr. Watson nor Sherlock Holmes. Elementary, maybe, and something a little more than observational. There's a feeling I get when a lie is told. A disgust that creeps up when a liar is doing her best to muck things up or, more likely, save her own ass. Oftentimes, I can't put my finger on it; I can only tell when I see it. And years in foster care honed this skill to an art.

Harrison Baichwal may not be a liar, but he's hiding something. A mother of two was gunned down in his convenience store and the kid whose family owned the gun is crying wolf. His wealthy parents want Melissa to rip Harrison apart on the stand, to spread doubt that it was their child in the store that day wielding a stolen weapon, but Harrison isn't playing the game. He has disappeared and the subpoena can't be served. And now I have to find him to figure out why.

# 6

I'M NOT GOING to lie because, like I said, I generally don't: the years after I officially became a survivor were particularly dark. There were three godawful relapses during that period and one morning, just a couple of weeks after I spiraled into the third, I heard a whisper of a sound just outside the back entrance of the office. At first I thought it was a manifestation of my hangover but after an hour of huddling in the corner, wrapped in a blanket, I got angry. Okay, that's not true. I got paranoid, drank a beer to calm my nerves, and then got angry.

When I went out, steel pipe in hand, I found a huge ball of matted fur sniffing distastefully at a carton of spoiled chow mein I had put in the garbage the night before. The ball of fur looked at me with baleful eyes and stretched out the kinks in her long, elegant back, but made no move to beat a hasty exit when I tried to shoo her away. I've called her Whisper ever since. And that day I quit relapsing because an alcoholic is a shitty caregiver, and I know this from experience. If someone chooses you, that's a damn honor and you'd better be ready to give it your best. It's not often that you get chosen in the world. Everybody, even a mangy mutt, has options.

Whisper is a gray that exactly matches the pavement below and the clouds overhead. She roams the city with me at all hours of the day and night, and sees what others refuse to acknowledge. Although I have no special fondness for animals, it's impossible to deny that we have a kinship. The best thing about Whisper is that she's a constant reminder that at least I'm happier than one creature out there. Every day she looks at me with mournful eyes. Even when she passes gas, it's a hint of a sound and a barely detectable smell, leaving behind only a sad trace of odor. Whatever it was that brought her to my door is her little secret, but it must have been a doozy for her to pick up and go in search of a new life in the worst part of town.

And she has proven her worth from day one. I take her with me when I'm looking for information because people walk their dogs at all hours of the day and night. It's an accepted truth of pet companionship that a dog needs exercise and the person has to make sure it happens. No one looks twice at a dog walker, especially if both the dog and the walker appear to be minding their own business. This makes Whisper the perfect cover for surveillance. She is precisely at that age when she's no longer as delightful as a puppy or as pitiful as an old dog. She's somewhere in between and doesn't attract much attention. She reminds me of me, except for her horniness.

The only downside to Whisper is that she is sex crazed, even though the doctor at the veterinary clinic down the road assures me that she has been spayed. She is part hound, part wolf, and all nymphomaniac. Matted fur aside, I can tell from her excellent physical condition that she was once well taken care of, but I imagine that her slutty ways got her kicked out of a good home. She will gleefully hump anything that sniffs at her for longer than five seconds. She regrets it afterward and spends the following week in a depressed slump. After the hormonal high comes the self-loathing. I don't get mad at her, because I've been there.

I see her as a cautionary lesson in indulgence.

"You whore," I say affectionately to her after each episode. Then she whines at me and puts her face in her water bowl as if she's trying to drown herself.

After Leo and Seb leave for the evening, I go to the basement and wake her up. Like me, she prefers to be out when the sun goes down.

"We've got someone to find," I tell her. Her tail lifts as though she is thinking about wagging it and then falls back onto the floor with a thud. She gets up and goes to the door. She hates to admit it, but she loves watching people almost as much as I do.

# 7

THE REFUSAL OF the average Canadian to procreate enough to meet replacement levels of 2.1 children has necessitated a progressive immigration policy. We hover under 2, and this isn't a good thing. We can't sustain an economy on sub-2 levels. Who will contribute to our gross domestic product? Racists and advocates for closed borders can scream all they want, but unless they start making babies at a much higher rate, multiculturalism is the wave of the Canadian future. Their social safety nets depend on it.

Which makes Canada a clash of cultures. However, being Canada, it is not so much a clash as it is a polite acknowledgment and a few snide remarks on the golf course. For the most part. As I sit outside the RB Mart in Surrey and watch the Indians go by, I am reminded of this. And by Indians, I mean Indians from India, or sometimes Fiji. The community here is largely South Asian, but patrons are a tapestry of ethnicities. Everyone needs gum and throat lozenges.

Whisper and I sit on a park bench across the street from the RB Mart and watch the woman behind the counter. She is middle-aged and round-bellied with long dyed-black hair tucked beneath a loose scarf. I admire the efficiency with which she performs her tasks. Economy of movement, slender hands ringing up purchases swiftly, answering questions in a perfunctory manner, no more or less helpful than necessary. When there are no customers, she moves on to inventory.

This is not a woman who appears to be worried about her husband's safety.

At exactly 7 P.M. a young man in his twenties takes over the shift and Bidi Baichwal goes home. I don't follow her. I know where she lives with her now-missing husband, her elderly parents, and her adolescent children. Professional surveillance is a team effort but, once again, Stevie Warsame is nowhere to be found and a forensic accounting case just landed on Leo's lap, so for the moment, I'm on my own. I take a chance that Bidi will go home because she just had a long day and I'm betting she'll want to spend the evening with her children. I stay and watch the young man, Bidi's cousin, just arrived from India this past year. From the file that Melissa dropped on my desk, I know his name is Amir. He's a good employee, but has a sorrowful gaze that could give Whisper a run for her money. He continues the shift throughout the evening, but his English is not as sharp as Bidi's and he takes twice as long to answer questions. People don't seem to mind, though, because there's something vulnerable about him, something that makes them either want to be patient or take advantage.

As the time passes, everything around me grows still and quiet. It reminds me of the moment just before dawn, when silence hangs in the air and sleep becomes impossible. When my monsters come crawling out from under their rock and go marauding into the world, in search of sustenance. I don't let myself think of Bonnie, though. I don't even know the girl. From many years of suppressing her memory, I wouldn't even know where to begin dredging her out again. What I see is my sister Lorelei's face. What would I do if she'd gone missing? I know instinctively that if it had been Lorelei, I would not be sitting here, on a case.

At 11 P.M., Amir closes up shop. I follow him to an apartment building that is six blocks away from the Baichwal home. Most of the windows are dark this time of night except for a few night owls. Two minutes after he enters the building, a shadow crosses a window on the third floor. The lights are on in that apartment. Someone has been waiting for him.

I watch until the lights go out, while the knowledge that there is a missing girl out there with my eyes festers inside me.

# 8

THE KERRISDALE HOUSE is dark. Everett and Lynn must be sleeping. There is no moon out tonight and no streetlights in front of this yard so it is especially bleak. But even in the dark I can see that it's a beautiful two-story home with a rock garden in the front and a dapper wooden WELCOME sign over the door. The sign is hand-made and I can tell that it's amateur woodwork. I assume that Everett must be responsible for it. Everett and perhaps Bonnie. Did they make it together? From the outside, it is the only evidence that perhaps a child might live there. But this is the address that was scrawled on the back of the photo Everett handed to me outside the café.

I'm so interested in the sign that I almost don't notice the man sitting in a dark sedan and watching the house. By the time I do see him, it is already too late to turn back, so I adopt a casual, out-for-a-late-stroll pace. The man isn't sleeping, so I know that he's not a cop. Also, he's eating an apple. I have never before seen a cop eat an apple and, though I suspect it must happen from time to time, I can't imagine it in a surveillance situation. Everett said that the police logged Bonnie as a runaway. Unlikely, then, that they'd maintain a presence.

I pass him with Whisper and, after an initial glance in which he has inventoried my features and strands of dark hair creeping out from beneath my hoodie, he dismisses me. I am clearly not a threat, nor whomever he is looking out for, so he returns his attention to the house.

It doesn't bother me that he has seen my face because he'll never remember what I look like come morning. If pressed, he might say "maybe native, average height, skinny." If he was going to be mean about it, he'd add: "flat chest, no sense of style, ugly dog."

I circle back around the block and find a place outside of his line of sight. I watch him watch the house for a while. I wonder if they have hired him to keep an eye out for Bonnie, in case she returns, but dismiss the thought almost immediately. They wouldn't need someone to watch the house when they're inside.

The picture becomes more complicated. There is a third party involved.

A light goes on in a bedroom over the garage. The window cracks open slightly and a cloud of smoke seeps through. A thin hand emerges and waves the smoke away from the window. Lynn is stress smoking in a room that's not her own, somewhere she hopes Everett won't see. From where I'm sitting on a lawn several houses down, I can't be certain if the not-cop in the sedan has observed this, if he has written it down in his notebook to include in his report. A woman, whose guilty conscience won't let her sleep, passes her night smoking in the bedroom of her missing child.

# 9

I GET HOME before dawn and sleep until ten. Seb and Leo work from home on Fridays and sometimes Mondays, Wednesdays, and Thursdays as well. Tuesdays are their only steadfast office days. Though Seb will most likely leave me alone with the hours of recorded interviews he left for me to transcribe, I know that Leo will call at noon for an update on Harrison Baichwal.

Seb's book on where the hell Canada's foreign aid goes and if it really does get there is a huge undertaking, one that he and I pick up on the side. He's recently had to take on some freelance projects just to pay the bills but that is the bucket and he is the crab. There is little value for seasoned investigative journalists, not with the Internet enabling just about anyone with a Wi-Fi connection to investigate and also to call himself a reporter. So Seb is also working on *The Crow*, his syndicated news blog, which is carried by a couple of papers. The work keeps us both busy and me employed, so I have no complaints about the time commitment.

I step over Whisper and go upstairs into the office. Our wing of the building is mostly empty. There is a small marketing services company next door that doesn't seem to offer very many services, as their door is always closed.

When I get to the office, I see that the red light on the office phone isn't blinking (as usual), but the red light on my mobile is.

I forgot it at my desk last night and had not missed its presence at all. Only Seb and Leo call me, anyway, and they aren't likely to do so much after office hours. I don't recognize the number on the missed call log—but there is a message.

The voice is one that I vaguely remember. Hundreds of cigarettes and countless cups of stale coffee have roughened it, but it's still the journalist I used to know.

"Nora—I'm sorry, I know you said never to use your name. Fuck. Mary, then. I had a hell of time finding you, lady, so I hope you're okay. Had to go through Crow, too, which I know you're gonna hate but it's an emergency. There's something I gotta tell you, but not over the phone. We need to meet. Tomorrow morning. Same place we spoke last time. Do you remember? Please, be—"

The message ends. Either he was cut off by the system or his battery died. Even though he was halted midsentence, I'm sure the last part was a warning. I play the message several times and then slump down in one of the stiff-backed chairs in the waiting room, left over from the previous occupants of the suite.

All of a sudden I'm scared of what's happening here. First Everett Walsh and now the journalist. It seems that my past has come looking for me. That its violent fingers have clawed up from the damp soil in the woods where I buried it and it has now returned to pull me back in.

And, just as suddenly, I need a drink.

# 10

SOMETIMES WHEN I wake up, I dig out an old hand mirror and stare at my reflection in it. My face always comes as a shock to me. Like a vampire, I avoid looking at myself in mirrors. Unlike a vampire, I expect a reflection, albeit one that is in serious need of an uplift.

All I see now is a dusky wraith descending into middle age but with none of the milestones that usually go along with it. I cringe at the woman staring back at me in the dim morning light that filters reluctantly into the room. There's not much that stands out, not much to show the passing of time, but I note that every year my buttocks descend just a fraction of a centimeter more. The general public is not aware of this decline. I've been told this is the process of "getting old" and there are injections that I can pay for that will provide some lift, but I have never valued money enough to keep it in any significant amount—rather, never made enough of it to keep it any significant amount. Also, my old bad habits of spending it on booze make it impossible to keep that kind of temptation around.

Seb and Leo think that I have no sex appeal, that it is a game for the young. I won't distract their clients or leave them for other men. They think other men don't pay attention. I can't argue with this logic, because they're mostly right. Also, this natural disguise of mine works well in surveillance situations so there is a professional bonus. There's nothing more invisible than the middle-aged woman, and there's no denying that middle age is creeping up in time with the descent of my ass, a sort of inverse gravitational relationship.

After I woke up in the hospital, I used to wear thick panties day and night as an extra protective layer, but a brief stint in a survivor's support group showed me that I must not punish myself and that I'm not to blame. So, in an act of rebellion, I have mostly discarded the use of underwear altogether. But now . . . now I think I need them. I fish around for a pair with the elastic still intact and I call my bosses to tell them I may have a lead on Harrison Baichwal, but I'll give them an update tomorrow. There is the transcribing of interviews to be done, but I can do that later.

Technology is a remarkable thing. It allows for so much work to be accomplished sitting in one's sweats at the kitchen table, which is what Seb and Leo are probably doing now.

"Sounds good, Nora," Seb says over the speakerphone. I hear Leo cursing the coffee machine in the background. "Everything else okay?"

"That depends on what you mean by okay."

"I just mean, do you feel all right?"

"Yes," I say, if only because all right is relative. Compared to some people, I am all right. Compared to others, I am an ex-alcoholic survivor, sober off and on for thirteen years, celibate for just as long, who owns no property, has no friends, and spends her nights wandering the city with no one to love except a dog that is perpetually in heat. Compared to those people, I am one country song away from leaping off a bridge.

Whisper is waiting for me by the door. She can smell my fear and is wondering if she, too, should be scared. If she would be better off taking her chances elsewhere. We never lie to each other, she and I, and we both know that she's in it for the food.

I spend the rest of the day surfing the net on the office Wi-Fi. I get three bars here in the basement instead of the normal five I get upstairs, but two bars less is a sacrifice I'm willing to make for free Internet. My mobile rings steadily for an hour. The journalist is desperate to reach me, but I've had enough of this shit.

I put on Nina Simone and her melody drowns out all ambient noise. The good thing about Nina Simone is that you can never think about anything else while you're listening to her. She commands all attention. You can pull the covers over your head and sink into that voice for days on end. After her, I put on Muddy Waters and then Percy and a little Tom Waits for flavor. I've had some personal experience with the blues, but for the past few years I've found it more useful to listen to others sing it than wallow in it myself. It allows me to be employable, which I am, but just barely. Lucky for me, Seb and Leo are excellent employers and don't ask many questions.

I need a drink so bad that my stomach is in knots. I'm shocked at how my body can remember how good it feels to be buzzed. How it's always the one escape that I long for when everything else that I touch turns to shit.

# 11

I WAIT UNTIL evening settles in and then I dial the number I'm not supposed to call anymore. He picks up after the fifth ring, the fear that I've relapsed overwhelming the urge to shut me out.

"I need to see you," I say. "One hour, the bridge."

"Nora?" His voice is thick with sleep. I stop to wonder why that would be at this time of day while he fumbles around for his thoughts. Probably napping at his desk with a cold cup of coffee at his elbow. "Goddamn it," he says when he finally finds them.

"It's important."

He sighs heavily in response but I know he'll be there.

I take the long route around with Whisper at my heels. I let her off leash because we're just using backstreets and no one will be around this time of the night to take offense.

They say a sponsor should be a shoulder to cry on, someone to share your burden with, to talk you down off that ledge. There were many nights my ex-sponsor and I shared a comfortable silence where we sat on the hood of his car parked in a lot near the Lions Gate Bridge, drank coffee, and watched the city go to sleep. I didn't talk about my problems and he didn't talk about his. We sat and drank until one of us had to pee and then we went our separate ways. Night is the worst time to be alone with your demons, as anyone with demons will tell you. The shadows deepen in your imagination, turn menacing as the sun drops out of sight. It's when you are most desperate and will make the little compromises with yourself to get that one taste, that one drink, and then what's another . . . and yet another couple of beers after that. He understood that intuitively.

One night he moved to pat my shoulder and I grabbed his wrist and slammed the heel of my hand into his nose. Blood spurted everywhere. That didn't bother him much at the time. He just reached for my hands, twisted them behind my back, and cuffed me before I realized what was happening. The cold metal slid over my wrists and I learned something then about keeping secrets. That some people are better at it than I am.

After that night he decided that we weren't the right fit. That he couldn't help me in the way that I needed. Whatever that meant.

My ex-sponsor is already waiting at our usual lot by the time I arrive. He unfolds his long body from the ludicrous MINI Cooper that he insists on driving. It's his singular prize from what I can only assume was a disastrous marriage to someone who enjoys confined spaces.

"I told you to find a new sponsor," is the first thing out of his mouth when he sees me. I haven't seen him since last year when he tried to put a hand on my shoulder, but the change in him is startling. His nose is still slightly crooked. I am unable to take my eyes from it. His hair is flying in every direction and his eyes are red-rimmed. I wonder if he has been hitting the sauce again. If his failure to nurture me back to health and well-being has driven him back to the bottle.

"I did. She asks a lot of questions. I think she might be a spy."

He sighs again, as if I'm the hugest pain in the ass he's ever encountered. The other cops called him Bazooka because of his name, even though there's nothing loud or forceful about him. They could have at least given it some effort. Then the World Cup went to Brazil and a soccer ball was named. Suddenly, Brazuca became "the Brazilian" even though he is actually Portuguese mixed with British and has lived in Canada for most of his life.

I search his features for a flash of the exotic but besides his dark eyes and a barely distinguishable tan, his demeanor is decidedly British. Reserved, self-deprecating. He's tall and lanky but walks with a limp that becomes more pronounced when it rains, which is seven months out of the year. At first I thought the limp was a ploy to get women to be nice to him but I asked him once if it still hurt and he didn't lie. Later on, after some snooping, I learned he took a bullet on the job. He is a detective, he explained to me the night he cuffed me, not a uniform man on the front lines, so I know there is a story there that he is not telling.

"You know, you don't have to work for an intelligence agency to want to get through to people," he says to me now. "Talking usually helps."

"Does it help you?"

He's silent for a moment because he knows that for people like us, talking accomplishes nothing. "Why am I here, Nora?" He eyes my worn sweatpants and the tears in my hooded sweatshirt. "Do you need money?"

I hold out a scrap of paper. "I need you to check this plate number." It would be a simple matter to ask Stevie to filter this through his contacts, but I don't want him or anyone else at the office to start asking questions about Bonnie. The less they know about my life, the better. For them, anyway. For reasons I have chosen not to explore, plausible deniability has always been a concern of mine.

He laughs quietly to himself. The paper hangs between us like a spurned offering. I don't remove my hand. He stops laughing. "You're serious."

"A girl is missing," I tell him. "That car was parked on the street last night watching her house and the man inside wasn't a cop."

"The police . . ."

"They don't give a shit. She's not blond enough."

He flinches at this and has the decency to look ashamed. He is with the force, after all. I should apologize, but I don't because we both know there's some truth to this. There's a whole highway in the north of the province stained by the tears of indigenous girls and women who weren't blond enough to matter, whose families are still looking for justice. This lack of justice isn't isolated to a single highway, either. It is more like a cancer that has spread through every segment of Canada's social and political systems, generating press during election times and buzzwords like "the missing" and "murdered."

"Why do you care?" he says finally.

It's a good question. I've been wondering the same thing myself. I don't tell him that she has my eyes, and that maybe that alone is enough to seal her fate. To deny her justice. So I shrug and wait. Part of me hopes that he'll refuse, if only because it means that I've at least made an attempt—even though I don't have to. The child is a problem I gave to people who were allegedly better suited to deal with her. It turns out that they have failed the both of us.

"How old is the girl?"

"Fifteen."

"Is she missing or did she run away?"

"The parents think she ran away, but now she's missing."

His grim smile confirms my suspicions. "I can see why they didn't take it seriously. That's not a good sign."

He hasn't told me anything that I don't already know. "I didn't come for a lecture. I just want to know who this car is registered to."

Brazuca takes the paper and blinks down at it.

"Make and model are at the bottom there," I point out.

"Fine, but after this you can't call me anymore. Let the police do their work. They're a lot better at this than you might think."

I laugh at this, quietly and to myself, and then realize he's serious. How quickly the tables turn.

# 12

I LOOK AT my past self with pity and more than a small dose of shame. The Nora of twenty years ago, that singing fool, was like a character in a particularly grotesque cartoon where dreams were possible and even dishonest people could help achieve them if they were getting something out of it, too.

Pathetic.

But now I am a survivor. There's a particular world-weariness that comes along with this. Don't get me wrong, I haven't seen it all—I still have within me the capacity to be surprised—but I've seen a hell of a lot. So it doesn't throw me to see a beautiful red-haired woman kissing a man who isn't her husband in the parking garage beneath her workplace. This is most likely why she lied about being at work the day that her daughter went missing. She was probably somewhere else, doing something similar to what she's doing now. I watch her and wonder, does she feel guilty that she could not provide a happy home for her daughter? That her family was not enough and she had to go looking elsewhere for satisfaction? Now that I am aware that Bonnie was so restless in their home that she ran away, it's not exactly something I can forget. Her unhappiness eats away at me.

Huddled in a dark corner, I don't even blink.

I look for pointers on technique that I will probably never employ again. He reaches his hand inside her jacket but she pushes him away and gets into her car. She drives off, completely unaware that she's being watched by the man she has left hanging, the cameras in the parking garage, and me.

# 13

PEOPLE THINK I should be some sort of tracker because of my father's bloodlines and my appearance. They couldn't be more off the scent. My heritage is so mixed I wouldn't know where to begin. I would get lost in a forest easier than a tourist with a malfunctioning GPS. I hate the smell of pine and damp earth. Not to mention the various bears, cougars, wolves, coyotes, snakes, spiteful plant organisms, and stinging insects. No woodland romps for me, thank you very much. Give me a dirty street filled with vagrants and littered with needles any day. I know the predators there and they don't bother me anymore.

I sit outside the apartment building in Surrey and watch Bidi's cousin Amir leave for work two hours before his shift. Through the thick glass windows of the lobby, I can see him glance around before coming out the door. Although cautious before he exits the building, once he is out he moves quickly, throwing anxious looks over his shoulder.

This time I don't follow Amir. This time I get a coffee from the shop down the street and wait for a glimpse of the bogeyman haunting his waking moments, causing him to cast fearful glances about and leave home so much earlier than he needs to. After an hour, I am rewarded. An SUV with tinted windows eases into the back parking lot. A young native man comes out of the building and hands a garbage bag over to the young white man in the driver's seat. Three Asian boys and a black girl walk by, deliberately ignoring the entire exchange. The two over at the car speak for a moment and then the car pulls away. I would bet my next paycheck that bag is filled with greasy money.

Even though I see that there is now an organizational element to this case, I have to give a grudging respect to what's happening here. Only in Canada can you find gangs not based on ethno-cultural lines drawn in the sand. These youth are embracing the thirst for commerce that unites us all.

I watch the kid saunter back into the building as if he owns it and wonder where his people are from. But if anyone could tell, it wouldn't be me. And I don't have the right to speculate, either. That connection was lost a long time ago. It's as dead as my father. And if my father were here today, seeing this native kid in his multi-ethnic gang, he might say that at least this boy seems to belong somewhere.

Look at how well assimilation can work.

If you think residential schools were the only way the Canadian government gutted indigenous communities, you'd be wrong. They went at it all kinds of ways, just to see what stuck. In the fifties, sixties, and into the seventies, they had a scoop, by which I mean they scooped up kids from indigenous families and put them up for adoption. Some of them even went to America, Europe, or as far away as New Zealand, with no real memories of who they were or where they were from.

So when my father eventually found his way back to Canada from Detroit he was as rootless as they came. He was born in Manitoba and he could have been part of any of the sixty-three First Nations communities there, or métis, or mixed in some other way, but I don't know if he ever found out for certain. Those records had been long lost, even before he returned to the country of his birth. I can't say that he ever felt as comfortable in his skin as that kid appeared to be and it's the one connection that we share.

He was just as much of an outsider as I am.

As I stand watching, the man in the SUV pauses to make a phone call and then drives off. Like Lynn in the parking garage, he doesn't notice me. He probably wouldn't care if he did. I walk away feeling like I've just found a key piece of the puzzle. These guys seem to be low-level dealers, part of a larger organization. Bidi's cousin Amir doesn't strike me as the type to be in a gang, so it might be that he's just an unfortunate tool who is merely being harassed by one. Because he knows something he shouldn't and, if I had to take a stab in the dark, I'd say Harrison Baichwal knows the same thing.

I get a text on my phone.

*Now.*

# 14

THIS TIME I get to the lookout by the Lions Gate first, even though I've just spent about an hour in the gridlock that usually wraps itself around this part of the city. I stare out at the water and wonder where the black current is. Where the warmth is. The rain has stopped for now, but it still threatens to fall with even the slightest provocation.

"Hey," comes a soft voice behind me. Brazuca is on foot this time and looks more tired than ever. What I initially thought were signs of a hangover when I saw him last now seem to be closer to extreme fatigue. If possible, he's even thinner than before. He's clearly spiraling, and taking it out on his stomach rather than his liver this time.

He grips the railing with his hands and stares over the edge and into the water below, as if it could unlock the mysteries of the world, if only he could speak its language. He doesn't, and again he is a failure. It is almost eight and the people of the city have scattered to wherever it is that they go when they're not clogging up the streets.

"Do you have it?"

He ignores the question. "Tell me about the girl."

I wasn't planning on doing anything of the sort, about Bonnie, Everett, or Lynn, but there's something calm and reassuring about the way that he asked. Up until now I was just a pain in the ass. Now I am a pain in the ass with something of interest.

Or maybe it's just the detective in him.

I shrug. "I don't know much about her. Only child. Parents are architects. Nice house in Kerrisdale. She took off a couple of weeks ago, but they think she never meant to stay away this long."

"Is this a Krushnik Investigations case or something you're running with for Sebastian Crow?"

Every muscle in my body goes rigid.

"Don't look so surprised," he says. "I've known where you work for a while. I wasn't going to bring it up, but you asking for this favor, out of the blue . . . not very anonymous, is it?"

I see where he's going with this. By giving him the plate number, I have invited him into my life. There is no more anonymity or privacy. Now we're just alcoholics.

"How did you know?"

"I followed you last year. After you broke my nose. I thought I deserved an apology."

"But you never got up the courage to ask for one."

"It isn't a matter of courage. I realized that an apology should be offered, not demanded." This is a pointed jab, but it's misplaced. I've never been one to hide behind manners. Good manners, though it can be wonderful to be on the receiving end of them, are deceiving. I have never forgotten that.

"Whose car is it?" I ask. I get the feeling that he's hiding something. That for him to be here instead of just picking up the phone and giving me a name means that what he found is unexpected. Or maybe he's lonely. I suspect the former.

He ignores my question once again. A massive tanker cuts through the sea in the distance, moving out with the tide. "Who's the girl to you?"

We stand there at the railing, not looking at each other, each staring out at the water. I consider lying but I can't. I could settle for bullshitting but I don't want to feel like an asshole. So I just stand and look over the railing until Brazuca shifts his weight and reaches a hand down to massage his knee.

"It's gonna rain again tonight," he says, like an old man whose greatest pleasure is to predict the weather based on the status of his various injuries. Brazuca is somewhere in his forties and though he likes to pretend that he's older than he appears, I know that this is merely a stalling tactic. I have to admit that there's a certain charm to it. How easy it is to disarm someone with simple conversation about the weather.

"It's a Vancouver winter." Meaning, get on with it, of course it's going to rain.

He doesn't take the hint. For now he's holding all the cards and is content to go his own pace, which, apparently, is glacial. "I'm thinking of moving somewhere hot. Where it never rains."

"I hear the Sahara is nice. Friendly scorpions."

A quick smile flashes across his face and then it's gone. "Nora, the car is leased to WIN Security. It's part of their motor pool."

"The private security firm?"

"That's the one. So, tell me. Is this really just about a runaway? Because I can't for the life of me think of why they'd be interested in this. When it comes to the security business, they're high-end. They do mostly corporate work now."

"But they also do private investigations?"

"I'd assume so, but mostly for their corporate clients. Finding missing girls isn't exactly in their wheelhouse. And they're not cheap, either. You said the car was watching the house? Their surveillance teams are top-notch and you'd be paying serious money for that kind of service. Just to see if a kid comes home."

Everett and Lynn seemed well-off, but nothing about them screamed serious money. "Can you find out what WIN Security is doing there?"

"No, that wasn't our deal, remember? I run the plates for you and you let this go."

"I never agreed to that."

"Fine, then let me help."

I look at him now. He meets my gaze and I can see that he's dead serious.

"Thanks for the information," I say, turning away.

"Where are you going—hey! Come back here!"

He calls after me and for a moment it looks like he's tempted to give chase, but I'm much faster than him. Besides, it's undignified for a man with a limp to run after a woman, especially if she is shouting, "I don't want to buy drugs from you!"

Though this statement is misleading, technically it's true. But I'm not proud of it, all the same.

# 15

A SEDAN IS parked outside the Kerrisdale house. Different spot, different car, but it's the same man slumped in the driver's seat. This time he is popping blueberries from a stainless steel container. How very eco-friendly of him. I take a moment to appreciate his commitment to the planet. He's listening to a replay of last night's Canucks game over the radio and only barely looks up when Lynn leaves the house, not bothering to lock the door behind her. As soon as Lynn pulls off in the Audi parked in the driveway, the not-cop yawns and searches for another healthy snack in the glove compartment. I take the opportunity to walk through the front door.

Canadians tend to be complacent when their loved ones are at home. As though the valuables should be locked up while everyone is out, but not while they are inside. If my intent was criminal, now would be the perfect time to strike. The shower is on upstairs, so I know Everett will make an appearance shortly, should I desire to assault him. Since I'm only here to snoop, I go to the basement, pass the laundry room, and hide in the storage area.

There I find row upon row of neatly organized shelves. Three lives, all packed away in a discernible order. I admire the precision it takes to sort through one's life like this. Taxes? Top left. Sporting gear? Bottom right. Winter clothes? Center stage.

One storage box on the top shelf is askew and upon closer examination, I find that it's the only one not labeled. Inside is a locked fireproof box. The lock on the outside is easy enough to pick. I always keep a few hairpins on me anyway, just in case a situation like this presents itself. Normally I have no desire to pull apart people's lives, though Leo says I have a certain knack for it. But when you give up on your dream of being a blues singer, you have to hang your hat somewhere. This is Vancouver, after all, and you're going to have a hat, or a hood on a sturdy raincoat that won't go flying about, or a decent umbrella. Fate presented me with the journalist, who led me to Seb and Leo. They don't ask where I learned to use these hairpins, don't know that during basic training in the Canadian Forces I used to sleep next to a degenerate like myself, barely eighteen, who could open any door she wanted instead of waiting around for it to open on its own.

The lock on the box has been tampered with, but from the scratches on the exterior of it I can tell that it was an amateur's work. Inside are adoption documents and copies of the application that Everett and Lynn sent in to the agency. Here I find letters about how well suited the Walshes would be for children. How in love and well employed they were. How much money they had in their bank account. Beneath these papers, I find Bonnie's birth certificate, the one with my name on it. Just as she must have found it when she went looking. Their self-delusion in keeping it here is astonishing. Of course if she were to start looking, she'd start here.

I stare at my name scratched on that piece of paper and feel the coffee I'd had this morning curdle in my stomach. I hadn't wanted to see her at the hospital when she was born because I hadn't wanted to have her at all. When the nurse swaddled her in a blanket and tried to hand her to me, I turned away and pretended that they—all of them, the doctor, nurses, orderlies, the baby—didn't exist. I have tried to forget everything about that day, but the memories are starting to come back in vivid flashes of sound and color. Her cries. My exhaustion. The overpowering numbness in my lower extremities. It was easy to give her away then, easy to pass her on to a better life than I had to offer. A better life with these people, whom I'd never met or even knew the names of. I had no regrets about this at the time. It was a relief. But now . . . now all I feel is anger that they didn't keep up their end of the bargain. If there is one firm rule in this world, it's that when it comes to children, promises must be kept.

This child was not supposed to be lost to the streets. She wasn't supposed to be like me.

I'm tempted to go upstairs and confront Everett but over the years I've learned a bit about self-control, mostly that it pays off in the end. Besides, he would kick me out or call the police and, other than Brazuca, I don't talk to cops.

On the main floor above me, I hear cursing as Everett frantically prepares for work. I feel absolutely no sympathy for him. A few minutes later, the back door upstairs slams shut, but I wait for an extra ten minutes anyway before I go up. In the laundry room, there's a man's shirt stuffed into the washing machine. I sniff it and find the faded scent of expensive cologne and something like jasmine.

Once I'm certain that Everett is too far away to return home for forgotten items, I go upstairs. I am angry, but not so much that I don't take a moment to admire their good taste. The house is as nice on the inside as it is on the outside. Everything is done in tasteful creams and cerulean, with strategic splashes of red and yellow accent pieces. On the mantel are the family photos and, for the most part, they are happy reminders of a loving family. Even Lynn is smiling in them, which interests me because I hadn't imagined her face contorting in such a pleasant way. The earlier the photograph was taken, the happier she seems. The oldest photograph on display is one where Lynn is holding baby Bonnie in her arms and grinning at the camera. In the photo, she's looking like her wildest dreams have come true. She looks excited and nervous and staring down at the sleeping baby with dark tufts of hair like it is the greatest prize in the world.

I set the photograph down carefully and retreat. Most people put up pictures to preserve memories of happier times, to keep them afloat when they need reminding, but I prefer to keep my memories locked away so that only I can dust them off and look at them when I can't help myself. And they are for me alone. Part of this is because Lorelei and I didn't grow up in a home with smiling photos and there sure as hell weren't any of us in foster care. The other part is that some of my memories are gone forever, gone because one night I sang at a bar and woke up in the hospital with hazy recollections of my blood on a sheet and what the earth in a forest smells like with my face pressed into the ground.

I move upstairs and enter the room above the garage. The bed is covered in a bright green comforter the color of a tennis ball.

If there is any connection to be had with my progeny it can't be found in this neon monstrosity. The walls are like a giant ad for a tanned, shirtless young man named Jacob. He looks somewhat familiar, but I can't place him. I've never met anyone that attractive in real life. There's one snapshot of Bonnie and another teenage girl tacked up on the mirror just above the dresser. They're both sticking their tongues out at whoever is behind the camera, though Bonnie is doing it in laughter and the other girl seems fairly annoyed at the whole thing. Below it is a photo of Bonnie in sweatpants and a crop top striking a pose for the camera.

I go to the desk and pull out her school binders. Here I find some genetic similarities. The binders are heavy on doodles and light on actual notes. I stare at the drawings in the margins. There's no talent to be found here, only the confused scribbling of a child with a fondness for a certain kind of expression. An angry face with one eyebrow raised. Some look demonic, but no real thought or effort was put into them. Though the face changes, the eyes are always the same. Almond shaped and turned slightly up at the corners. Her eyes, as inscrutable as mine. I put the binders back and search through the closet and chest of drawers for anything of interest. Everything is in order, which means that the girl is at least too smart to leave clues behind.

Everett and Lynn's room is airy and bright, but there is a noticeable formality here. Everything is put in its place, even though they work full-time and have both rushed out of the house by seven this morning. No clothes left strewn on the floor or on the bed, no cosmetic jars open or tubes left uncapped.

These are clearly people who are very careful with each other. I try to imagine them having sex on this bed but the thought, which usually makes me uncomfortable, in this case leaves me indifferent.

I move on.

I sniff all the scented toiletries in the room and in the master bath and find nothing that resembles the smell of jasmine. I'm standing just to the side of the bathroom window when out of the corner of my eye I see a hooded figure pause in the large backyard below. At first I think it's the not-cop, but after a moment of watching the figure survey the yard and look up at the window to the room over the garage, I realize that it wouldn't be him. The shape is too lumpy and too furtive. It is not the fluid stealth of a private security agent, but the darting sneakiness of a teenage girl.

Downstairs, I remove the screen from the back door and, being somewhat compact, squeeze through. It's not an elegant escape, but it's effective. I put the screen back, careful to align the edges, and sidle over a dip in the fence. The girl had come in and left the same way.

I cut across the park three streets down, following the girl. She walks quickly but I am quicker so I'm able to head her off before she reaches the school grounds. With a swift motion, I pull her into the trees. She opens her mouth to scream but I step back quickly and hold my hands up to show I'm not a threat. Her mouth hangs open as she relaxes somewhat to see that I'm a woman, even though that means nothing in regard to her safety.

"Who the fuck are you?" she says, blue eyes narrowed. It's the other girl in Bonnie's picture above the dresser. Straw-colored hair with platinum highlights frames her face, which is caked with foundation to cover the acne that dots her broad cheeks. She is wearing a skirt hiked up to her thighs and her hoodie is open so that I can see a tight white T-shirt underneath. Even though she's dressed like a prostitute, her clothes look high-end so she must come from money. She would have to, to go to this school, in this area.

"I'm looking for Bonnie," I say.

She snorts and eyes me. "What, she owe you money or something?"

"I'm her mother." Saying this out loud is like a jolt to my system. I force myself to stay calm. To keep my panic to myself. "I hear she's gone missing and I saw you in the yard back there. Were you getting her stuff for her?"

Her jaw hangs open again, but snaps shut as a fly buzzes nearby. She laughs at me and I resist the urge to smack her. I know this kind of girl. Even though she has affected an abrasive personality to get attention, underneath is an insecure little gremlin, just hurting for love and acceptance. I try to remember that as she continues. "So she found you, huh? She's been looking online for a couple years."

"No, I was contacted by her parents."

"Mr. Cheerful and the Ice Queen?"

"You know them?"

"Sure as shit I do. Bonnie was my best friend for, like, eight years. I'm Mandy," she tells me, matter-of-fact. She studies my face. "You don't look anything like her. 'Cept for your eyes. But hers are, like, prettier."

I ignore this last part. "The camping trip she was going to go on . . ."

Mandy spits out her gum on the ground and scuffs some dirt over it. "Was with my family, yeah. She was really sneaky about that. Didn't even tell me she was gonna take off, even though she knows I totally would have covered for her. She just calls late the night before, crying, and says that she can't go anymore, but don't come over because everything is super fucked up and she'll talk to me when I get back. Then I find out she told her parents that we're gonna pick her up an hour later, *after* they've gone to work, but don't worry, she'll call from the road. And then *I* get in trouble because now everyone thinks I was, like, aiding and abetting or whatever. What a bitch."

She has gone pale beneath the layers of foundation. That Bonnie has lied is not the issue. That she has lied to *her* is the problem. "And I wasn't getting anything for her, since you asked. I was just checking to see if she was back yet. She borrowed some money from me and my dad cut me off this week because, well, just because, so I need her to pay me back."

"How much money?"

Mandy shrugs. "Like, two bills. Not a big deal, but I'm gonna be dry for the next couple weeks, so . . . whatever. She probably gave it to her asshole boyfriend. She's been leeching ever since she met him 'cause everyone knows he doesn't have any money. That's probably who she's with, by the way."

Everett and Lynn didn't mention a boyfriend, so he must have been one of Bonnie's dirty little secrets. Her room didn't show any evidence of a particular male presence in her life, except for the shirtless young Jacob. Somehow, I don't think he's involved. "Who's the boyfriend?"

Mandy's eyebrows knit together. Her distaste is obvious.

"Tommy Jones. He was here for a semester living with his aunt but her husband hated him so she got rid of him quick. He's like a quarter Inuit or something and all of a sudden he's the key to Bonnie's life. She really digs that native shit, you know? Apparently Mr. Cheerful told her that her real mom was part native and she couldn't get over it." The girl eyes me, hoping I'll be offended. I'm not. When you spend as long in foster care as I have, these blatant attempts at baiting cease to have any effect, positive or negative. What does strike me is how little I thought about what her adoptive parents knew about me when they took her away. It never occurred to me to ask. It never occurred to me that she'd be interested in the woman who abandoned her.

"Did you tell anyone else about him?"

She shrugs. "Just the second cop that came by. The first one that showed up at my house was so clueless. How the fuck was I supposed to tell him about her boyfriend with my mom's freaking knitting circle hanging around. I told the second cop, though, because he just showed up after school and had the decency to, like, pull me aside on the street where there were no parents around."

"What did this second cop look like?"

Her eyes narrow. "What are you, writing her life story?"

I smile. She showed her cards just moments before and now it's too late. Now I know that she's hiding something. "No, but if you don't help me find her, I might tell your parents about Tommy. You don't want them to know about him for a reason, right?"

A flush creeps up her neck. "Fuck you, bitch."

I reach her in a single step and manage to pin her arms to the tree behind her. She tries to knee me in the crotch but I turn my hips to the side. She pants, taking in frightened gasps as our eyes lock. Her breath smells of cigarettes drenched in mint. Even though she is a good five inches taller than me and outweighs me by twenty pounds, she is no match for my strength.

"They don't know you and Bonnie are both sexually active, do they?" I whisper. "If you bring up Tommy and they find her, you're scared that she'll tell them who you've been sleeping with."

Mandy coughs in my face and a blast of saccharine breath assaults my nostrils. "Please, maybe she went off her rocker but she would never spill about me. She's my best friend."

Suddenly, I sense her reluctance, at least enough to guess at the cause. "Ah, it's Tommy then. You two aren't as close. What does he know? That you got rid of the baby?" It's just a hunch I have, but very suddenly her expression changes from defiance to fear. "You know they have records, right?" I say. "I could just call around."

"They . . . they said I didn't need my parents to sign anything. It's confidential."

"Nothing is completely confidential when you're a minor. They keep the records and your parents can file for your medical history." I especially hate lying to kids, but I've come too far now to let her get the upper hand.

Her face crumbles, perhaps at the thought of her allowance being cut off for good. "Bonnie made him . . . she made him pick me up after. He never would have done it if it wasn't for her, but she doesn't have her license so she made him take his uncle's car. Tommy hates me. Now even more because he got kicked out when his uncle found out about the car and he couldn't live with them anymore." Tears form at the corners of her eyes. I had forgotten how fragile children are.

I step back, but am careful to keep eye contact as she collects herself. "What did the second cop look like?"

She thinks for a moment as she wipes the tears away, leaving black streaks of mascara behind. "Hot, but in a professional dude kind of way. White guy, maybe in his thirties or something. Short brown hair. Way nicer body than the first cop. He was eating one of those, you know, seaweed snacks while he was waiting for me, which was so, like, out there because you'd think they'd be eating donuts, right?"

"I see." Mandy just described the not-cop in the sedan. So it's gone beyond watching the house. A private security agent impersonating a police officer to get information out of a teenager sounds more than a little shady, even to me. "How long ago was this?"

"About three days ago. Look, I gotta get to school," she says. "We done here?"

"One more thing. Do you have a photo of Tommy?"

She hesitates.

"I'm just looking for Bonnie, that's all. Just the photo of her boyfriend and I'm out of here, okay?"

She wants nothing more than to end this conversation so she reaches into her bag for her phone and scrolls through it. Children these days are so quick to document their lives. She turns the phone toward me. There on the screen is a photo of Tommy and Bonnie, smoking a spliff and mugging for the camera. Another reason why Mandy wouldn't want her parents knowing about Bonnie's boyfriend. I look at the photo. He's just a child, really. The camera is looking down at the two of them and all I get from him is a forehead, dark eyes, and hair so blue-black and shiny he could be in a shampoo commercial.

"Do you have another picture?"

"Here, you can see him better in this." She snatches the phone away and opens a video log, pausing on one video. "They met at a dance thing. Bonnie, she's a pretty good dancer and Tommy is, too. There was a group of kids at her studio that wanted to form a crew and do shows, but Tommy didn't have the money to join so she paid for him."

She hits play on the video. I see a group of break-dancers start in on a choreographed routine. I recognize Tommy right away, but Bonnie is harder to pinpoint. And then I see her. She's some-where in the back. A solid dancer, holding down the routine. The video zooms in on Bonnie for a moment and even though she's buried in the back, she's got the kind of attitude that makes you pull up short. Good. If she really is on the streets, it's better that she's not some kind of delicate flower.

Mandy smirks as the video comes to an end. She puts the phone back into her bag. "She shoulda known from then he was a loser. She isn't supposed to be paying for him. It's the other way around."

She turns to go, but I step closer, blocking her exit. "Just one last thing."

"Hey, you promised!"

"No, I said one more thing, and this is another. But it's the last."

"Whatever. What do you want?"

"Where can I find Tommy?"

"He went back to live with his mom. She's in Ende-something, I forget the name but it's near Kelowna. She works at some kind of mill. Just so you know, that's probably where Bonnie's at. If you find the bitch, tell her to call me. I want my effin' money back!" Her chafing persona slides back into place. She turns on her heel and stomps away.

As I make my way back to Whisper, who waits patiently in the Corolla a few blocks away from the Walsh house, covering the back window frame with thin slivers of drool, I remember the sheer madness of trying to talk to a teenager. I haven't had reason to attempt it in years. Teenagers are impulsive, emotional, reactionary. It is impossible for them to lie well, though they do it constantly. For example, to their parents. About their sex lives.

But it doesn't matter how much I bend the scenario, the existence of a boyfriend doesn't explain the private security guy sitting on the Walsh house, or why someone who isn't a cop pretended to be one in order to extract information from Bonnie's best friend. Even if Everett and Lynn hired them to look for Bonnie, the one who went talking to Mandy would have no reason to lie about who he was. None of this adds up, but I now have a place to look for the girl. Trouble is, whoever is also looking has three days on me. The not-cop still maintains a presence, so I know that he has not gone to Kelowna to look for Bonnie. Whatever this assignment is, it truly is a team effort if they can afford to leave him here to monitor the house. So it's more than just a throwaway case to WIN Security, more than just routine surveillance work.

The why of it gets me every time. Sometimes the why is immediately obvious but here, I can't find any motive for a security firm to be this interested in an adopted girl from a good home.

Whisper greets me with accusing eyes. She smells the sweat and the adrenaline from my earlier chase and wants to know why I went running without her. "Not everything is about you," I tell her in a brisk voice that is meant to reaffirm that I am the leader of this two-member pack. She refuses to drink the water I brought for her and continues to drool out the window to punish me. When I cruise past the house, I see another discreet sedan parked a few houses down.

The why isn't becoming clearer, it's full of too many loose threads, so I'll have to try something different to figure out what the hell is going on here. When a girl goes missing, it's usually a simple matter. A dark but simple matter. But this seems to get more complicated by the hour.

If the why is too muddled, then maybe I'll have more luck with the who.

# 16

WIN SECURITY IS housed in an innocuous three-story brick building on West Broadway, just off the downtown core. I can walk to it from our east side offices and, for this trip, don't think it wise to bring Whisper along. She doesn't whine or make a sound of protest that I'm leaving her behind this time; she just glares at me and returns to her careful consideration of the threadbare rug on the floor. But from her posture, I know that she's upset. You can't live this long with a female and not recognize her moods.

"I'll bring you a treat when I get back," I say, to lighten the mood. She lifts her gaze and her eyes hold no hope that we will ever see each other again. She is preparing for the worst, but still, her lack of faith in me stings. "I'll be back this afternoon." From her dubious expression, she doesn't think it's likely. She walks away.

"You should be a cat," I call to her retreating back, as a parting shot. She doesn't acknowledge that she's heard it, the bitch.

Outside I see a vagrant rifling through the dumpster and I surreptitiously survey the Corolla to make sure that he hasn't touched it. Not a scratch, well, except for the ones that I have made, so I pass him and try to ignore that he is sniffing at the moldy remnants of a sandwich that someone has tossed without finishing. Desperation makes some things easier to swallow. It's hard to look into the eyes of someone who is in need. Desperation made me an addict for a while and nobody could quite meet my eyes. Can't say I blame them.

"Spare some change?" asks the man. He avoids my gaze and I avoid his. It's better for the both of us this way. He looks to be about sixty years old, but on the streets that would place him anywhere between forty and fifty. As a rule, people don't age gracefully living in back alleys and rifling through dumpsters.

I toss him a granola bar I find in my pocket and he stares at it suspiciously as I beat a hasty exit. Whether or not he eats it is his prerogative. I'm not trying to make any sort of statement with handing out food rather than money. I just don't carry cash on me. That way, if I get mugged, all the asshole will get is something to snack on while he thinks about his life choices.

The streets are busy as I walk down East Hastings in leggings and a dark jacket with reflective stripes, a reluctant thrift store expense. Along with the bicycle helmet and ratty messenger bag, the bill came up to twenty-two dollars, which was twenty-two dollars more than I would have liked to have spent, but after pondering my options this seemed to be the best one.

The drizzling starts just as I pass Main and turn onto Broadway, and I pick up my pace. I doubt anyone in my path has stopped to wonder why a bike messenger is sans bicycle, but I power on just in case. It's just after lunch when I approach the squat three-story building. People are slowly getting back to work. Likely they are stuffed with carbohydrates and sodium and are looking for a quiet corner to take a nap so that their digestive systems can recover. Actually, I'm betting on it, that they just might be distracted enough to let an errant bike messenger slip past their defenses.

The building itself is innocuous. Its weathered brick façade fades into the background and the neatly landscaped walkway is pretty enough to be pleasing to the eye, but doesn't draw unwanted attention. I wait until I see two men wearing slacks, collared shirts, and glasses go up the front walk and then I sidle in behind them, close enough that I'm just a blur on the various subtle cameras pointed in our direction, but not so close that they notice before we're in the doors.

"Oh," one of them says when he sees me enter behind them. He holds the door open awkwardly while balancing a tray of takeout coffee cups. The other one holds a tray, too, so I presume by the way they're dressed that these must be the gofers of the IT department. As I pass by, my shoulder jolts the tray and the man holding the door loses his grip. Tsk-tsk. How clumsy. The other reaches over to help and his own tray gets away from him. Scalding liquid splashes on me from both directions.

"You morons!" I shout. "Look at what you've done! If you ruined my packages I'll sue all of you! I need this goddamn job! How am I going to pay my bills?"

The receptionist hurries over, in full damage control mode. "Are you okay?" she asks me, sending a glare over at the two IT guys.

"No, I am not okay." I muster my finest impression of an imperious messenger, holding up my dripping bag. "Do you have a washroom I can use to sort this out?"

"Oh, our facilities aren't really for public use . . ." she says, her eyes flickering upward to the two cameras set up over her desk.

One is pointed at the door and the other at the second receptionist at the desk. He's watching with undisguised interest.

"Do your employees normally accost the public with scalding hot beverages?" I say, giving her a stare worthy of Medusa,
implying with my eyes that this could be a potential lawsuit if
she's not careful.

She blinks, wants to get rid of me, but sees that I'm not going
without a fight. "But, clearly it's an emergency, so . . . follow me."

Smart lady.

She crosses to a set of double doors just past the elevators.
"Frank, get maintenance in here, please," she says to the other
receptionist at the desk. Almost as an afterthought, she turns to
the two IT guys. "You two better go back and refill your order.
And not on the expense account this time, Walter." The receptionist gives the one named Walter a knowing look and continues on, completely ignoring the other IT guy, whose name she
probably can't even recall.

The two IT guys look crushed, but what are they going to
do? Complain that *I* bumped into *them*? Which, of course, is the
truth. These young men are a decent sort, however, and just
accept that their day has gone from normal to shitty in mere
moments and they're out of pocket for two trays full of designer
coffee.

Past the welcoming wood-paneled reception area, the building is much more sophisticated and austere in the interior than it
appears from outside. This is more in line with what one would
expect from the city's biggest security firm. The hallways are
spacious enough that people can walk comfortably side by side,
but not so spacious that the mounted cameras that are at every

turn will miss you. I thank my good fortune that the peak of my bicycle helmet is long enough to cover the top of my face. How much can someone tell from a chin, anyway? Behind the camera, I feel that someone is watching. It's always better to assume that someone is.

The receptionist swipes her key card at the entrance of the washroom and a light on the black box flashes green. She moves to follow me inside, but I jerk my head toward the trail of coffee drippings that I've left in my wake and say, "Look at the mess! Hope you guys don't have too many appointments this afternoon."

The receptionist frowns and glances at her watch, now concerned about the afternoon appointments. "I better go make sure Frank got in touch with maintenance," she says. "Please wait in the washroom until I come back for you. You're not really supposed to be here, you know." As if it is somehow my fault that coffee got spilled all over me. Which it is.

I wait until the clicking of her heels round the corner before I exit the washroom, my bag hastily wrung out in the sink and the bottom of my shoes dried with paper towels. I sidle down the main corridor and try to look lost, even though I've never met a messenger with a poor sense of direction. The hallway has the sterile feel of a medical research facility and branches out in several directions. I follow along, pretending to check messages on my phone whenever I spot a camera. All doors require a key card to open and I am running out of time when a door opens in front of me, almost knocking me to the ground.

"I have no idea what's taking them so long. Freaking newbs," a harassed woman with tired eyes announces to the room behind her. She is dressed in slacks and a striped shirt, the feminine version of what the IT guys I bumped into were wearing.

"Excuse me."

The woman looks at me, surprised to see me waiting behind the open door. A quick peek inside reveals a large office space crammed with cubicles.

"Yes?" She takes in my helmet and messenger bag. "Aren't you supposed to leave packages at the front?"

"I'm a singing messenger," I tell her. "For Walter. It's his birthday today and his grandma wanted him to have a special surprise."

I'm sweating with the effort of the lie, and my voice has increased a decibel or two, but she is apparently nonplussed by the idea of a sweaty singing messenger, a natural contralto who has suddenly turned mezzo-soprano, because she doesn't seem to notice. She blinks for a minute as her mind processes this all, holds on to the most juicy tidbit of information I've offered, and then turns back to the room. "Hey, guys! Walt's *grandma* sent him a singing messenger for his birthday! A granny-gram!"

The room behind her erupts in a gale of laughter. "I could just wait at his desk, if you don't mind. It's better when they're surprised," I say when the laughter subsides.

"Yeah, yeah, okay. I gotta go pee quick before he comes back. I can't miss this." She points to an empty cubicle at the corner of the room. "Hang out there, but don't touch anything."

I head for the cubicle, nodding at the IT gnomes as I pass by. Their benign faces are eerily lit by their computer screens and they appear like a bespectacled ghastly horde of the digital era. There is an underlying hum of excitement at the prospect of Walter getting serenaded publicly at the behest of his grand-mother by a damp singing messenger in tights.

By my calculations, I have a few precious minutes to get something out of this trip. Walter's laptop is open on his desk, but a swipe of the trackpad on the keyboard shows me that it is password protected. It takes only a few minutes for the IT de-partment to become distracted by their screens again, and when I feel confident that their attention has moved away from me I lean over, placing my bag in front of the computer as a make-shift guard, and type in "password." Not accepted, but it was worth a try.

I search the cubicle for clues to Walter's personality, but either he has none or he is an extremely hard worker. I feel the tick-ing of the clock, even though there are no clocks in the room apart from the ones on computers and phones. His workspace contains only paperwork and detailed to-do lists. No personal effects. Poor Walter.

The door to the office opens and I catch a glimpse of the re-ceptionist with the IT woman that let me in trailing behind her. They both look confused and flustered. The IT woman points in my direction. I'm out of time. I slip the laptop into my messen-ger bag and step out of Walt's cubicle as the receptionist heads straight for me. The door opens again and the two IT guys I met at the entrance of the building appear, carrying trays of coffee. They were quicker than I expected. Someone must have called ahead to order.

I have never liked the improvisational nature of early jazz because sometimes you can stray so far away from a song that it's hard to find your way back. You can get lost, and lose your audience while you're at it. But the good thing about it, the very best thing, is that moment when you don't know what happens next but you know it's going to be good. Looking from the receptionist to the room full of expectant IT workers, who are now waiting slack-jawed for something to happen to turn this into a day that deserves the effort they put in ironing their collared shirts and putting on clean underwear, I feel a sense of daring burst through.

As the receptionist opens her mouth to speak, I make eye contact with the plaid-shirted IT worker named Walter and break into a very loud "Happy Birthday." A rich, husky contralto escapes from my lips and bathes them all in a birthday song like they've never heard before. I have not sung in more than fifteen years, but my vocal cords remember what to do before my mind processes what's actually happening here. The room goes quiet, stripped of sound and breath and movement that do not emanate from me. A tremor in Walter's hand shakes the tray of coffee as I move toward him. I hit my stride and hold the final run for several seconds longer than anticipated. It feels like it will never end and I'm soaring with the headiness of it.

When I was a child, Lorelei, the beautiful one, the baby, could smile at you and if you happened to drop dead the next moment, you would feel blessed that hers was the last face you'd seen. Me? Well, you could stare at me for an hour straight, look away for a minute, and not be able to describe my face. But if I sang to you . . . you would never forget it.

My mouth closes but my last note floats there in the air, the reverberation in the room keeping it alive. And I wonder if the people in this office know that the high ceiling, hardwood floors, sparse office furniture, and shoe-box shape of the room have created a perfect sound chamber if any of them wanted to hold an impromptu concert. The acoustics in here are incredible.

They stare at me, stunned, and I feel perversely happy that I've still got it, even though it has been more than a decade since I last wanted it, and that it still has the power to make closed jaws hang open and cold hearts turn to putty in my hands. The note dies out and I take their shock as an opportunity to tell Walter that his grandmother loves him and head for the door. Behind me I hear Walter finally protest that it isn't even his birthday and his granny is on a cruise, but then the door closes and I'm too far away anyway to see the outcome. I feel a twinge of pity for poor Walter; he's never going to live this one down.

The receptionist, no slouch herself, catches up to me moments later with long strides that could put a Kenyan marathon runner to shame. Boy is she quick. "I thought I told you to stay in the washroom?" she says, without breaking her pace.

"It smelled really bad in there. Won't happen again."

We're practically sprinting now, both of us wanting me to be gone as soon as possible. "No, it won't. You never told me you were a singing messenger. I thought you were a courier. When the coffee spilled on your bag—"

"Those were the words to the, um, songs," I say as we reach the doors leading out to the front entrance.

"You need lyrics to 'Happy Birthday'?" She puts a hand on the door, blocking me from opening it. I tense, preparing to push her aside. She's thin, but in great shape, and I see her bicep flex underneath her sheer blouse. She looks at me, frowning. "You have an incredible voice, but you can't just go wandering about people's offices, okay? It's quite unprofessional. What is the name of your company? Is it Singing Sensations?"

"Mmm," I say. She takes this as affirmative. I duck under her arm and pull open the door.

"You'll be receiving a complaint!" she shouts at my back.

I see a security guard approaching from the elevators and I make a beeline for the entrance. He's also fast, but nothing compared to the receptionist. I am close now to the doors and make it out and down the walkway by the time he clears the lobby. I weave through traffic and horns blare in my wake. There is not much time, so I hail a cab.

"Waterfront Station, please."

The cabdriver stares at me in the rearview window, taking in my attire and the messenger bag I'm clutching to my chest. "Stole your bike, eh?"

I don't reply. I have lied enough for today and can't stomach yet another. There is stolen property in my bag, property that can easily be traced. Or so it seems to my overactive imagination. I pull out my cell phone and send a text, *911, Waterfront Station,* and then bury the phone deep into my pocket.

The cabdriver takes my silence as an affirmative and shakes his head as he changes lanes without signaling. Horns blare behind him, too. This is hardly the smooth getaway that I had planned but, in all fairness, I hadn't anticipated stealing the computer. "This city is going to shit," says the driver, who I can see from the laminated card on the back of the seat is named Maurice. "All the junkies and crackheads. You wouldn't believe what I see every day, lady. I came to Canada for a better life, but it's the same old shit everywhere."

"Free health care, though. Right?"

"You think I don't pay for it with how much they tax me?"

I study his profile and try to place his country of origin, but in the end it doesn't really matter because he's right. It is the same shit everywhere. I wonder whether Bonnie has had a better life with the Walshes. She lived in a big house with two parents who cared about her. It's more than I could have given her, even if I'd wanted to. And still, look at what happened.

The cab pulls over and I'm forced to pay this additional expense. They aren't kidding when they say having children is financially draining. "Hope you get your bike back," Maurice says to me before he pulls off.

I unzip my jacket and leave it, along with my helmet, in a pile just outside the entrance to the busiest station in the city. Then with my hood up I slip inside to wait.

# 17

SHE SHOWS UP dressed entirely in black and wearing a heavy black wig and dark makeup. She has chosen to keep her jewelry light, however, and sports only her basic eyebrow and nose rings. This is by far the cleverest disguise I have ever seen. She is a mixture of Dutch and Japanese, but by her current appearance you'd never know what she really looks like underneath her mask. People pay attention to the outfit, not the person.

She sits beside me on the bench. "What's the emergency?" she says in a husky voice, only slightly deeper than mine. "You know I dance tonight, right? These legs ain't gonna shave themselves, babe."

I hand her the sleek laptop. "Password protected."

She frowns, but takes it regardless. "I thought you had a job. Never pegged you for a thief—ooh, this is nice." She flips the top open and runs her hands over the smooth keyboard. She's wearing leather driving gloves, leaving no fingerprints in her wake.

"I do have a job. This is for something else. And it's from WIN Security."

She stills. "Honey, you stole a laptop from a security firm? You know they can track this."

"I wouldn't ask if it wasn't important."

"I wouldn't have come if I thought otherwise," she says,

eyeing me. Her gaze is unflinching. Out of all the sad sacks at the meetings I used to go to, she was the least sad sack of them all. And she took pains to mask her real identity by using her onstage persona, which seemed to be a prudent step. A drag queen named Simone by night, the creator of web-based security software named Simon by day. She was the one who suggested Brazuca as my sponsor, though I suspect this might have started out as a private joke on him—and possibly ended that way as well. "I do a lot of shady shit, babe, you know that, but this is a bit much even for me. Why?"

"Someone might be in danger," I tell her. You don't get something for nothing. For someone to break her own code, there's got to be a damn good reason for it.

She stares at me for a good thirty seconds and I use the surplus time to wonder how she's able to wield a liquid eyeliner wand like a precision instrument. My few attempts at that sort of thing when I was just out of adolescence only resulted in me looking like an astonished raccoon.

"Okay," she says. "Give me some space. We should be fine for a little bit as long as it's offline. You're lucky I know a thing or two about WIN."

I take a walk while Simone does what she does. I have no clue what that is and would never interrupt her concentration to ask. But I am curious. This kind of skill has always fascinated me. My own computer abilities were gleaned mostly from public library workshops. Librarians don't teach you how to hack and, in my experience, tend to take offense when you ask them.

"I'm in," she says, when I return. "What are we looking for?"

"Last name Walsh. First name Everett, Lynn, or Bronwyn."

She runs a search of their database for each of their names, but nothing comes up. "You sure they're in here?"

How else to explain the not-cop in the company sedan? "They should be."

"We don't have much time," she reminds me. A security guard saunters by, hands on his hips. From the deliberate way he's not looking at her, I know he'll be back.

"Pull up their client list."

She taps a few keys and a list of names appears. I take pictures from my phone's camera as she scrolls through. This takes far too long and we're both sweating by the time I snap the final picture. Without another word, she puts the laptop on the seat next to her and walks away. I slip it back into my bag and head in the opposite direction. Outside the station, I lean against the railing overlooking the ocean and slide the bag off my shoulders. The marina is so busy that you can hardly hear the splash.

I don't wait for it.

I walk as quickly as I can away from it and resist the urge to look over my shoulder. I learned that bravado from Simone. Stealing, however . . . that's just something I've always known how to do.

# 18

I STAND OUTSIDE the apartment block in Surrey with a steaming pizza box warming my hands. It's busy. People are just returning home for the evening. They cast ravenous glances in my direction. The window on the third floor that I'm looking at is fully illuminated, so at least there's one lucky break for me today.

An elderly woman in an oversize trench coat hobbles toward me from the sidewalk, up the paved walkway, and moves, very slowly, toward the door. Her concentration on where she will place her foot next is complete. Once she fishes out her keys and opens the door, I help her prop it open with my foot and shrug apologetically, nodding to the pizza box as if to say, Look, my dinner is compromising the safety of our building. Whatcha gonna do. She glares at me and shuffles away. Apart from the entrance, accessible only by key or by being buzzed in by someone inside, there are no other security measures. I take the elevator up to the third floor, knock on Amir's door, and listen as quiet footsteps approach the entryway. There is some motion behind the peephole and then another pause.

"Pizza," I say.

"I didn't order pizza," comes the soft, accented voice behind the door.

"It says here this is for Amir, but I'm a little late." I hold the pizza up to the peephole so he can see it, and wait for his stomach to overpower his will. A few seconds later, it does.

Harrison Baichwal opens the door to Amir's apartment and stares at me. His eyes are drawn toward the box in my hands. "Amir just left for work. How did you get up? I didn't hear the buzzer."

I shrug. "Someone was coming in and I took my chance."

Now that the door is open he gets a clearer picture of me and sees that I'm not a pizza delivery person. I'm not dressed for it. I don't have a warming bag or a uniform. His fear pulses outward from his body like a magnetic field. "W-who are you?"

"Someone who's as hungry as you are and knows your name, Harrison. Do you want to talk out here about that night a woman got killed at your store or can we have some privacy?"

After a brief hesitation, he waves me in. Once inside I see that he has been spending his time cooped up in the apartment cleaning. There is not a spot of dirt on any surface. The furnishings are sparse and cobbled together from mismatched garage sale pieces, but I can't fault their cleanliness. I wonder if Harrison Baichwal would be willing to share his skill set with me but Whisper would never let him into our basement. She's very private about her space. Since we've been living together, no one has ever been in there but the two of us.

Harrison disappears into the kitchen and returns moments later with two plates. "I told you people that I'm not going to testify, all right? I've done everything you asked. Nobody even knows I'm here."

"I do."

He frowns at me and grabs the pizza box. One slice per plate and a plate dutifully handed over to me.

"I was hired by the kid's lawyer," I say.

Harrison freezes, a slice oozing with cheese halfway to his mouth. "You're not with—"

"Nope."

He puts the pizza slice back down on his plate and removes the plate from his lap. "Have you told the police where I am?"

"Not yet. Dodging a summons to appear in court is serious business. Just wanted to give you the chance to make it right on your own."

Baichwal isn't moved by my attempt to manipulate him. He gets up and paces the room. "You think I don't know that? I've been in this country twenty years, work fourteen hours a day every day, always pay my taxes, always obey the rules. You think I would ignore my obligations if I had any other choice?"

"So what? The gang that operates out of this building, they threaten that if you get on the stand they're going to tank your business? You've got insurance, right?"

He shakes his head in disgust. "You people. Always about money, always about work. They don't threaten my business. They don't have to. They know where I live! Do you see what I'm talking about?" He looks away, tries to compose himself. There is a quiet despair in his eyes when he turns to me and I'm reminded of Everett Walsh and our meeting at the café. It is a father's plea. "Please . . . please don't tell the police I'm here. I promise these drug dealers that I won't testify. I even hide here in Amir's apartment so the lawyers can't find me. I have to protect my family."

"That kid that went into your store, that killed that woman. He didn't act alone."

"What does it matter if he was alone or not? He walked into my store with a gun!" He paces five steps from one wall to the other, and then back again. A hand rakes through his hair and he comes to a decision. "Okay, you want to know? There was another one of those thugs waiting at the entrance, just outside of where the cameras are, but that boy was there to rob me! I was giving him the money, but the lady was in the back. He didn't see her and then when he did . . . He got scared and the gun went off. It was an accident. But he made the choice to be there."

"Why wasn't Amir there? That was the plan, right? The dealers around here knew the store, knew that Amir was supposed to be on shift that night, so why wasn't he?"

"Don't blame him. He's a good boy. They follow him one day in the staircase, tell him that they gonna come in and they don't want no funny business from him. They say they will come back when me or Bidi are working instead if he doesn't do what they tell him. They don't want to scare us because we're old, we have children, so they gonna come when he's there. He . . . well, he's not used to this kind of thing. He can't sleep when he gets home the night before it was supposed to happen and he takes a few sleeping pills."

"And misses his shift."

Harrison nods. "He never shows up to relieve me, and that's when they come in to rob me."

"If you tell them what happened, the police would try to protect you." Normally I wouldn't say something like this, but when mothers are murdered, the police usually pay attention. Still, the words feel stiff coming out of my mouth and Harrison Baichwal isn't fooled.

He scoffs. "Yes, because the police are so reliable in our neighborhood, right? No, I don't trust anyone with the most important thing in my life. My family. My wife, my children. They are what matters. I came to this country to give them a better life. What kind of man would I be if I didn't do everything I could to keep them safe? What kind of person? After the trial, I come back to my store and everything's gonna be okay. That's what they tell me."

"The drug dealers?" I don't even try to keep the skepticism from my voice.

"So what if this is what they are? I have no choice but to trust them! Do you see?"

We sit there without speaking for a long time, me and this frightened man. I know what it's like to be scared for your life. I wonder if he has nightmares, if his subconscious plots against him when he closes his eyes, bringing back memories of what he saw that night.

We are both immersed in the past and our mistakes. The pizza gets cold, but neither of us makes another move to touch it. When my uncertainty of what to do next becomes absolute I get up and leave. I stop outside of the building and look up at his window. The light is now off in the apartment, but the curtain is lifted slightly to one side. I can feel his eyes on me, watching, waiting for what I'll do next. His fate is in my hands. He knows this as much as I do.

# 19

WHEN I GET to the office, I can tell that the Seb and Leo are still here, putting in a late night, but something is wrong. Leo's door is closed. Leo's office door is never closed. Through the opaque glass window covering the top third of the door, I see three outlines moving inside the office. Two are the familiar shapes of Seb and Leo and the other looms over them, even though they are all sitting down. The voices in the office are muffled, but if I edge close to the ficus near the wall between my desk and Leo's office and put my ear to the door, I can hear almost every word.

". . . You're saying she's an expert in lie detection?" the stranger in the office says. There is genuine surprise in his voice. I can't place the accent, but something about it seems familiar.

"Amateur," Seb says.

"An amateur expert?"

"The most talented amateur we've ever seen. Puts some of the expert lie spotters we consult with in this country to shame," Leo adds. He's lying, of course, but the stranger doesn't notice because he's not an expert, amateur or otherwise. They've never consulted another lie spotter because they get me, at a special discounted rate.

"So her duties are not merely secretarial?"

"We're not discussing her duties." I can tell by Seb's voice that his patience with the conversation is at an end. "Can you please tell us what this is about?"

"Do you know who this woman is?"

"What do you mean?" says Leo. "Of course we know who she is." He's outraged on my behalf, but I can hear his restraint.

"Nora Watts, born in Winnipeg. Father dead by suicide. Mother's whereabouts unknown. In and out of foster care as a teenager. No fixed address since she left the Canadian Forces, arrested once for assault during a bar fight."

"Convicted?" Seb asks.

"No, the charges were dropped."

"And when was this?" This is what I love about Seb. You can't win him over with an emotional appeal until he has all the facts. It's what makes him a brilliant journalist, but a shitty romantic partner. It's almost impossible to manipulate a person like him.

"Six years ago," says the stranger.

Leo rises from behind his desk and paces to the window. "So why are you here now? What do you want from her?"

"She's a person of interest in a break-in."

"And you're from WIN Security?"

"Yes."

"Was the break-in at your establishment or at one of your clients'?"

The man hesitates, as though he doesn't want to admit that WIN's own security had been breached. "I'm not at liberty to say. I'd appreciate any information as to her whereabouts."

"Well, she doesn't really do much work for us anymore," Leo says. "Cutbacks, you know. Our office isn't exactly flooded at the moment."

"We call her when things get busy but we don't ask her to come in very often," Seb adds. If this not-cop has had any experience whatsoever in interrogation, they aren't fooling him. "We haven't needed her in weeks."

"What's the number that you use to reach her at?"

Seb hesitates. "If the police contact us, I'll share that information. But for now I have to ask you to leave."

There's a pause as the men in the office size each other up. But there's really no legal requirement for Seb to give out my number and the man knows it.

"I see," the stranger says. His voice is still measured, but has gotten softer, the way an outlaw speaks in the few vital moments before dawn, when his gun is loaded at his hip and the gunslinger across from him has twitchy hands. "Ask her to call me when you speak with her next." A card is exchanged and a shadow moves toward the door.

Oh, shit. I edge away from the ficus. The only place left to go is into the open kitchenette or out the door.

"Wait a minute."

The shadow turns at the sound of Leo's voice. Leo, who isn't sure what's happening, knows that whatever it is, he doesn't like it. It gives me enough time to slip out of the office and up to the second floor, where a massage clinic has rented the entire level. The door to their offices is locked, so I'm trapped on the landing. From the stairway I hear footsteps traverse the hallway and come to a stop in front of the main entrance, at the bottom of the staircase up to the second floor. These footsteps are not in a hurry to leave. They seem pensive, as if Seb and Leo have given the owner of the feet plenty to think about. What else did they tell him and why does he want to know? That he has information about my past has thrown me off balance.

I risk a peek around the corner and see the figure of a large man with a shaved head open the front door. He is about to step out but something makes him turn his head in my direction. I duck and wait for several breathless seconds as he looks toward the massage clinic. I glance around for a weapon, but there's nothing around here. As quietly as I can, I extract my key ring from my pocket. On it are five keys. One for the Corolla, one for the main entrance, one for the back entrance, one for the office itself, and the last is for the basement, where Whisper is waiting for me. I arrange each of the keys between my fingers and close my fist over the ring. Crude, but it's the best I have.

Only a few seconds have passed.

"Anybody there?" the stranger says. He takes a step toward the staircase.

With no door between us I can hear him clearly now. My breath catches in my throat, lodges in there like an errant fishbone, and I feel the bile rise up from my stomach to meet it. Fifteen years has not altered it in the least. I now know where I've heard that voice. Quiet, almost muffled orders as they wrapped my limp body up in a sheet. Flashes of red that I mistook for my blood, but no, I remember now that I had lost most of that on the floor. The red stayed with me, though, and the timbre of the voice that ordered the disposal of my body.

The fabric of my shroud, and this man's voice.

I have this feeling now, this feeling that knocks the breath right out of me, that my past has not just come looking. It has found me. It's no coincidence, then, that now that the girl is missing, this man is the one who shows up asking questions. That from whatever grainy security footage WIN Security has from my break-in, this is the man who recognizes me. And I know that wherever he is, the other will not be so very far behind. The other with his smooth, manicured hands that pressed me into a bed, dragged me along a hardwood floor, then pulled me into the woods.

And I can't help the tiny, mirthless laugh that sneaks up on me just then. That I just barely manage to hold in my throat so that it doesn't escape my lips. Because maybe Everett Walsh wasn't so far off when he asked about Bonnie's biological father. Maybe I shouldn't have been so quick to dismiss the possibility. Maybe this is all connected somehow and I'm only just now starting to see it.

I hear another set of footsteps approaching. "Let me get the door for you," Seb says.

The stranger hesitates.

"Thank you," he says finally. I listen to the door closing behind them and wait on the landing for ten minutes afterward with the keys to my life stuck in my fist and the ring sweaty in my palm.

# 20

I CAN FEEL Whisper staring at me and I know what she must be thinking. She's wondering why her personal food provider is sitting in the dark with four full bottles of painkillers in front of her, caps off. They are your basic over-the-counter painkillers, nothing close to fentanyl or Percocet, though I could get them if I really wanted to. The over-the-counter stuff will do the trick if taken in a large enough quantity.

It is nearing midnight and my phone is somewhere across the room, where I have flung it after going through the images from the WIN Security laptop. The absence of three names on their client list confirms what I have begun to suspect. No Bonnie, Lynn, or Everett Walsh. Whatever is happening here, happening with Bonnie, has spun out of control. So much so that WIN's surveillance of the Walsh house is officially unsanctioned but unofficially present.

I'm tempted to reach for the bottles, but something holds me back. Still.

Do you know what post-traumatic stress disorder is? Not the term that they bandy about on television, but the actual reality of it? Post-traumatic stress isn't just reserved for soldiers that experience emotional turmoil because of what they've seen in combat. It's when something is so disruptive to the mind that a person can't compute what has happened. You know when you feel it that some part of the human experience has gone off the rails. Some part of you will recognize that.

In the time I was enlisted, which, admittedly, wasn't very long, I never saw anything that could compare with what happened after I left. I don't know how to explain the horror of waking up from a long sleep filled with nightmares to find a child growing in your belly, a reminder that sometimes nightmares occur when you're awake, too. A huge, distended stomach as evidence that something happened to you several months before, but you can't remember what or when, though the how is pretty damn obvious and you only have hazy visions of the who. You don't know the rest, but there, taking root inside of you, is proof that something horrible, something that you did not say yes to, did in fact occur. And you search your memories in desperation, hoping for anything that will shed light. But you just can't remember. All you want is for the evidence to slip away quietly in the night, and you're willing to let yourself go along with it.

But the evidence does not slip away and she does not do it quietly, either. She runs, setting off a chain of events that brings me here, now. At the edge.

Whisper rises from her vigil across the room and slinks toward me. As she passes the table, her tail brushes the bottles and pills go scattering across the floor. Though it seems an innocent enough mistake, it can't be an accident. Because I know her. Because she's the only guardian angel that I've ever had. The bitch did this on purpose and even if I allow for her heart being in the right place, as opposed to her unwillingness to find another food provider, she has just forced my hand. I won't guzzle pills off the floor. I'm not that far gone yet.

I retrieve my phone, mercifully intact, from the far side of the room and listen to my old messages. The ones I have pretended don't exist, but can't seem to erase, either.

I feel like seeing a ghost from my past, but not tonight. I send a text. The reply comes almost immediately, as I somehow knew it would. *Tomorrow.*

# 21

THE NEXT AFTERNOON, I wait for my ghost at the most beautiful building in the city. Elliptical on the exterior and built to resemble the Roman Colosseum, the Vancouver Public Library is nine stories high and part of a complex that takes up an entire block. Two doors on either end lead onto a covered sidewalk with the glass-encased library along one side, and little indoor shops and attached office building on the other.

I stand on the sixth floor and watch as the birds that get caught in this pretty glass case swoop past, searching for the exit. Opposite me, just above the covered shops, I look at the art banners and feel, like I always do, a sense of deep reverence. On each banner there's an outstretched hand, each in a slightly different position, but every one of them held out in welcome.

Because I like the view, I don't mind waiting the hour and a half it takes me to finally accept that he stood me up. That's when I know that something is seriously wrong. And just as this realization sinks in, I see a lithe, muscular man weaving his way through a tour group and toward the library entrance. He doesn't match the other patrons in their heavy raincoats and studious expressions. Because he's not in a car and because he's not munching on a healthy snack, I don't immediately recognize the not-cop from outside the Kerrisdale house. He stands in the center of the concourse and looks up. His eyes meet mine, briefly, but long enough for me to register a flicker of recognition on his face. It could be he remembers me walking past Bonnie's house, or perhaps from WIN's security footage. Or maybe it is simply the intensity with which I am staring at him. I don't stop to give it much thought because now I am moving swiftly through the stacks.

The elevator would be foolish, would leave me at the mercy of whoever was on the other side of the doors when they open, so I take the central escalator down to the fourth floor, which still has areas under construction from the big centralized move the library has undertaken.

I crouch between two carts of unsorted books. I have found surprise to be the most important factor when dealing with an attacker, especially if he is bigger than me. Surprise and an offensive strategy that uses my low center of gravity to subvert his higher one. A smaller person never wants to play fast and loose with the element of surprise. That sort of laissez-faire attitude can leave her naked and unconscious in the woods somewhere.

There is the sound of oncoming footsteps and, sensing his location rather than seeing it, I send a cart careening in the direction of the sound. The not-cop dives out of the way, but the cart smashes into his shin and he falls to the ground with a grunt. I push a row of shelves over, but it doesn't budge. It is bolted to the ground because this is a big and important library that leaves nothing, even unsecured furniture, to chance. I swear lightly and grab another cart, which I use both as a shield and a weapon as I sprint directly at him. His leg buckles under him as he tries to shuffle out of the way, his eyes comically wide, like in a cartoon. And, like a cartoon, there's a sickening crack as the cart strikes him, but I have no interest in pausing to see the outcome.

A middle-aged security guard is bounding up the escalator two steps at a time on creaky knees.

"There's a man over there—I think he's causing some trouble," I say, gasping and pointing in the direction of the fallen WIN Security agent. I can hear him shouting into his phone, describing me. Luckily, the aging security guard's hearing isn't as finely tuned as mine. "He tried to harass a lady and she ran him over with a cart." There is no point mentioning the lady is me. Again, I don't stop to see what happens. I make for the escalator going down and hope an altercation with the security guard will buy me a head start out of the building.

At the entrance to the library, I spot a trim man with an athletic gait striding through the north plaza directly toward me. It can't be a coincidence, not with the not-cop presumably still up on the fourth floor. This newest poster child for a well-used gym membership hasn't seen me yet. I move quickly through the south doors, but there is yet another male fitness model powering his way up from Howe Street into the south plaza and a friend on steroids approaching from the other side. I'm blocked in all directions but up, so I take the staircase to my left, going into the attached office building of the complex.

There's a shout as they spot me.

I can hear them behind me, closing in. They're in better shape, with longer legs, and are right on my heels by the time I reach the next landing. I push my way onto the walkway leading to the office building. The not-cop I'd seen on the library concourse makes his way toward me from that side. I am sandwiched between the two at my back and the one in front of me and there's nowhere to go but down. I slip my belt free of its loopholes. It's not much, but it's all I've got.

"Don't be scared. We just want to talk," says the not-cop in front in dulcet tones, as if he's talking to a bad puppy. His eyes flicker to the two others closing in behind me. They move cautiously, though, just in case I've got something other than a belt hidden away.

"You're perfectly safe with us," the one immediately behind me adds in an unconvincing voice that spans about three decibels.

"Just come with us quietly and we won't report the break-in to the police," growls the one on steroids.

What do they think I am, a novice?

Every single one of them is lying.

Thankfully, none of them belongs to the voice that I heard at the office. I don't think I could handle that. I narrow my eyes at the one in front of me. "Don't be scared," he said. But that's the worst thing you could say in this situation. Fear is our warning system. It's what keeps us alive. He should have said, "Be very afraid, the odds are against you." I would have respected that.

There was a woman in the States who had damaged the fear center in her brain and was constantly having near-death experiences because of it. She couldn't judge dangerous situations because she'd become inherently fearless. Her life was consistently in jeopardy. Fear, despite what various self-help gurus seem to think, is a perfectly healthy response. And right now, a necessary one. My spine stiffens and my shoulders hunch in on themselves. Even if I don't remember the violence done upon it, my body does. It's protecting me, because I've done such a poor job in the past. The violence is absent from my mind, other than a few snatches of memories that come at night when I relax and close my eyes, but my body never forgets. It stands vigilant, ready to protect or to run at any sign of danger. It doesn't trust my judgment. So I'm not totally to blame for what happens next. Some of it is just my body, weighing the options and deciding on what kind of pain it would prefer.

By now, everyone with a seat at the glass window opposite gapes at us from the library. The visually open architecture of the building has led several library patrons to believe that there's going to be a spectacle. They pull out their cell phones so that they can share it with their friends later. The not-cops are as uncomfortable with this as I am. The security guard posted at the entrance of the library way down on the ground floor is as shocked as the rest of them. Any second now he's bound to pull out his own phone.

On the art banner hanging from the wall there is an out-stretched hand depicted in beautiful reds, yellows, and blacks. A symbol not only of welcome, but of reconciliation as well. This gesture is mimicked by the man in front of me, whose bland ex-pression has twisted into a glower as he reaches for me in a move that is so opposite from reconciliation that it's almost obscene.

"There's nowhere else to go, sweetheart," he says.

I think it's the "sweetheart" that does it for me.

There is a collective gasp from the library patrons as I loop the belt over the railing and launch myself over the edge. The not-cop closest to me grabs a fistful of my jacket, but his hold is too tenuous and it slips through his fingers. The belt doesn't give me a lot of reach, but it's enough to just barely grasp a corner of the art banner in my gloved hand on my way down. I release the belt from my other hand, hear a loud tearing sound as the banner is ripped from its restraints at the top, and as it falls, I fall with it. I was aiming for the concourse below but the ground rises fast and I don't let go in time. Instead, I go swinging back toward the wall and the banner is now hanging off only on the bottom rung, but it's enough for me to slide down the length of it as I go swinging toward the second floor and execute a bracing roll as I hit the ground.

"Damn it!" comes a shout from above.

The not-cops above me don't dare follow my route down; their joints are far too precious for them to consider such a thing. My ankle buckles under me as I run for the staircase in the north plaza, but I don't feel the pain yet. I know it will come, but not until the adrenaline has worn off. That stunt has given me a slight advantage, but they're in better shape and will catch up unless I pick up the pace.

There are more barked orders as the not-cops scurry back for the fire escape but, even limping on a badly sprained ankle, once I'm out in the city I can disappear as if I'd never been there at all. Out on the streets, I have the advantage. I know the roads and the alleys, the dark nooks and secret passages. I have slept on these streets and walked them at all hours of day and night. Light and dark. Nothing scares me out here anymore because this is my playground. I am transparent, like the rainwater that falls down on us now in a fine mist, and so I melt into the damp pavement and flow through the city, keeping to the dirty puddles and stench of human waste. The places no one else would think to go.

# 22

I SIT IN the alley at the back of the Hastings office, near the dumpster, until dark. Earlier, at a convenience store down the street, I bought garbage bags, a newspaper, and an ACE bandage. After bandaging my ankle, I use the bags as a barrier between me and the ground and crumple the pages of the newspaper. These balled-up sheets go in my clothes as insulation.

The rain has been relentless today, but it somehow feels like it has always been this way. Because I'm in a terrible mood, I think about my sister.

I don't remember exactly how old I was when I realized that Lorelei and I were not the same. That we would never be. Same mother and father (I think). Roughly the same genetic material. But throughout our lives, the sun shone down on her while a damned rain cloud seemed to hover over me. Wherever I went people would step aside to avoid being drenched, whereas with her the exact opposite was true. They would move closer and she would shine brighter. Me, though? My cloud still won't give me a rest. It follows wherever I go and I've come to expect it, even enjoy how the damp air feels on my face. When there's no rain, there's snow. I am a harbinger of precipitation. But the sky isn't weeping for me; it's just letting me know that I shouldn't get too comfortable. That a dark cloud overhead is biding its time, sending a little squirt down every now and then to let me know that it's there. So I'll be ready.

I watch the back of the building, my whole body clammy, even with my newspaper insulation, and with a right ankle that is on fire. The same vagrant I'd given a granola bar to wanders nearby, picking through the litter. "Got any more of those bars, sweetheart?"

What's with this sweetheart stuff? Because his tone isn't patronizing, I fish around in my pocket and hand him one. He unwraps it right in front of me and breaks off half, returning the rest. With a tip of his grimy hat, he shuffles off and I am left with a soggy half of a granola bar in my hand, wondering how long it's been since someone legitimately looked at me and thought "sweet" and "heart" in the same breath.

The rain amplifies and in this sudden deluge, I can wait no longer. Whisper is probably up by now, thinking about urinating indoors. I slip through the back door and am about to go straight through to the basement when something, I'm not quite sure what, makes me turn toward the main hallway instead. The door to the office is closed, but there is a light on inside, visible by a strip just at the bottom of the door. No one but me usually stays at the office this late, and that is only because I happen to live in the basement underneath.

Inside, I find Seb going through the bottle of whisky he stashes in the bottom drawer of his desk, and making some good progress. It was full the last time I checked and now it's almost half-gone. He stares at me as I come in, eyes red behind his glasses. I see my name scrawled on a manila envelope on the desk.

He doesn't comment on the fact that I'm favoring my right leg or that I'm dripping all over his floors and there's a wad of garbage bags and balled-up newspaper under my arm. "Sit down, Nora."

Though he hasn't said this loudly or forcefully, I know he means business. Normally I take offense at this kind of tone, but I owe Seb, and he knows it. So I sit and watch as he leans back in his chair and gathers his thoughts. He pushes the bottle of whisky toward me and for a second my fingers reach toward it before I remember that this is my greatest weakness and that for Whisper and the girl, I can't afford to give in. Not even a little bit. Not even once. My fingers retract and find their way to the arm of the chair, where I dig my nails into the wood and then run the pads of my fingertips over the scratches I made.

Seb puts the bottle back in the drawer and I am able to breathe deeply again. It occurs to me that he has just tested me and I am once again in awe of his cleverness. I have never admitted to him that I'm an alcoholic, but somehow he must have known.

"We've known each other a long time," Seb begins. This is his standard interview technique. Start with something irrefutable, preferably something light. Make the other person comfortable. I nod, but say nothing in return.

"Now, I never asked where Mike Starling from the *Post* got your name. He just said that he knew someone who might be able to help me with that piece I was doing with Rebecca Pruitt. You remember?"

After relapse two but before three. Yes, I remember, and probably better than he does. "The sex worker assaults in East Van."

He smiles. There is genuine warmth there, warmth that I have not always felt that I deserved. "You did a great job getting me those interviews."

I say nothing. He wouldn't have hired me on afterward if I hadn't.

"I wouldn't have given you the job afterward if Starling hadn't gone to bat for you."

Oh.

"That being said, I've never regretted the decision."

There's that smile again.

"Then Starling goes overseas, becomes a foreign correspondent, and I don't hear from him for years. Last week, he calls me out of the blue looking for you. He won't come to the office, ranting about how he's being followed. I give him your number and then . . ." Seb pauses here and his friendly demeanor turns cold. "He goes missing. Know anything about that?"

I hesitate. This is not a matter of trust. If anyone has my trust, it's this man. It's a matter of bringing him into a story that I don't fully understand and one that might, judging by what happened at the library just a few hours ago, put him and Leo in danger. "He wanted to meet with me but he never showed up."

"Why did he want to meet with you?"

"I don't know."

"Why did you break into WIN Security? What were you looking for?"

"I'm not sure yet."

"Was it this?" He nudges the envelope to me. I see that it has been opened. There's a single key inside.

I stare at the key, perplexed. "Who sent it?"

"Starling," he says, just as I realize it for myself. "When we worked together I'd seen enough of his notes to recognize the handwriting on the envelope. What does this key open, Nora?"

"I don't know. I've never seen it before."

"There seems to be a lot you don't know lately," he says, an edge to his voice that I hear only when he's talking to Melissa. Just like that, I'm relegated to the ex-wife level on the pain-in-the-ass spectrum. He takes off his glasses and cleans them with the edge of his shirt. For a moment we just sit there in his office and stare at the plaques from his three Canadian Association of Journalists awards, proudly displayed next to his degree from Queen's University and his certificate of completion of French pastry, level one, from a culinary school in Montreal.

He rakes his hand through his thick dark hair and gazes at me from over the top of his glasses. "My work is very important to me," he says finally. "For a long time, it was the only thing I really had in the world to call my own. Only thing that made me happy."

With the advent of the Internet, everybody fancies themselves a journalist. Everybody has access to a camera on their phone. The old news institutions are crumbling because people no longer want to pay the price for information if they can get it for free. But there is an art to dedicated reporting, to the research it takes to give a full picture. Seb is an artist in the way he processes information, in how he relays it to others. Whatever is sensationalistic in his work gets there naturally on its own merit. His work ethic is what has kept him employed and respected. And, apparently, I'm now a liability to that sterling reputation of his.

"A research associate who's breaking into places and lying about where she is and what she's doing . . . I don't know what to think. If you'd just told me . . ." He trails off and looks at me with a desperate plea in his eyes. With a child he only sees on the weekends, a broken marriage, and a lover he doesn't quite understand, he's a man who takes simple pleasure in examining an issue until he lays it bare, exposes its bones, losing himself in the minutiae of research that would drive most academics mad. What he's dealing with here is out of his comfort zone.

"I'll leave," I say, after a moment of silence. I put the key in my pocket.

"No, that's not what I meant. I'm trying to . . . what the hell is going on here, Nora?"

I shake my head. "I don't know." It's the truth, but not the one he wants to hear.

"You can trust me."

"I know," I whisper. "But you can't help me with this."

Seb's voice stops me before I cross the threshold. "I called my old editor. Mike Starling hasn't been seen or heard from for a week. He was supposed to come in for a meeting today, but he never showed up. Has something happened to him? What do you know about his disappearance?"

"Nothing."

"Nora, if the paper doesn't hear from him by tomorrow, they're going to file a missing person's report. And if the police come to me, I will tell them he was looking for you."

I turn to go. He says nothing to make me stay, and I walk away slowly on my bad ankle, like a spurned lover waiting to be called back into welcoming arms. For a brief moment it makes me sad, makes me angry, that this has never been my story.

I'm in the basement, running my hands through Whisper's fur, when an address is texted to my phone. Though he may not approve of what I'm doing, or the secrecy with which I'm doing it, Seb has decided to give me a chance to make things right. As far as employers go, he is quite possibly the best someone like me could ever hope for.

"Come on," I say to Whisper. "We have work to do."

The Corolla doesn't start but the place we're going isn't too far away. Only about an hour and a half on foot. We walk in the rain, Whisper happy to stretch her legs, completely at ease in this weather and on these streets.

# 23

I DON'T ENVY investigative journalists. They have to employ their own bullshit detectors, with varying degrees of success. If they're lucky, they uncover a massive plot of some sort and win prizes and accolades and eventually get to write the definitive book on how *this* really happened or *that* came tumbling down. They place themselves in the role of impartial observer with nerves of steel and impressive moral compasses. They are defenders of justice and, come hell or high water, they're going to give you the truth because, for them, the truth is paramount. For others, not so much. It's an exciting career because even though they don't make much money, investigative journalists work hard and get to look busy and important. If they're unlucky, they're thrice-divorced alcoholics suffering from PTSD from reporting on the front lines of war, haunted by stories that got away because of singular sources.

This particular journalist has had it rough. For a hard-nosed, chain-smoking reporter to be relegated to human interest pieces about women is insulting. When I think about him doing extended coverage for my story, I'm embarrassed for him. He must have been devastated when the assignment came down.

At the apartment address Seb texted me, I try the key from the envelope in the lock. It doesn't fit but, no matter, because the door is unlocked. Someone has been here before me, tracking dirt over the threshold and into the room. Good. The dirt from Whisper's paws will fit right in, but we pause just inside the door anyway. There's something not quite right here. I don't sense another person, another presence, but there is a feeling of disquiet nonetheless. I listen for any unusual sounds, but there's nothing out of place. Whisper moves ahead of me, following a scent. She disappears into the bathroom. Naturally.

I look around Mike Starling's apartment, with boxes of old files and stories haphazardly stacked in every available corner, and I can see that he hasn't given up on his ghosts. He's let them into his home and they haunt his private spaces. There are dishes piled in the sink and the garbage is overflowing with takeout containers. The milk is at least a week past its expiration date. There are reminders stuck to the fridge about appointments and meetings. Two appointments for this week: one with a chiropractor and the other with his divorce lawyer to sign the papers. Over the latter he scrawled: *For Amy . . . Where the fuck is the fuchsia duvet?*

I continue on. A cursory look through the files reveals an obsession with corruption in the housing market, corruption in the medical profession, corruption in the political machinations of the extraction industries. His notes are categorized by date and fill dozens of journals and notepads strewn about.

I move away from the files, stand with my back to the door, and look at the room. There is no art on the walls, no furniture save for a mounted television, a desk where there should be a kitchen table, and an ancient leather couch that presumably serves as a bed. There is a lived-in feel here, and the smells that go along with it, but it's nothing that anyone would call a home. Bare walls, stacked boxes. A threadbare blanket on the couch.

Not very much in the way of furniture. A fuchsia duvet would be an affront to the minimalist decor.

Whisper appears at my side. She rubs her nose against my hip and leaves a wet smear from her snout. It is only then that I notice that the smell in the apartment isn't only of must, garbage, and dying dreams. Opening the bathroom door has released a scent into the room that I've been too preoccupied to notice. A smell of decay.

In the bathroom I find Mike Starling naked in a bathtub full of bloody water.

When I used to live in shelters and needed a night of not sleeping with one eye open, when it wasn't raining too hard, I'd head over to Stanley Park and spend the night huddled in the underbrush or at the foot of a tree. I had a few places that were so deep inside the park that I felt relatively safe. Safer than a shelter, anyway. Once, I found a man dressed in rags nestled between a shrub and a tree root. He had such a peaceful expression on his face that I knew immediately he was dead, because you don't sleep in the park if you're the sort who has nice, happy dreams. His eyes were closed and his facial muscles relaxed in repose. There was a half-empty bottle of Johnnie Walker next to him, so I know he went the way he wanted to. I snatched the JW before I left him there—I'm no angel—but stumbling on a dead body like that in the woods wasn't as horrible as you might think. Plus, I had a good half a bottle left to help me get through the trauma. Whoever that man was, he died warmed from the inside out in the company of his beloved.

Mike Starling is a different story. He did not go well. As easy as it seems to slash your wrists and bleed out in a tub of water, the breaking of skin, severing the ulnar artery, is a big step that, no matter how much I turn it around in my mind, doesn't seem like one he would take. If he was going to commit suicide, it would be pills at his desk or a pistol in his mouth.

His eyes are wide open and staring at me as I stand just inside the bathroom. I'm not a forensic expert and I haven't watched enough television crime procedurals to guess with any precision as to how long he has been there, but if I had to take a stab at it, I'd say it was somewhere between our text message exchange to arrange our library meeting and when those not-cops showed up in his place.

Whisper and I retreat from the room, from the apartment. Once we're far enough away from the stench of death, I find a bench to sit on while I collect my wits. My sprained ankle thanks me for the rest, but it's not going to last for very long. On my phone, I pull up a search of storage lockers in the area. The closest one is four blocks away from this apartment complex and it happens to be a twenty-four-hour access facility.

On the way there, Whisper sees a stray mutt across the street in an empty parking lot. She pulls the leash out of my hand with a swift jerk and rushes to meet the mutt. They circle each other warily. I don't call to her, because she damn well knows that what she's doing is wrong and I don't want to draw any attention. It doesn't take long for the other dog to pick up on her energy and before I reach them, he mounts her and humps away for several exuberant moments. It is over just as soon as it starts and she returns to me with her tail between her legs and her head hanging low. I don't punish her for it, though, because we all cope however we can. I just dust off the other end of the leash and hold it tighter in my grip to prevent another episode. We still have a lot left to do tonight.

# 24

"EXCUSE ME, MA'AM," says the young security guard. We're standing outside of a storage facility and he's several feet away, shining a flashlight into my eyes. "You're not, um, supposed to be doing that."

Whisper moves out of the shadows and growls as the guard approaches. She's feeling guilty about what she has done earlier with the stray mutt in the parking lot and is trying to make up for it by being especially protective. When the guard catches sight of her, he slows and comes to a stop just outside of lunging distance. I quit trying to shove the key from the envelope into the lock of the exterior storage unit on the first floor of the building and put a steadying hand on Whisper's back. This is the fourth unit that I've tried, in hopes that the security guard in the front office was taking a nap. Apparently not.

I decide to come clean. "I'm looking for a unit registered under the name Starling. Mike Starling."

The guard eyes Whisper. The hand that's not holding the flashlight moves unconsciously to cover his groin. "We're not supposed to give out that kind of information. Are you his, um, emergency contact?"

Maybe this is his first week on the job or maybe Whisper has rattled him, but the adorable young guard only wants to help. It is refreshing, but silly. He has just inadvertently given me what I need.

"Amy Starling?" I say, hoping he won't notice that I haven't said that I'm Amy Starling. There is only so much outright lying I can stomach. But if I'm to access this storage unit, sacrifices have to be made. A girl is missing and a journalist is dead. Both are connected to me. These two things can't be coincidences.

The guard pulls a slim portable tablet from his pocket and scrolls through it. "Oh, yeah. Here you are, Ms. Starling. We're really supposed to take ID, but . . ." He glances down at Whisper. "Maybe you can stop by the office on your way out and leave your dog by the gate. I'll take a copy of your ID then."

"That sounds like a plan." My voice is so falsely cheerful that I'm sure he can tell something is wrong . . . But he doesn't seem to. He's too busy keeping an eye on Whisper, who is, in turn, busy keeping an eye on him.

"You're looking for unit 108, Ms. Starling. It's right this way." He points to a unit on the far side of the lot, farthest away from the security office, then looks down at Whisper. "You're fine to get there on your own?"

"Yup," I say. My face contorts into a bright smile. Damn that cheerfulness. Damn it to hell. Sneaking around a storage locker in the middle of the night is nothing to be cheerful about. Raising suspicion by trying to get access to a murdered man's storage unit before his body is found is no smiling matter. If I'm caught, how will I explain this?

"Great," the young guard replies, clearly relieved to put some distance between us. "Make sure to stop by the office afterward."

Whisper relaxes and trots along behind me as I head for unit 108. The key fits perfectly into the lock. I open the door and switch on the light.

Like his apartment, Starling's unit contains boxes and boxes of files, but instead of haphazard piles strewn about, these files are stacked neatly and appear to be organized by date and story research topic. There's a desk with a work lamp plugged into the unit's single electrical outlet, along with a space heater. On the desk is a laptop and a portable modem. So this is where he'd actually been working on his private projects.

Before we start, Whisper and I share a bottle of water, me first on account of her drool. I sit at Starling's desk and, careful to keep my gloves on, go through his laptop. His most recent searches were not about corruption. He was looking at bone marrow transplants. Some private research into embryonic stem cells. The curative powers of stem cell treatments. I wonder if Starling was sick and needed a transplant; if so, a divorce might have pushed him over the edge. But illness isn't what killed him. I'm almost certain of this. Though putting him in a tub and slitting his wrists was a deft touch, it will not hide the fact that he'd been murdered. In my mind I play his message on my voice mail and I know that I'm not mistaken. It was real fear coming through.

I continue searching. After an hour or so, I hit the jackpot.

It takes me a while, but now I have a rough idea of what he was looking into, just not why. Starling's interest in corruption and industry bribes to political bodies seems to zero in on Syntamar Industries, a Canadian mining outfit. For the most part it has been operating quietly in the province, hardly making the splashes that the pipeline companies have. There were a few joint ventures overseas, but these too seemed to be under the radar.

British Columbia is one of the most beautiful places in the world. Mountains and oceans and lakes and nonrenewable resources. The draw of the west coast is bigger than the hype of Vancouver, the main economic center of the province. Most of the indigenous territory here is on unceded land, and most of this land supports entire ecosystems that shelter and protect, by a truly perverse twist of fate, these valuable resources. Lorelei has been encouraging me to go to her anti-mining protests for years, but she's never able to find me when the date approaches. Not that she's ever tried very hard. Starling had probably rubbed shoulders with her a time or two and I wonder if he had any idea that one of the leaders of the province's environmental movement is none other than my sister. If he were alive, he would have salivated at the idea of that story.

A photograph of the board of directors for Syntamar Industries from twenty years ago is circled in a newspaper clipping that I find on the desk. Seated around a conference table, the board is composed of Caucasian males of varying shapes and sizes, but all over the age of fifty and sporting the requisite dark suit and subdued tie. They are grinning, presumably happy to be wealthy and important. At the far end, either at the head of the table or at the foot of it, is a slim Asian man, also in his fifties. His expression is polite but inscrutable. Whether or not he is pleased to be wealthy and important is not immediately obvious. I do a web image search on the photograph, but nothing comes up that identifies the Asian man.

There's a name written in the margin of the old paper. I fold the clipping and slide it into my back pocket.

Along with the Syntamar research, Starling has also pulled details on Canadian immigration from Hong Kong during the nineties. Something about it rings a bell, but there isn't much there.

Just after 3 A.M. I wake Whisper up and we leave the unit. I lock the door behind us and slip past the security office. I don't tie Whisper outside and I don't go into the office to speak to the nice young guard. Someone has to teach him to be more thorough in his enforcement of the access policy and it looks like that someone is me.

It's not raining as we walk home but the streets are still slick from an earlier shower. They glisten in the places where the streetlights hit them and then fade away into the darkness. For a while I hum some Howlin' Wolf because I'm in that mood, but don't get much further than a few bars of "Back Door Man." No matter how much I try to push the other voice out of my head, it persists. It has been in there since I saw the journalist in the bathtub with his wrists slit—no, who am I kidding? It has been there for years, hiding away in some dark corner of my mind, but replayed incessantly since I heard it while cowering on the landing of the office. Was it just yesterday? I don't know. My memories are being particularly intrusive tonight.

"*Get rid of her,*" the voice said, some fifteen years ago. Or was it sixteen? I lost so many months in the aftermath, I can't quite remember.

Someone on the other side of the room said something in return but I couldn't hear it clearly, not with my head covered.

*"I don't give a fuck. Wrap her up in that sheet, no need to spread her blood around any more than you already have, you imbecile, and throw her in a ditch somewhere. I don't care where, just as long as it's past the city. And stop giving them that shit. Someone's gonna catch on sooner or later. What will your father say if he finds out?"*

The other person was muffled, pleading, as the man with the voice that haunts my nightmares turned away. Footsteps moved down the hallway. Quiet, confident footsteps. The steps of a man who knows his orders to dispose of my body will be obeyed.

And they were. In a ditch somewhere, out of the city, where no one would stumble upon me.

But someone did.

Mike Starling did.

# 25

WHISPER AND I get home just as dawn breaks. I make a fresh cup of coffee because I'm too jazzed to go to bed. My hands are shaking. I don't remember them ever doing this before, but I realize that it's been a long time since I've seen a body with violence done upon it. I'm shaking because of what I've seen tonight.

Starling is dead.

His eyes, wide open and unseeing, follow me even here. Would anyone even blink twice at the idea of him committing suicide? Divorced, broke, living in a shithole, an old-school reporter in a world where social media and the Internet have turned the old boys' club of journalism on its head. Who wouldn't be tempted to slash their wrists? But Starling was too miserable and argumentative to go out like that. Would anyone else pick up on that?

I pull out my laptop and start searching. Whisper has been somber since we got home and refuses to meet my eyes. Now that we are back to life inside our basement, she's likely regretting her tryst with the street mutt and is cleaning herself with an intensity bordering on obsessive, starting from her front paws and working her way back. This isn't unusual for her and I'm not worried because I know it will pass in a few days and she'll remember that she's the boss.

It only takes a few minutes to find that Syntamar, once based out of Vancouver, is now defunct. There isn't much more information about it online, other than what Starling had found. There's an article talking about its diversification of mining tenures, a few joint ventures in Canada and a rare earth minerals mine in the Congo, but nothing that points to why Starling was so interested in it before he died. You would think that if you're leaving dire messages on someone's phone, the last thing that you research might have something to do with your sense of danger.

I look up the name written on the newspaper clipping and find that it belongs to an associate professor at the Environmental Sustainability Center over at the university. Fancy. I find him on the staff pages of the institute's website and call his department. It takes only a minute for the call to be transferred. I brace myself because I know that, once again, I'll have to be more evasive than usual. But Starling is dead and the girl is still missing. I don't have much of a choice now.

"You work with Sebastian Crow?" the warm, masculine voice says, when we're connected.

"Yes," I reply. "I assist him with research." (This is true.)

"And you want to know some specifics about a particular company?"

"Syntamar Industries." (Also true.)

There's a brief pause. "Well, yes, I could help you out. Anything for Mr. Crow. I really enjoy his work."

It's interesting when someone knows a particular investigative journalist by reputation, enough to say that he's familiar with Seb's work. But, of course, this man lives in the world of ac-

ademia, where knowledge of things outside of the public scope
is part of his job description.

We arrange to meet on the university campus the next
morning before his classes. I'm excited by this, despite the nature
of the visit. I've walked through that campus many times. It's a
world of its own, set within university endowment lands near
some of the priciest views in the city. The elitist area is a turn-
off but the campus itself is something special. There's a different feel to the air there and even my frigid heart can't help but
be moved by it. Youth. Thirst for knowledge. Hope. Possibility.
The things that wither and die when time gets its hands on you.

"So," he interjects, before we hang up. "Will Mr. Crow be
there?"

"No. He's away at the moment, but he asked me to reach out.
He read your last paper in *Science* and found it illuminating." (A
big, steaming lie. I'm getting better at them, at least.) *Science* is
one of the most prestigious journals around. You can guess the
subject matter.

The flattery works to disarm him. His voice takes on a full,
throaty note of anticipation for a rewarding professional—
maybe even personal—relationship with one of the country's
most dedicated journalists. There are speaker's fees to collect.
Interviews and panel discussions to participate in, all of which
he is well aware of. "Well, it will be a pleasure speaking with
him when he gets back. In the meantime, I look forward to
meeting you, Nora."

Okay, there are some things you realize about journalists like
Seb if you know anything about them. The first is that even if
they do have research help, they rarely have other people con-

ducting interviews for them. They prefer to do the legwork personally. Second, only the most unscrupulous in the field need to resort to shameless flattery to get in the door. Third, and perhaps the most important point on this list, they can hold grudges.

By using Seb's name to get this man to talk I have firmly crossed a line that I will not be able to uncross, with one of the only people in my life who has consistently given me the benefit of the doubt.

# 26

I SLEEP FOR the rest of the day and wake up just as evening sets in. Since I need to be presentable for my meeting with the academic, I slip upstairs after Seb and Leo have gone home for the night. They haven't changed the locks, which I'm grateful for. After leaving Seb in the office that night, I've proceeded onto the premises with caution. He didn't say I wasn't welcome, but he expects answers that I don't have.

As I step into the room, I'm acutely aware of the bottle of whisky that may or may not still be in Seb's office. I let out a deep breath and turn left instead, into Leo's office. He has a dark green cardigan draped just so over the back of his chair and a gray scarf that is soft as butter hanging on the coatrack. I snatch both and, on my way out, I also snag the leather wing tips that he leaves by the door for when he removes his rain boots.

Back downstairs, I put a steel pipe the size of my arm on the cot next to me and then crawl under the covers. Whisper jumps up and arranges herself at my feet. Even though it's a small cot, there's still room for the both of us. Maybe she senses how scared I am or maybe she's seeking out my warmth. Whatever it is, I'm glad she's there. And then I sleep.

The next morning, after I walk Whisper, I slip into Leo's shoes and throw the cardigan and scarf on over my cleanest shirt and jeans. I am pleased by the result. Studious butch is what comes to mind here, but that isn't necessarily a bad thing.

I say goodbye to Whisper, who ignores me because this is her nap time, and leave through the basement door. Leo's clothes have pleasant top notes of sandalwood and leather and they give me a peculiar feeling that I'm someone else, off to meet a respectable individual for a cup of coffee. I manage to catch a bus just as it's departing and settle into a rear window seat. For the bus ride to the university, this fantasy takes over, fueled by Leo's good taste in cologne and shoes. There is little traffic this time of day, and it has started to rain, but people are still out on the streets going about their business.

I'm in such a good mood that I think about my youth, which is rare for me. I usually think in terms of Before and After. I've mostly drunk the After away, and I'm not ashamed to say that I really don't remember too much about it. Before, naturally, is a special place where I am so innocent that those memories lie in my gut like a lead ball, pinning me down with shame. My father's sister, before she got sick, was employed by a wealthy family in Winnipeg who ran a chain of grocery stores. She was a cook and sometimes a nanny. She would bring home old books for me and Lorelei, though I always let Lorelei have at them first because I knew she would eventually ask me to read them to her. Some of my fondest memories were of opening a carry bag and pulling out the castoffs from these rich kids whom I never met but only glimpsed from a distance every now and then. For a while these secondhand books and toys were treasures, until Lorelei got old enough to realize that they were just charity and didn't want anything to do with them. I agreed with her at the time, but would still read the books when she went to sleep, to avoid any arguments. These old books with their torn bindings and stained pages were the best we ever got. Well, the best I ever got. Lorelei always expected better for herself and, through sheer force of will and natural good looks, she has managed to achieve it.

The bus glides along the well-maintained roads toward the university. The fantasy of being someone else evaporates as I disembark from the bus and stand on the pavement to get my bearings. It's important to get my story straight. I walk into the coffee shop we agreed to meet in, which is also an art gallery. The art on the walls consists mostly of bright landscapes of the city in the summertime, which is a cruel joke on the patrons, considering that we haven't seen the sun for weeks. I spot the professor, whom I recognize from his staff photo. He pumps my hand vigorously when I get to the table, which is already filled with binders stacked neatly, three deep, and a cup of coffee.

"You must be Nora. I'm Angus Holland," he says, still pumping away. He has a broad forehead and pale Nordic features to go with his equally pale eyes. They are either blue or gray, but even in this well-lit space, designed to give you a good view of the coffee and art, I can't tell. Everything about him blends into the white walls behind him, the spaces in between the art, everything but his red cheeks, which make him look like a naughty schoolboy. When I squint, he even appears to have a twinkle in his eye. Imagine that.

I give him a professional but still friendly nod, meant to indicate that he should let go of my hand but keep up the high spirits. "Nice to meet you."

"Pleasure, *Ms.* Watts?" He trails off, covertly glancing at the front of my cardigan for signs of breasts. He comes up empty, as I have been for the past twenty years. If you want fleshy on me, you have to look to the back. Even there you'd have a hard time of it, but you'd eventually find something to reward you for your efforts.

"Yup."

"You've got a very deep voice there, Ms. Watts."

I'm not a contralto for nothing, but people usually don't comment. Holland looks somewhere over my shoulder as we sit down, and I turn to see a student stride in, wearing makeup, with two pigtails peeking out from under a bicycle helmet. The bicycle shorts that the student wears leave no doubt of anatomically male genitalia, but the makeup and pigtails tell a different story. I suddenly understand the *Ms.* comment and the observation of my voice. For some reason, my vocal cords are thicker than the average woman's and he thinks I'm trying to pull the wool over his eyes. He's not wrong. I am. Just not about that.

"The campus is a very safe space," he continues, seeing that I've noticed Bicycle Shorts. "No one has to hide who they are here."

"Except if you're a large mining company, right?" I say cheerfully, seeing that this meeting is quite close to being derailed by my apparently ambiguous gender identity. Perhaps studious butch wasn't the way to go after all. I pull Leo's scarf off my neck to show a little clavicle. It's not much, but it's the best I've got. "They must be persona non grata around these parts."

He clears his throat, all business now. "On the contrary. We have a robust mining engineering program here at the university. It is the job of the center to look at issues of, among other things, the social and environmental impact of the extraction industry. So is Mr. Crow doing a feature article or are we looking at a book?"

"We're just at the research stage of some feature work at this point, but we're open to expanding the project if we get the money. We won't know until he pitches it to his publisher."

"Why Syntamar, though? There are quite a few Canadian companies doing damage overseas and in country. I wouldn't put it at the top of my list."

I shrug. "I'm not sure, either. There are a lot of moving pieces here and I just do what I'm told." Enough of Seb's work over the past few years has had the byline *With contributions from N. Watts* for me to sell this line to Holland.

Something I've said amuses him. He chuckles into his mug and his cheeks turn even redder. "Sounds a lot like my job. Teach this but not that. Research this with our money, but the other stuff you do on your own. Would you like some coffee?" He gestures to his cup, as if he's about to share.

"No, thanks. I've got a bit of a deadline to get this in to Mr. Crow."

"Right, of course. Syntamar, then. What do you want to know?"

"Let's start with the Congo mine." It was the company's only project outside of Canada.

"Okay." He glances down at the binders in front of him but doesn't move to open them. He doesn't need to. I get the feeling that he knows this material inside out. "Syntamar had a tough time getting off the ground outside of Canada. They went in a couple of times with shady promoters who were raising money for projects that were never viable. This was before

Canada implemented the NI 43–101 . . . Sorry," he says, off my look. "Not sure how much background you've already got here. Basically, mining can be shady and Syntamar lost a lot of money in ventures that were never going to pan out, projects where the promoters would raise the capital two times over, make twice the money in different markets, and then leave their investors high and dry. Syntamar had a couple of successful projects in Canada but they made some bad choices before going in to the Congo."

"So they were desperate to make it work."

"Yes, they were." He stares at a painting on the wall. In shades of red, a couple in love, mouths intertwined, hands clasped. "Do you know what the most difficult part of the mining process is?" He doesn't wait for an answer because he's gearing up for full lecture mode. I lean back in my chair. His mood has changed, going from pleasant to unexpectedly grim in a matter of seconds. "It's not getting the permits or acquiring equipment or skilled technicians. It has to do with the human and environmental cost of this process of digging deep into the earth and bringing out raw materials that some say may be better off left there. Extraction can ruin the environment around the sites that are being used. There's no denying that. And they are most toxic and harmful in the immediate vicinity of where the mining or the drilling or the fracking takes place."

"The local populations."

There's that twinkle again, but it disappears almost immediately. "Exactly! Nobody wants a damn mine or drilling op in their backyard, but sometimes they're steamrolled by governments that are in the pocket of industry. Some jobs are thrown their way. People are initially cautious but need to eat and there's no denying that some income is better than no income at all. It's when the animals start dying, the people start getting sick, and the water in the area is not safe to drink that turmoil happens."

I nod. "And they don't always treat local employees well, do they?"

He sighs and drains the last of his coffee. "No, they can't even get that right. In Canada, not so much. We're not perfect and unions don't really have the bargaining power they used to, but we have some safeguards here. Overseas is a different story. Our mining companies in particular have a horrific record of human rights abuses. Just terrible. A report from a nonprofit think tank several years ago showed that Canadian companies are some of the worst offenders. Not exactly in line with our polite, peace-keeping reputation, is it?"

This is all very interesting, but I don't see the connection. "Where does Syntamar fit into this picture?"

"Like I said, it's not the worst, but how can you qualify what is bad abuse and exploitation and what isn't? The Congo had more than a few companies operating there. In the region where Syntamar had their gold mine, there were also two American projects and one Chinese. The Canadian outfit was smaller than the others and ran into some trouble both with their workers and the local population. Strikes, protests, general unrest. They were losing money fast and, by chance, a militia that was used to quell unrest in another mine suddenly appeared at Syntamar's a few months later. Many local reports suggested that the perpe-trators were the same. The protesters and striking workers were brutally treated in a manner that is too horrific to speak of here within these walls, my dear." He looks away for a minute, lost to his thoughts.

I don't look away, though, because I'm suddenly flustered. What I had initially thought of him over the phone was very wrong. I seem to have misjudged him terribly.

"So both Syntamar and this other company used the same militia to get a handle on the situation."

"Yes. The mine was profitable for a little while and then Syntamar suffered a hostile takeover by an American company several years later. All of its existing rights were handed over, except for two, both in Canada. Both became joint ventures, with Syntamar taking a backseat role. One in the northern tundra, which has become a hotly contested region since that time, and one for a copper mine on Vancouver Island."

"Wasn't this unusual, that they sold the company but someone else got the other two projects?"

"Not really, but there was something about it at the time that made it stand out for me. Backroom deals happen all the time, but those two projects had the potential to be very profitable in the long run."

"You're saying Syntamar offered up those projects to another company in return for help with the Congo mine."

He sighs. "There's no way to know for sure because there are no official records of who financed those militias . . . but I strongly suspect that's the case."

"If there was bad blood with the Americans, then that leaves the Chinese company."

He smiles. "You're very good. When they needed help in the Congo, they turned to their only other option. Zhang-Wei Industries. They moved their headquarters to Vancouver in the late nineties. Up until then they weren't publicly traded so we didn't have a lot of information on them."

He meets my eyes and suddenly his gaze becomes intense, almost pleading. "I do have a student waiting for me to go over her thesis, but please, feel free to contact me if you need any more information. I am a great admirer of Mr. Crow. He appreciates the finer details and for someone like me, that's a valuable quality in a journalist. You see, people here are upset about our pipelines and our in-province extraction projects, but it's a very unique situation where local populations can make themselves heard. No company is going to sanction mass murders and rapes here in Canada. But they do in other places in the world where people aren't as protected. I hope you and Mr. Crow can help us get the word out."

I shake his hand and leave him there, his ruddy cheeks flushed with altruism and purpose. My mind is filled almost to bursting. What I am able to dredge out and examine is how badly I've misjudged this man. Maybe I've seen too much darkness or just dwelled in it for too long, because I missed what was happening here. What I thought was an opportunist's enthusiasm to increase the value of his speaker's fees by being the talking head for an exposé was in fact a crusader's genuine concern for the well-being of others.

I think of my sister, how these two would immediately take to each other. They would have a lot to talk about. Saving the environment and all that. They would be on the same page, bonding over the things about the world that bother them and need to change. And, as a side note, he would not mistake her for a man.

# 27

MY SISTER IS a do-gooder in the worst sense of the word. She has been an activist for most of her life and does it out of a true belief that her actions may directly obstruct the construction of a pipeline carrying bitumen and other nasty toxins dug up from the bowels of the earth, transporting them from the tar sands to the lovely coastline that she now calls home. Lorelei looks at pictures of whales and bears and wolves and salmon and pleads for their rights. They move her to tears.

But she does not budge for me.

When she opens the door to her East Vancouver house, the startled, curious expression on her face becomes hostile. Her stance turns to rock and her shoulders subtly block the entire doorway. She looks at my paint-splattered jeans and my ratty sweater. "Salvation Army is down the street" are the first words out of her mouth.

We haven't seen each other in a year.

It has always been this way with her. She has an angel's face but a tongue like a shrieking harpy. If anyone could stop an immovable force like pure, unadulterated greed, it would be her. She knows this and has equipped herself with a bland trophy husband, academic laurels, and carefully cultivated relationships with key environmental organizations in the province. There's a new kind of political engagement within local communities and Lorelei wants to be at the front of it. She's grooming herself for something big and I am the wrench in her gears.

Naturally, she mostly pretends I don't exist.

"Did the pipelines collapse yet?" I ask politely.

I've learned that if you want something, you have to give something in return. For her, this is civility and maintaining her carefully constructed appearance of someone who is untainted by the social ills that are part of our colonial legacy, what some call cultural genocide while others omit the "cultural" part. She is a shining star, one who escaped, completely aboveboard, with a sharp mind and well-turned ankles. While she is busy connecting with parts of our father's heritage that she has decided are hers, my connections to the same have slowly been eroding over the years. Because she ignores what I refuse to, which is that he is only part of our story. The other part is our mother, whom we know nothing about except that she was a foreigner and that she left us long before our father died. And never looked back.

Now my sister's mouth is set in a grim line. I have that effect on a lot of people, but no one more than my sister. "Why are you here, Nora?" She steps onto the porch and closes the door behind her, putting herself between her home and me. "Do you need money?"

Why does everyone think that? I consider investing in new clothes.

"I need to borrow your car." I look over at the new SUV in the driveway, gleaming silver. Though her husband, David, is a lawyer, he goes camping all of twice a year and thinks that it's enough of a reason to justify a gas guzzler like this. But I don't hold it against him. Nobody's perfect.

It takes Lorelei a few seconds to process the request, then she laughs. "Come on, Nora. Be real."

"I am real." Her disapproval pins me to the porch. I'm suddenly seven years old again, and she is four. I remember the stolen chocolate bar melting in my hand as she goes crying to our aunt about how I am a thief. Staring at me accusingly through an ocean of fake tears. I remember being beaten with a belt in the yard, hot tears streaming down my face. What I wanted to say was that I never even liked chocolate, but the words never emerged. Lorelei did. She loved chocolate.

"Nora," she continues, in a voice full of false concern, as if I haven't spoken. "You're an alcoholic. You don't even have a driver's license. I can't lend you David's SUV. He needs it for work."

I look at her through the veil of distrust that has always lingered between us. She's lying about David. He's a junior partner who mostly takes the train into the city to avoid the impossible Vancouver gridlock. He doesn't need the car. She's not aware that I am up to speed on the events in her life, though, and I don't cop to it. I've been keeping an eye on her since she was born, but she'd never know it.

"Okay." I turn to leave. Did I really expect her to say yes? I could tell her about Bonnie, could tell her that I'm in trouble, but something stops me.

"Wait, Nora."

I stop, but don't turn. It hurts to look at her too long.

"Why do you even need it?" She is genuinely curious now,

though not because I need help. She's always taken that as a given. Because I've never asked *her* for help.

I consider telling her the truth. Coming clean. But I realize now that some things never change. "It's not important."

But we both know that it is. We both know that me standing there, asking for a favor, is a pivotal point in our relationship. Her turning me down is her attempt to put me back in my place, and to keep her in hers. I don't blame her for being the way she is. Grasping at whatever she can control, trying to fit in wherever she can. I gave up on that a long time ago. We are a patchwork, Lorelei and I, stitched together from different fabrics. Hers are more beautiful, but the edges are just as jagged. She doesn't allow you to see her seams and I may be the only person in the world who knows she even has them. This is why we are barely on speaking terms. I have always let my seams show.

That night, after the lights go out in the house, I pick the lock on the side door, sneak inside, and grab the spare keys for the SUV from the garage and a loaf of bread from the kitchen counter. A girl has to eat, after all. Lorelei doesn't know that I figured out her alarm code, or else she would have changed it by now. It is the date of her wedding, backward.

# 28

I KNOCK ON Seb's door with a red feather boa that someone left behind on the bus scrunched up in my hand. He's shocked to see me when he opens it. I don't do home visits and neither does he.

I hand him the boa. "A present."

"Thank you, this is . . ." He's not quite sure what to say. He thinks I'm stereotyping him but, despite our recent spat, he values me as an employee and is weighing his response.

Leo elbows him out of the way and wraps the boa around his neck. "Nora, I love you! How did you know I lost my boa in the last move? It was blue, but still. This is *awesome*."

I didn't know, but I take the credit anyway. They motion me inside. I stay where I am on the porch. "I'll be going away for a few days," I tell them.

Seb frowns. "Nora, I think we need to talk and I'm glad you came over. Mike Starling was found dead yesterday and I think . . . I think you might be in danger. Who was that man who came into our office?"

"And did you really break into a security firm?" Leo adds, not wanting to be left out.

Seb glances over at him. A look passes between them. "If this is about you living in the basement, we can find you a safer place to stay."

"No," I say, surprised. I didn't know that they knew, but now that they do, I decide this could work to my benefit. "But if you could look after my dog . . ."

I whistle. Whisper bounds through the open hatch of David's SUV and lands on their lawn. Leo gasps. "Is that a wolf?"

"Hang on," Seb interjects, involuntarily backing up a step. "You've had a dog all this time?"

Leo stays where he is. He stares at Whisper, enchanted. "In our basement?"

"She's very quiet." I look at Seb. "You said I could trust you."

Whisper approaches, cautious. Seb kneels and stretches out his hand. Whisper sniffs it and then gives it a cursory lick. She buries her face in Leo's crotch and susses out the situation there.

Seb stares at me for a long time. "I did say that, but I wasn't talking about a dog."

"I get it." I try to keep my voice even, but can't hide my disappointment.

He sighs. "Do you, Nora? Sometimes I wonder. We'll keep the dog for you but if you're not back in a week, she's going to the pound."

Leo opens his mouth to protest but Seb puts a hand on his shoulder to quiet him. "You have one week."

I scratch behind Whisper's velvet ears. Seb would never put my dog in the pound and he knows that Leo would never let him. What he's telling me is that I have one week before he comes looking. One week to find the girl. It's plenty of time, considering that I could be dead by nightfall. With my luck. I pull her leash from my back pocket and hand it over to Leo. "Okay. Her name is Whisper and she's not picky. She'll eat whatever you do, but she likes steak and roasted chicken mostly."

Then I make a decision to extend the trust that I can. "What do you know about immigration to Canada in the nineties?"

"That's a pretty big topic," Leo says. "Any way to narrow it down?"

I think about what I learned from Starling's storage locker and from my meeting with Angus Holland. "From Asia, I suppose."

Leo shakes his head. "We've always had a Pacific connection here on the west coast with Asian communities. Can you do better than that?"

"No, not really. I don't really know what I'm looking for. Just anything that stands out."

Seb is quiet for a moment, then looks at me. "There is something I remember from my time at the *Post*. It was a big scandal back then. The Los Angeles Canadian consulate was notoriously corrupt. They approved immigration applications without doing background checks. Some people with criminal connections wouldn't be vetted, if they provided the right bribes, and would get approved. They would bring their families over and be free to go on with their criminal activities in their own countries, and sometimes here, too."

"Anyone in particular? That maybe Starling was interested in?"

"A man who was allegedly the head of a criminal organization in Taiwan faced most of the heat, but there were others. That consulate continued unchecked for quite a few years. It became well known in criminal circles. Some speculate that the west coast triad connections were born from the applications that were approved in that period, and from that consulate."

Seb pauses as something occurs to him. "Mike Starling did a

lot of coverage for that story. He even investigated some other potential criminal ties and was obsessed with another Hong Kong businessman who he suspected was deeply entrenched with one particular triad. But he got stalled. I remember he couldn't get sources on it, was just spinning his wheels and wasn't handling his other stories very well. It was around the time he was put on leave and when he came back they gave him human interest stuff for another year. He wasn't happy."

"Oh, yeah!" Leo says. "I remember he did a string on sexual assault victims, one in particular who he found in the woods. It was a great series of articles. You were pretty jealous of him, babe. What was it that he won? A Canadian Association of Journalists award?"

"He was nominated," Seb says, his expression dark. He is careful not to look at me.

"That's why you asked him for research help when you were doing your piece with Rebecca Pruitt," Leo continues. "That's when you met Nora."

Leo smiles over at us, then the smile on his face dies. Seb and I are studiously looking everywhere but at him. He sees a new connection that he's never noticed before, one that has been right in front of him for several years. "Oh."

It is always hurtful for me to look at someone's face when they realize. The pity, then the false cheerfulness. It changes relationships, not that I ever had many After. Starling was careful not to reveal the truth about my past when he introduced me to Seb, and I've never said anything, but I'm sure Seb figured it out a long time ago. Leo is silent now, as my behavior and my habits click into place.

Seb clears his throat and tries to smooth things over. "Before you go . . . What about Melissa's case? Did you find Baichwal?"

I shake my head. "He's long gone. Stevie might have better luck."

"He's on something else and you know how he can be." Leo sighs. "We really could have used that money."

Seb just stares at me, a peculiar frown on his face. Despite my quirks, I have always come through on cases. But I can't forget the look of fear on Harrison Baichwal's face. Fear for his family. It moved something in me.

I walk away from them then, without a second glance at Whisper. I'm afraid that if I say anything to her or look into those sad eyes, I'll change my mind. Before I met her, this kind of affection for a dog would have been unthinkable to me. I leave her there on the porch and get into the SUV. My foot aches as I press down on the gas pedal but the pain feels good and I use it to focus on what's ahead, rather than what I'm leaving behind. As I drive away, I decide that I'm imagining the long, desperate howl that fills the air.

# 29

THE GIRL REMEMBERS her name now.

It has eluded her all this time she has sheltered, cold and exhausted, in the heart of the tree. Since she crawled from the rocks and into the forest, she has not known her name or where she came from. Just flashes of the glass castle nestled in the forest, glimpsed from her frightened looks behind her, as she willed herself to dip the oar into the water, to keep her weak arms moving.

Her name . . . well, she doesn't have the strength to say it, but at least she knows what it is. She feels a sense of accomplishment at this, but it's short-lived because now that she knows what she's called, she has to figure out the other parts of it, too. Questions, always questions. Running around in her head, stabbing at her brain. She huddles in the hollow tree and closes her eyes. And then opens them again. There's a noise outside. The girl curls into a ball and waits, frightened. She's starting to remember who they are now, the people who took her, the room with no windows in a house full of them, the high-pitched cries that seemed to come from inside the walls . . .

If they find her now, they will take her back to that place. Her exhaustion soon overwhelms her fear, though. She knows the fear will be back, but for now she is so tired.

# TWO

# 1

AH, THE OPEN road. Canada is not the second-largest country in the world for nothing. Open road here leads to open road, and then to an empty highway and back onto some more open roads where you can see mountains so high, forests so green, and lakes so crystal clear you'd swear they were something from a picture come to life. If you're on the coast like I am and drive inland for more than two hours, you'll see so much unused space that your vision will start to blur from the vastness of it all. When the terrain turns from damp and gray to sunny but covered in snow, I am grateful for the foresight that prompted me to steal David's SUV, equipped with sturdy all-season tires, instead of trying my luck with the Corolla. Though the not-cops have a definite head start on me, I hope that they haven't reached Tommy yet. Unlikely, I know. But I've been in a dangerous mood since I left Whisper.

I feel like taking chances.

I wipe the sleep from my eyes, drink so much coffee that the corner of my mouth develops a twitch, and play I Spy to pass the time. Lorelei and I attempted this once, when we were taken from our aunt's house and on our way to our first foster home. I knew somehow that our lives had just changed forever, but she was still too young to understand the feeling you get when someone gives you away. She was only five years old. She kept spying the same thing over and over again, red stop signs, and after twenty minutes of this, I ignored her. She got angrier and angrier and pinched the skin on my forearm until it became bruised and swollen. She eventually kissed the skin that she'd pinched so hard, just to see if she could heal it, and was quiet for the rest of the trip.

On this trip, in her husband's stolen car, I play by myself. It is a long drive to Kelowna.

I spy some more trees. On the west coast, trees are not in short supply.

I spy a blue five-wheeler in front and a silver sedan behind.

I spy a mountain to my right and a lake to my left, as I take a winding pass at over a hundred kilometers an hour. David's SUV is a beautiful thing, meant for hard driving at high speeds. I give it some lead and feel like I'm soaring.

I spy a stretch of road so straight that I can see for kilometers ahead and behind me.

I spy the silver sedan slow down until it is barely visible in my rearview mirror. I reach the end of the long, straight stretch of road and a mountain rises up from the earth. The silver car plays peekaboo as we spiral up the mountain.

I spy the green landscape turning snow covered before my very eyes the farther north I go.

There are few gas stations on this road, so the necessity is always to fill up when you see one or else you'll be stranded on the side of the road with an empty jerry can, cursing your stupidity and relying on the kindness of strangers. At the next fuel stop, just outside of Merritt, I park behind the station and wait. I think about Whisper and wonder if she's happy with people who can give her more than I can. Fine, upstanding people like Seb and Leo who take things like proper nutrition and regular checkups seriously. I imagine her sprawled in front of their fireplace—even though I'm unsure as to whether they even have a fireplace—sleeping peacefully. Seb passes and gives her a little belly scratch while Leo takes her supine position as an opportunity to wrestle a brush through her mane. The thought of Whisper being groomed and cuddled is so appealing and I almost lose myself in this fantasy except . . . except.

Except because of Bonnie, I know better. I know that the only way to make sure that someone is safe and warm and happy is to have eyes on them at all times. Do not trust caretakers, no matter how many hopeful letters of recommendation they bear. That I have left Whisper to Seb and Leo is an act of faith, but faith only goes so far.

About fifteen minutes later, I see the silver sedan pull away from the station and get back on the highway. I pull David's car around, fill up my own tank, the price of which leaves me feeling unsettled and violated the way only being overcharged can do to a person, and then ease onto the road. I speed up until I see a speck of silver in the distance ahead and then slow until it is out of sight again. No need to be too eager here. It's always easier to be the hunter than the hunted. I know that I will catch up to my prey. This road is too long and bare for games.

Just as dusk falls and the needle approaches empty yet again, another gas station appears like a mirage, nestled at the foot of a mountain, and the road leading toward it is shaded by trees. I slow to a crawl and through the glass I see that there is only the attendant in the station itself. Parked in the back is the silver sedan. I take a picture of the license plate, text it to Leo, and, on second thought, also send it to Brazuca. Then I rummage through the SUV for supplies. Thank goodness for David's road safety preparedness. After finding the journalist dead, a girl can't be too careful.

I approach the back of the building on foot. There's a single light on over the bathroom door. Just as I reach it, the door opens and a man emerges from the dimly lit single bathroom, eyes on the illuminated screen of his phone. I have one quick second to approach but before I start, he pauses, mutters "Shit," and turns back to flip the switch.

Then I move.

The tire iron glints in the dim light the moment his hand hits the switch. My face and outstretched arm are eerily captured in the mirror for one brief, frozen moment, but he has no time to figure out an escape or room to maneuver in the tiny bathroom. He falls against the automatic hand dryer, knocking it off the wall. It crashes to the ground. He groans and writhes around on the floor in the darkness. I turn on the light again, mostly for his benefit. No one should roll around on a gas station bathroom floor blindly, without at least having some idea of the germ content.

He pulls himself into a sitting position, back against the wall, legs stretched toward the small sink, and clutches his head. I take a deep, fortifying breath in.

The man is Brazuca.

# 2

"FOR FUCK'S SAKE, Nora," he says after a minute of us staring at each other, him squinting in the harsh glare of fluorescent lighting and me trying to hide my surprise.

But it's late at night and I've been driving all day so all I manage is a half-assed glare. "Why are you following me?" This comes out as an accusation, but it isn't my intention to push him away just yet. For some reason, I'm absurdly pleased to see him, that he's the one that I find underneath my tire iron.

"Because I'm worried about you!"

"You should worry about yourself." The blow was hard enough to send him to the ground and leave a nasty bruise, but not enough to do permanent damage. At least I don't think so, but really, what do I know? I'm hardly an expert.

"Yeah, no kidding." He tries to get to his feet but his legs are jelly and won't hold. I tuck the tire iron into the waistband of my jeans and help him up.

"If you're concerned I'm relapsing—"

"Oh, just shut the hell up for a minute. Jesus. You hit me with a goddamn tire iron." He clutches his head and groans.

"I could have hit you harder."

"But you didn't because you wanted information, right? Bloody hell. You thought you were being followed and you snuck up behind me, hit me with a fucking tire iron, but not hard enough to maim me, no, because you're not afraid that I'll get back up and go batshit on you. You're not afraid of getting hurt. All you want is information! Do you have no bloody human compassion in you at all, woman?"

I stare at him with undisguised fascination. I've never heard him curse this much before. In my experience, sponsors usually have been quite responsible with their language. With his hair standing on end, his eyes bloodshot, and a nasty bruise forming at the base of his skull, Brazuca looks like a madman. A line of spittle dribbles out of the corner of his mouth and he swipes at it with his sleeve.

I lead him to the sink, where he scrubs at his hands and his face with soap and hot water. I keep a hand on his back to steady him, and feel that there are no holes in his wool coat. Two very discreet zippered pockets add an element of style to the ensemble. I keep a hand on his back because he is also a survivor, like me, and it inspires just a brief moment of tenderness toward him. A survivor of alcoholism, of a bullet wound, of divorce and now a vicious attack with a blunt instrument. He needs all the support he can get in the world.

"Why are you following me?" I repeat, after I have given him a minute to recover.

He sighs and looks at me in the mirror. "Just get me some ice for my head and I'll tell you all about it."

The gas station attendant has been patiently waiting for me to show my face and purchase goods from him. I get a bag of ice, the smallest I can find, and an energy drink, and prepay for a tank of gas. The time I take to pump the gas clears my head. When I return to the bathroom with the ice, Brazuca seems to be more himself. Leaning on the edge of the sink and watching me with tired eyes. There is a small smile on his face and I wonder what the hell he could be amused at. Being assaulted by a woman half your size doesn't seem to be particularly funny to me.

He takes the ice, wraps it in a white T-shirt that I assume to be his undershirt, freshly removed, and then arranges it over the back of his neck. "Ah, that feels good."

"Get hit a lot, do you?"

"Mostly by women."

"That shit's supposed to end when you get divorced, you know?"

He laughs, but it's just a bit pathetic coming from him.

"I got you the ice," I say, locking the bathroom door behind me. "Your turn."

"Where are you going?"

"No, that's not how this works. You first."

There's more silence, more staring deeply into each other's eyes. It would be romantic if I hadn't just assaulted him with a weapon that I stole from my brother-in-law's SUV, also stolen. "WIN Security reported a break-in last week," Brazuca begins, turning away from me.

I pick his phone up from the floor, touching it with only the tips of my fingers, and slip it into his coat pocket, along with his car keys. And pause for a moment there, my hand resting lightly just above his hip. Then I remove it. He hasn't noticed the hesitation or the touch. "So?" I say.

"So when I heard it was the same company you were looking into I asked a buddy of mine on the case to show me the tapes." He looks away for a moment. There's something odd about the way he says this. Maybe he feels guilty for checking up on me or maybe he's got a concussion. Whatever it is, the moment soon passes. "The intruder on the security cameras looked a hell of a lot like you dressed up like a bike messenger. I didn't know you could sing."

I wave the comment away. "Doesn't explain why you're here. Why you're following me."

He sighs. "You were looking for information on why they're staking out that house, right? Looking for a client list, a case file? Did you find anything on that laptop?"

"No," I admit. I am suddenly tired of playing these games with Brazuca. The long day of driving has taken its toll and I want nothing more than a cold compress for my ankle, a hot shower for the rest of me, and the greasiest pizza I can get my hands on. He is what stands between me and my few creature comforts in life.

"Well, sometimes the only way to find what you need is to look straight into the horse's mouth." He smiles and relaxes back into his normal charming but effusive self. His teeth are pristine and white, shining out at me from at least two days' worth of stubble. Dental hygiene must be very important to him if this is the kind of fluorescence he can achieve and still be a coffee addict.

"I thought a break-in would accomplish that."

"Nope."

"No?"

"Didn't help, did it? This is a security firm we're talking about. Half of what those companies do is off the books and borderline illegal."

His method of making a point using rhetorical devices has become tiresome. I cross my arms over my chest and wait for him to continue.

"So, sometimes, before you look inside the horse's mouth, you should probably also have a little chat with the guy who the horse belongs to, just to get an idea of what's going to be in there. When it comes to WIN Security, the guy you want to talk to is either one of the owners. James Whitehall or Lester Nyman. One of them is going to be up at that fancy new ski resort they built just past Kamloops in a couple days. The big chalet. WIN is working a small, exclusive business function. A few heavy hitters. Might be some people worth talking to over there."

"I'm not good at talking to people."

"Then you're in luck, because I am." He says this without a shred of modesty.

"Which one will be there, Whitehall or Nyman?"

"What's the difference? I don't know for sure, but I hear that one of them has to go to shake hands or kiss ass, or something in between."

You learn some valuable lessons in foster care. Eat everything on your plate. You never know when they will feel like feeding you again. Beware of footsteps outside your bedroom door. For obvious reasons. Don't trust people who are nice to you and ask nothing in return. These are the people who want something and usually you have to figure out what it is. So I stare at him and wonder what he wants. I don't know what his angle is and consider the possibility that perhaps he doesn't have one. Nothing he's said has read as an outright lie. Then I consider what he's offering. A Sherlock and Watson scenario. Butch Cassidy and the Sundance Kid. Nancy Drew and the Hardy Boys. A partnership. Someone to help share the burden. I look at him, with his gimpy leg and his tired eyes, and I am all at once moved and frightened by this unexpected show of support. In the past half an hour we've exchanged more words than we had in the first year that he was my sponsor. This time he's not trying to talk me off a ledge; he is offering to climb onto the narrow precipice with me. Out into the cold.

"Come on," he says, staring at me with eyes so kind that I can't look away. "What do you have to lose?"

I nod to the makeshift compress he has strung over his neck, which has started to turn soggy. "Take care of that, will you? I'll wait outside."

He grins. "Okay, I'll be right out."

When I'm clear of the door, I take a deep breath and run my fingers over the car keys that I have snatched from his pocket. After a moment's hesitation, during which I think about the shitty person I have become and weigh my habitual suspicion against the desire for company on a road trip, I throw Brazuca's car keys deep into the woods bordering the little gas station.

As David's SUV kicks up gravel from the road leading back to the highway, I feel a momentary twinge of disappointment. In myself, mostly, but life has a role to play in this as well. Hopefully the treacherous connector highway will be open for me and closed for Brazuca. With the stiffness in his bad leg and the head trauma from my blow, he's probably an unsuitable candidate for this kind of journey, anyway.

But I hope he makes it out of here okay. You know, from one survivor to the next.

# 3

IDENTITY IS A slippery thing. You think you have a hold on it and then whoops, it slides right out of your hands and shatters on the ground in front of you. And no matter how much you try to put it back together again, somehow the pieces don't seem to fit. I saw from Bonnie's pictures that she was happy as a child, but as the years went by, her smiles became thinner, more guarded. Maybe self-awareness affected her ability to make good choices in life. Or maybe she just became a teenager and, the natural extension of this, a hormonal little bitch looking to get back at her family by running off to be with her boyfriend. Whatever it is, the more I learn about her, the more of myself I see, and it scares the hell out of me.

Tommy Jones strides out of school dressed in black, with longish hair that falls over his brow and an easy, confident gait. I know it's him from the video on Mandy's phone, which doesn't do him one lick of justice. This is a good-looking kid and a clever one, too, considering that he's only been back to his hometown for a few weeks and is already flagrantly skipping school and saluting the teacher who watches him go from the window. If he can get away with that bullshit, it is about more than looks. He's the kind of trouble that teenage girls love, but hopefully grow out of before they get pregnant and move with him into his mother's basement.

In the cold SUV that has been waiting outside the school for a good three hours, I watch him take off in the old pickup truck that he arrived in. There's only one high school in Enderby and, by some stroke of luck, he just so happened to show up today to make my life easier. So I won't have to go searching in town for a single mom and her teenage son, and possibly Bonnie hiding out in his bedroom.

This town has only one main road, and it leads out to the highway. The exit is clearly demarcated. But Tommy isn't heading for the highway or for his house. He crosses the Shuswap River and drives down Mabel Lake Road. I know now where he's going from a map that I picked up at my last gas stop. He's going to the cliffs. From what I know of small Canadian towns like these, this is where kids go to drink beer, smoke shitty weed, and lose their virginities. It's also, I remind myself, the kind of place that bears go to forage when they're hungry.

When I get to the private lot at the trailhead to the cliffs, I drive by the old pickup. Tommy isn't in it. I park at the opposite end of the lot so as not to draw too much attention and take the path deeper into the woods. I have clothes for Vancouver's mild, wet winter, but nothing that holds up to the frigid air that drifts down from the cliffs and settles like a blanket on me now. I am cold to my bones, and through them, too. Surrounded by wilderness, away from the grimy streets that have become my home, I feel out of my element. I wonder why I've kept going and think about Bonnie, this girl I don't even know. Am I looking for her because I care or because I think no one else will?

If I'm completely honest with myself, this question has been rattling around in my brain since I found the not-cop watching the Kerrisdale house and I'm no closer to an answer. In all likelihood, grilling Tommy Jones about Bonnie's disappearance won't bring me closer to the truth about what's going on inside me, but maybe it'll help me find her. Maybe I'll find the answer then.

Less than fifty yards in, I hear the sound of a gun cocking from a stand of firs to my right. I crouch and move quickly into the tree cover to my left.

"Just tell me who the fuck you are and I just might let you live," comes the voice of a teenage boy, trying to sound older and tougher than he is.

I weigh my options and decide that I'm going to have to come clean, because young men with guns should never be ignored. "Just want to ask you some questions, that's all."

"Yeah? Well, I don't want to answer your questions, lady, so stay the hell away from me! Stop following me! You and those other assholes!"

So the not-cops are here, and he's noticed. It makes sense now why my presence at his school tipped him off. He knows that he's under surveillance and thinks that I'm part of their game. "I'm not with them, I swear."

He fires into a tree nearby, the shot so loud it rings in my ears for several seconds afterward.

"You gonna shoot your girlfriend's mom, Tommy?" I shout back, careful to keep still. This is the second time I've called myself Bonnie's mother in front of one of her friends. There's no denying that the panic is still there, but the gun pointed at me might be a contributing factor.

The silence that follows that statement sits for almost a full minute, until I hear rustling from the trees he is hiding behind and boots crunching on snow. He's trying to be quiet about it, and would have been successful if we weren't alone in a forest, less than fifty feet away from each other, judging by the sound of the gunshot. I slide farther into the woods and double back around. I am smaller than he is; quieter, too. He doesn't see me come up behind him, is too busy creeping up to where he thinks I am. I'm in the periphery of his vision too late for him to do anything before I grab his gun hand and slam my elbow out and into his face. The gun goes slack and I pull it away from him before stepping back. It's a Browning 9mm, and feels familiar in my hands.

His nose is sitting at an odd angle on his face, but I feel no remorse. I hate guns, even though I'm not bad with them, and there is an irrational anger building inside me that this boy had the nerve to point one at me. To fire one in my vicinity. Tommy looks up at me with blood pouring down his chin. A few crimson drops stain the snow in front of him. "You broke my nose, lady!"

"You'll be okay. Where's Bonnie?"

"I don't know!"

"Has she tried to call you lately?"

He stares at the blood on the ground and a low moan builds at the back of his throat. "Christ! No, okay? Give me back my gun."

I step out of his reach. "Guns are not for children. Do you know where she is?"

"I'm not a kid," he says, his eyes starting to tear up. "You have to take me to the doctor."

"Where's Bonnie?" I repeat. I lower the pistol, though, and hold it just at my side. "I'll help you, but you have to help me first."

"Fine, okay, whatever. She's—" He pauses and glances behind him. At first I think he's stalling, then the sound becomes apparent to me, too. Footsteps on packed snow.

We're not alone.

I move to Tommy's side and haul him closer.

He flinches. "Give me back my—"

"Is anyone meeting you here?" I hiss into his ear.

Smart boy that he is, he picks up right away. "No. But lots of people come here, just not usually when it's so cold out. Sometimes dog walkers in the morning."

But it's afternoon now. I lead him deeper into the woods, away from the footsteps. He notices my steady grip on the gun and frowns. "Do you even know how to use that?"

Of course I do, but I don't tell him that. I put my finger to my lips. I have the irrational thought that perhaps we've woken a bear, but that's silly. They're hibernating. If four-legged, it's probably a wolf. And if it's a hungry wolf, lean from slim winter pickings, we're in a bad place. Isolated, and with only one gun between us.

The average North American gray wolf runs between 31 and 37 miles per hour. The fastest human alive, the current Olympic record holder for speed, runs at just under 28. An out-of-shape woman on the cusp of middle age and a teenage boy with more bravado than sense couldn't even come close to 28, especially not here in the snow, running through a forest. For me to shoot at a wolf in motion, at the speed it would attack, I have to know the direction it would be coming from. If it's a pack, then we're really screwed. After a few moments, I don't hear anything else, but I feel something or someone out there. Human or animal, I still can't tell.

I lower my voice to a whisper. "You said there are other assholes following you?"

He nods. "Saw them outside of school and then at my mom's place. But they've just been watching. I thought Mom's dumbass boyfriend did something stupid. He was in a motorcycle gang awhile back."

"Whoever it is, looks like they're doing more than watching now."

Tommy touches my arm and points to a small parting in the woods. A narrow pathway, leading through a dense copse of trees. "Different trail. Back to the road."

As we head toward the path between the trees, I spare a glance behind me and see a red beam cut through the snow. It arrives at a tree branch just over my head as I step into the sights of a rifle. When I duck, I feel a blast of air just past my ear and a spray of bark erupts outward.

"Holy shit!" Tommy cries, stopping to look at the smoking perforation in the tree, but then I'm pulling him deeper into the woods. "Who are those guys? Hunters or something?"

Something tells me that these are not your average hunters looking for some venison for dinner. It's the same something that tells me that I look nothing like a deer and neither does Tommy, for that matter. I push Tommy ahead of me and we run through the woods, not caring anymore about the noise or stopping to check who's after us. The pathway opens up, but

Tommy heads to an even narrower trail that is more densely covered by tree trunks. In the summer, when the foliage is in full bloom, it would be difficult to pass here. But now we're both able to slide through, both being smaller and lighter, presumably, than whoever is hunting us.

I have to give the kid some credit. His cardio is exceptional. He's barely even breathing hard while I feel as though an asthma attack is imminent, even with all the adrenaline in my veins. The winter air is so crisp up here that it hurts my lungs. If this is what fresh feels like, I think I'll pass.

Tommy stops suddenly at a thick stand of ice-covered brambles that towers over the both of us. I look up at the tangled branches and hope that he doesn't mean to go over, then he gets on his knees and starts to dig under the brambles. The snow, hard packed, is difficult to pull apart and we're losing precious time. "The road is right behind here," he mutters. "Come on . . ."

I kneel next to him and we are both digging frantically, hearing crunching snow somewhere behind us, getting closer . . . until finally the snow gives and a tiny tunnel leads us through to the other side, Tommy first and me behind. I hear a bullet whiz nearby and know that they're close. I push Tommy the rest of the way through and then scramble to my feet. My ankle, the one that I sprained jumping off the balcony at the library, crumples underneath me, but I manage to get back on my feet. I don't feel the cold anymore, but I know I will soon and I try to put some distance between me and the people shooting at us before that happens. David's car is parked just a few yards ahead, far closer than Tommy's pickup, with a black SUV pulled over in between. From this direction I can't see if there is anyone in it, so I raise the pistol and shoot the back tire, the one closest to me, out. Another bullet gone, but it can't be helped.

"Get in!" I shout to Tommy, who is looking at me like I've suddenly grown a pair of wings and am about to take flight. If only I could. I jump in David's SUV and Tommy doesn't waste any more time. He slides into the seat next to me. Two bullets hit the back of the car as we drive off.

# 4

IT'S NOT UNTIL we're on the highway, scenery flying by in a blur of snow and trees, that Tommy is recovered enough from our near-death experience to speak again. "Who the hell are you?"

"I told you, I'm—"

"Bonnie's mom is a redhead. I saw her once when she dropped her off at Metrotown." He stares at me for a moment. "You're . . . you're her birth mom, right?"

"Yes." It's snowing again, and I'm going as fast as I can because there's nothing more upsetting than being shot at. First in warning by Tommy and then by the men in the woods. But the highway here is treacherous, and becoming more difficult to navigate by the minute, even with a four-wheel drive.

"Where did you learn to shoot like that?"

"That doesn't matter—"

"Yeah, it kind of does," he says, his eyes bright. "You shot that tire out from almost forty feet away without even stopping to aim—"

"I aimed."

"You're . . . you're like a *pro*."

Where I come from, this means something completely different. "We can talk about that later. But for now I'm looking for Bonnie. Did she come to see you?"

He's silent for a moment. "Is that why those other guys were watching me, too? What did she do? Because I know her and she wouldn't get into trouble this bad on her own. Her friend Mandy probably messed up somehow."

I glance over at him. He's shivering, coming down from the adrenaline rush, feeling the cold in his hands and feet. "I'm pretty sure it's not about Mandy and I don't know what it has to do with Bonnie yet. Maybe nothing. Far as I know, she just ran away. I don't know why those guys are looking for her."

"But she's in trouble."

"I think so." Then I hesitate. I don't want to scare him, but if anyone is good at picking out when adults are lying, it's kids. Before life scrubs away their natural instincts for it. "Do you know why she ran away?" I check the rearview mirror. No black SUV, not yet. If I'd been in less of a hurry, I would have shot the other tire out as well. But now I'm thinking they must have had a spare. How long would it take for them to change a tire?

"Yeah, she was having a hard time with her moms and pops. Found out her mom was cheating, and her pops was too stupid to even notice or do anything about it. Her dad was always gone on business. It was messed up in that house, man. Those two hated each other. Bonnie thought her mom even started to hate her, too. Her other mom, you know."

The highway narrows to one lane for a winding stretch and the car in front of us is crawling along. I try to keep my voice steady, try to stay calm, but anxiety still spreads. We've lost time going this slow because of the weather and now I'm stuck behind grandpa. Figures. "Did she come here to meet you?"

"She was supposed to, maybe a couple weeks ago, but she

never showed up. Figured she just bailed on me. It was weird, though, because she said she had some news and I thought she was . . ."

"Pregnant."

He blushes. "Yeah, I guess. But we always used . . . you know, when we . . ."

"I get it."

"I figured it was a false alarm when she didn't show up and she was embarrassed or something."

"So you haven't heard from her?"

"Nah. Mandy texted me a bunch saying she was missing and her folks were freaked out, but I figured that's just Mandy being a drama queen. She'd do anything for attention. But this don't make any sense. Why did those guys shoot at us?"

The road opens up again to two lanes and I accelerate as fast as I dare. It's below freezing out so the snow is sticking to the asphalt, turning it hard and slippery. "I don't know, but you'd better keep a low profile from now on, Tommy." I glance over at him and he meets my eyes briefly. "You understand what I'm saying?"

He nods. "Stay away. You don't have to tell me twice, lady. Started keeping my mom's boyfriend's gun on me when I noticed those guys watching me, but I don't really know how to use it like you, anyway. Maybe you could teach me?"

He continues on about this for a while, but I hardly hear the words. This time I don't have to play I Spy to know that someone is on my tail. The black SUV is careful to keep three cars behind at all times. Even with the bad roads and being stuck behind slow cars, it's still too soon for them to have changed the tire, unless they're Formula 1–level mechanics in addition to being guns for hire.

I was afraid of this.

The SUV doesn't make much effort to disguise its presence, leaving me to presume that fear is their goal. They want me to make a mistake of some sort, to panic, to let my imagination run wild. We pass the next exit and the two cars ahead of the SUV take the off-ramp. We're now the only cars on the road.

"Is that them?" Tommy's panicked voice brings me back. "I thought you shot their tire out!"

"They're called run-flat tires," I tell him. "They come in armored cars and some high-end vehicle brands."

"Holy shit!"

"Listen to me very carefully. We don't have much time. When I say so, I'm going to slow down and I want you to jump out, okay?"

He stares at me, wide-eyed. "What the fuck are you talking about?"

"Listen! There are no exits coming up and it's about to get winding. I can only go so fast. They will catch up and you can't be with me when they do. They've already shot at both of us. Do exactly what I say and you'll live. Do you understand?"

He shakes his head, but I know that he does. "When I slow down, open the door, jump, tuck, and roll. Stay tucked and out of the way until you hear them pass you and then run like hell in the opposite direction."

"Back to town?"

"Wherever. Take the battery out of your phone as soon as

you get moving. Borrow someone else's phone, or steal one, I don't care. Don't call your mom; call her boyfriend to pick you up and then get the hell out of town. You said he has connections, right?" Tommy nods. "Good. You need to use them. Stay away for a couple of months." I don't know how much surveillance they have on Tommy Jones, but I'm starting to suspect the worst.

"But school—"

I laugh. "You don't really care about school, do you?"

His eyes are wide and frightened. "I don't understand what's going on—"

"Someone is looking for Bonnie and they're not satisfied with just watching anymore. That's all you need to know."

"But . . . Is she alive?"

"I don't know. But I'm gonna find her either way, okay?" The promise surprises me. In a way, it has always been leading to this. The inevitable. This is what Everett Walsh had wanted from the start, had hoped for when he placed the call that morning.

A mountain rises up in front of us and the road gradually elevates. I speed up and take the first curve swiftly. David's car goes careening around the bend. The SUV disappears from my rearview mirror. The second curve, I slow down as much as I dare. "Now," I say to Tommy and give him a little shove with my right hand.

As soon as his body hits the snow behind me, I spare him one glance in my rearview mirror to make sure that he rolls out of the way, and then I speed up. The door that Tommy jumped out of hangs open, buffeted by the wind, then a sudden gust blows it shut. It's not closed all the way, the open-door light still blinks at me from the dash, but it's enough to avert suspicion from the car tailing me.

I drive for a minute, suddenly tense, staring into the rearview mirror and then relax when I see the SUV behind me. Good. It means Tommy has a chance now. What follows is not so much a high-speed chase as it is a trip through the mountains, slowing at bends in the road and speeding up for the short, straight stretches. They are relentless in their pursuit. Ahead of me is the longest straight stretch that we have had yet and the SUV speeds up. I see a glint of metal in my rearview mirror and then David's car swerves suddenly. They've shot out one of the rear tires. I grapple with the wheel, trying to hold the vehicle in place, but the speed is too fast and the car bucks in protest. They use the distraction to gain several car lengths on me and now they are almost on my bumper. The road here is dangerously narrow, with a single lane for cars traveling in each direction.

The road curves up ahead and they have mere seconds to catch me before I disappear again. Another gunshot rings out and the other tire blows. The SUV, difficult to control with one tire gone, is damn near impossible with two. Whoever is in charge of the gun right now is doing a hell of a better job than the guy after us in the woods. The smart thing to do would be to stop right here, raise the white flag, and let these armed thugs, who seem to have gone guerrilla, do with me as they may. But I've never been a white flag kind of girl. In fact, I don't think I've ever owned a single piece of white fabric in my life. And, besides, you don't shoot out the tires of a vehicle in this kind of terrain in order to just question somebody. Not me, not

Tommy. They're tying up loose ends. Here on these roads, with winter ice and gusts of wind so strong that they can rattle vehicles twice the size of David's SUV right off the road, they're not interested in talking anymore. The moment for raising a white flag has passed. What I do instead is speed toward the bend in the road coming up, slow down just as I take the curve, and follow the exact instructions that I gave to Tommy.

A blast of icy air slaps me in the face as I jump out and then the air is replaced by a mouthful of snow. A searing pain jolts up my already aching legs, legs that have taken the brunt of a fall not even a week ago. There's a loud, sharp noise as David's brand-new SUV goes over the road barrier and plummets to the valley below. I lose my grip on Tommy's gun, which goes skating after the car. And finally a distant crash.

I'm just in front of a ridge of snow between the road and the protective railing, so I crawl as far out of sight as I can and then burrow into a snowbank. Just seconds later, the SUV screeches to a halt and the doors open. I huddle there, freezing and silent, and force my ragged breathing to even out. Heavily booted feet take off to the edge of the barrier where the car has gone hurtling over.

"Fuck!" a man exclaims. "Crazy bitch. That was her in the woods with the kid, right? The one that broke into our office? You sure of that?"

There's a pause and then the voice that haunts my dreams breaks the silence. "I'm sure," he says evenly. Like he's in no hurry at all. Like women and children go careening over the side of the road every day and Tommy and I are just today's casualties. "Let's go."

"Don't you want to see if she's dead . . . and the kid, too?"

"No. We can't be seen here. We'll stay close by and wait for news."

They get back into the car. I stay put until the sound of their engine recedes before climbing to my feet and staggering onto the highway. There are no cars for miles around and I am so cold that I have to will my tongue to the back of my mouth so my chattering teeth won't pierce it. Then I start walking.

# 5

AFTER THE ATTEMPT on my life, my mind refuses to rest. What about my investigation of a missing girl is worth killing over? Drugs, sex, and alcohol is the path that Bonnie went down. She ran away to be with her boyfriend, not to escape private security operatives that act more like thugs or mercenaries than anything else. The more I know, the bigger the picture becomes, and it makes me nervous because if there is one thing that is becoming clear to me, it is that she is in danger. And that it matters to me.

I wait for several hours just outside Kelowna, until the authorities have picked through the debris of the crash. They'll know by now that I'm not in a bloody heap at the bottom of the ravine. My first call is to Seb. I suspect that they, whoever they are, are most likely monitoring the office line, so I tell him that I'm calling from a hospital, I can't tell him where, but I'm hurt. I won't make my week deadline. When Seb collects himself enough to shout some profanities in my ear before pleading with me to know where I am, that he'll come get me, I just say west and hang up. Then I take the battery out of my phone.

With any luck, they'll come looking for me. The more time they waste on me, the better the odds are for Bonnie.

If she's alive.

A sad old husky wails at me from the window as I drive away

[2]

from the animal hospital and rescue facility in the old Honda I found in the yard. I'd walked him, let him roam around with me in the clinic unencumbered, and left him with enough water and food to last until whoever is out on emergency calls returns. A sign on the window says that the hospital isn't open on weekends except for emergencies, but they had left the spare keys to the Honda in an office drawer.

And technically, I haven't lied to Seb about the hospital or being west. West is relative to a fixed point that I chose not to mention.

I think about the road I'm about to take, and wish in vain for the damp air and overcast skies that I am most comfortable with. Endless rainy days and soggy streets are usually nobody's first choice, but they are a far cry ahead of what I'm headed toward now. To more snow.

# 6

BONNIE, THAT'S WHO she is.

She's even said it out loud a few times, her words weak, scratchy and alien in this place. She hasn't heard another voice since she's been here, nothing but the birds in the trees, calling to each other. Fallen twigs and branches have made her a decent enough barrier to her new home. Enough to keep most of the chill out, and the larger animals, but Bonnie knows that it is foolish to rely on sticks for protection. They won't keep away any creature that truly wants to get inside. But here, sheltered and alone, drinking from a nearby creek, Bonnie finally feels some measure of safety. Not from the four-legged animals—she isn't stupid—but two-legged ones at least.

She wants her mother and father but they wouldn't even know how to begin to look for her. The last thing she ever told them was a lie. She didn't even say goodbye to her mom, she remembers that clearly. Lynn, that's what she'd taken to calling her lately. Not even Mom anymore. Lynn was in the kitchen with a cup of coffee, waiting for Bonnie to come down. There was a single place set at the kitchen table with a stack of pancakes. They ignored each other as Bonnie ate, but when she turned her back to put her plate in the dishwasher she could feel Lynn's gaze roving over her. This was not unusual. Lynn preferred to look at her when she wasn't watching, but when Bonnie turned,

Lynn was staring at the cup in her hands. For more than a year now, she hadn't been able to meet her daughter's eyes.

But Bonnie has another mother. She even wrote her a letter once when she was twelve, though she didn't have an address to send it to. That letter took her so long to write that she remembers each word, remembers them because she'd thrown away draft after draft. She'd spent hours composing it and in the end threw the final letter away with all the others. But she knows what she'd written.

> Dear Mom,
>
> I know you don't know me. My name is Bronwyn, but you can call me Bonnie. I like music and sports, but that's about it. My parents (the ones that I live with) are Everett and Lynn. They're not so bad, but they just don't understand. Like, nothing. They just don't get it. People always stare at us. Sometimes I don't want to go out with them because I can't take all the staring.
>
> You never looked for me, but I looked for you. I don't know why you gave me away, but I'm sure you had a good reason.
>
> I don't blame you, okay? I just want to talk.
> Your daughter,
> *Bronwyn (Bonnie)*

And then she had scribbled her email address and phone number at the bottom of the letter, just in case.

Bonnie is glad that she threw away that letter. It was full of lies, anyway. She never really liked music or sports and she sure as hell blamed her real mom for giving her up. Who wouldn't? The only one who understood her was Tommy, whose dad walked out on him and his mom when he was just a baby, but Tommy's so far away now that it might as well be another planet.

She closes her eyes and goes to sleep. Curled up on her side, her cheek pressed against the dirt, she doesn't hear the quiet footstep move closer. She doesn't see the eye pressed against a hole in her makeshift barrier. She doesn't see the person step away, mobile phone in hand.

# THREE

# 1

SOME THINGS ARE just too easy for the fabulously wealthy.

Like a regular ski resort where there's a road that you can drive your Bugatti right up to the door on, tip the valet to park it for you, and then walk inside to enjoy a hot beverage before hitting the slopes. No, because that's too simple. That kind of ski resort is only for your garden-variety millionaires. If you're truly wealthy, you'll go to the ski resort that is referred to as "the Chalet," which only allows you to shuttle in from the nearby private airport for personal aircrafts, helicopter in directly, or, alternatively, have your driver take you to the bottom of the road where a hotel vehicle awaits you. Because your Bugatti will not get you past a treacherous access road reserved only for shuttles and hotel staff that must necessarily be live-in or fished from a nearby town. The only way they could make the resort harder to get to would be to surround it with a moat filled with dying peasants.

I pull into the small town near the base of the access road with a sore body, throbbing headache, an ankle that is probably permanently sprained (if not broken), and a shoulder that's possibly dislocated from my jump out of a moving vehicle. And, to boot, I'm dressed for a wet Vancouver climate and not for a place that holds the record for highest snowfall in the country two years in a row. My poor rain gear simply can't take the pressure and has frozen on my body, not even able to muster up a wind barrier.

I park the caretaker's Honda in front of a diner, in between the two cars already parked there, one of them a repair truck, and shiver my way to the front door. All noise is sucked into a vacuum as soon as I enter. The woman behind the counter pauses her coffee making to stare and the two middle-aged male patrons turn to get a good look. The men are in thick jackets and snow pants and the woman is bundled up in a red woolen sweater.

"You the new cleaner?" one of the men asks, sliding off his stool. "For the big shindig?"

"Ah . . ." I want to nod, but all I can manage is to stand there making unintelligible sounds through my chattering teeth.

The man frowns, taking this as an affirmative. "They usually hire younger, with bigger . . ." He trails off, then looks to the lady behind the counter for support.

"Tits?" she ventures.

"Hair?" offers the other man.

"Both?" I say, when it's my turn. I'm slightly warmer now, and actual syllables are manageable.

The man shuffles his feet and mutters something inaudible in reply.

"What was that?" I say loudly. "I couldn't hear you."

"I said, I'm heading up there just now, I'm night maintenance supervisor, so if you want a ride . . . that car ain't gonna make it on this road, especially without snow tires, lady." He glares at the Honda. "What the hell were you thinking driving that thing up here? I'm Carl, by the way."

I take this as some sort of apology for the insult to my tits and hair. He's not exactly the finest physical specimen himself.

"Carl here gets his foot in his mouth at least twice a day, honey, so don't take him too serious. He'll be all right to take you up," says the lady behind the counter.

"You really ain't gonna make it in that old shitpile. No offense," says the other man.

I turn to Carl. "You're not going to kill me and dump my body somewhere in the snow, are you?"

Carl, bless his simple heart, turns bright red. "Of course not!" The question is so outlandish that there's no way he could have fabricated that kind of indignation within mere moments of hearing it unless he was telling the truth. Part of me acknowledges that even if those were his intensions, I would still take my chances for the ride. There's a horse man on the mountain that might know a little something about Bonnie's disappearance. Or at least why WIN Security is so concerned about it.

The lady behind the counter giggles. "Carl," she says, shaking her platinum blond curls. "Killing somebody and dumping them in the snow." She smirks and goes back to wiping down the counter.

"Come on," says Carl, downing the rest of his coffee and heading for the door. "Lucy from HR said you weren't gonna make it today after all, but I thought I'd wait around just in case."

I park the Honda out back and then follow Carl to his old pickup truck, outfitted with winter tires. We start up the mountain in silence, my favorite kind of companion.

# 2

CARL WASN'T KIDDING about the road. I thought the highway to get here was bad, but this access road is a sight to behold . . . or would be, I'm sure, if I could see more than a few feet in front of me. What I do see is enough to make me grip the armrest between us like a lifeline.

He doesn't speak much during the treacherous drive that seems to wind its way up and around the mountain. To make matters worse, it starts to snow and our visibility is now limited to just in front of the headlights. Carl puts on a country radio station and hums along while I think about renewing my faith in a higher power. But it seems selfish to invoke one only when I need it, so I put all thoughts of faith behind me and breathe a sigh of relief when a building rises up in front of us, lights blazing, illuminating the dark valley around it. Carl parks around back.

I have no idea what time it is. It could be evening or the dead of night, I can hardly tell.

Carl's voice intrudes. "We got a team of five day cleaners and two night cleaners. Maria used to be a swing shift, but she quit last week. It's hell to get people up here to work. Most of 'em stay in the staff quarters 'round back or in town but I only live a couple hours away and my wife don't like me to be gone all the time. You do your paperwork yet?"

I shake my head. We get out of the car and fight our way through the icy mountain drafts to the service entrance.

"Arright," Carl says, once we're inside. He keeps walking, but a blast of warm air hits me and I need a moment to melt. He glances back when he sees I'm not following. "You'll get used to it, don't worry. Come on."

I force my feet to move. They're clunky, attached to legs that have recently jumped from a balcony and out of a moving vehicle.

"Lucy," Carl continues, "our HR gal, she's off today, so I'll get you a key and a uniform. You can talk to her in the morning when your shift is over. You know, they usually don't start new people on the night shift but, hey, guess they gotta make some adjustments when the corporate people book the whole place."

"Corporate people?" I ask, following him down a long hallway to a small office at the end of it.

"For some big meeting. VIPs and all that. Bought the whole place out, if you can believe it, though, to be honest, it ain't such a large place. I think they use that to jack the prices up. All the people who can afford to stay here are VIPs but management's been tearing their hair out for this weekend. Helipad on the roof's had traffic like you wouldn't believe. And everybody's got their own security, which usually ain't so much of a bother all the way up here." Carl has become a real chatterbox once he got out of his truck, and the extra effort seems to have tired him out. He rummages through a wardrobe off to the side of the room and pulls out a pair of black pants and a black monogrammed shirt.

"Bathroom's just across the hall there. Why don't you clean

yourself up a bit and come back when you're ready. I'll have a key programmed for you by then. Oh, and is that all you got?" He nods to my backpack.

"Yes."

"Well, we can store that in here for the time being. No sense wasting time in the staff quarters right now. Shift starts in about ten minutes. They, uh, prefer the ladies have their hair pulled back." The last sentence was uttered with Carl staring at a point somewhere to the left of my shoulder.

A minute later, glancing into the bathroom mirror, I see the problem. Matted on one side, like a rat's nest on the other, and looking like it would scare away even the most industrial of combs, my hair has seen better days. It takes me a full ten minutes to wrestle it into a bun. After that, I wash in the sink and apply two fresh coats of deodorant. A girl can never be too prudent when it comes to deodorant. Then I put on my new uniform. It's made of warm, soft material. A lot nicer than my clothes, that's for sure. I make a mental note to keep them once I get out of here.

Carl is already changed by the time I walk back into his office. He has noticed my limp and the tender way I hold my shoulder. He's too much of a gentleman to say anything about it, but I can tell what he's thinking. Lucy must be desperate to hire someone like me. Carl, however, is not in charge of hiring, so he shrugs it off and moves on. He hands me a key card and walks me through the building. I take stock of the most luxurious chalet this side of the Pacific. High, vaulted ceilings, wood accents, and floor-to-ceiling windows overlooking the valley below. We move through the lobby, meeting rooms, bathrooms, and kitchens. Tones are warm and soothing but each room still gives the sense of being in a large space. All guest quarters are occupied, Carl explains to me with a shrug, but the day cleaners are responsible for attending to them. Everything but the guest quarters gets cleaned at night.

I ask if he has a guest list with room numbers.

"No, we don't clean rooms on this shift, remember? Plus, they don't give us that information. Every morning day shift gets room numbers they have to take care of."

With that, Carl introduces me to the four floors of guest quarters. All guests have separate elevator cards that will take these fancy people to their designated floor only. Only the first floor of guest quarters is set up like a regular hotel, with fifteen standard rooms. "For the assistants and bodyguards," Carl explains.

"What's the event?" Brazuca had never said outright what it was.

"Some kind of annual thing. Asian Partnerships in Holding Hands and Taking Over the Country or something."

He smiles, but there's some confusion and anger there. Given the nature of the housing crisis in Vancouver, immigration has been a hot-button issue in this province. Vancouver has become a hedge city where rich foreigners park their assets, drive up housing values, and price out the middle class, all while underreporting their overseas incomes to relieve their tax burden. Some of them don't even live in their expensive mansions for much of the year, even though they're the only ones that can afford to live well in the city and have luxuries like a yard. Even though Carl doesn't live in Vancouver, he might have wanted to at one point, until his bank account balance put him out of the running.

"Damn government lets everybody in," he continues. Maybe he's venting, or maybe he's hoping I'll take the bait. But I've never been able to afford property, prime or otherwise. So immigration doesn't bother me. Although before Bonnie disappeared, I had been saving for a deposit to move with Whisper into an apartment of our own, maybe something with a balcony.

I just nod like it's the most interesting thing anyone's ever said and keep my mouth closed. Carl eventually gets bored of hearing the sound of his own voice and shuts up. He gives me a swipe card to open doors to everything but the guest quarters and I spend the rest of the night cleaning the public spaces. I am not much of a cleaner but I compensate technique with the liberal application of cleaning solvents. Carl has left me with a cart and a to-do list. He's presumably back in his office, napping, while he has delegated all of the dirty work to me. I'm so tired that I can barely stand, but I haven't yet figured out how to find which of the WIN partners is here and how I'm going to get to him.

It's the early hours of the morning and I'm mucking out stalls in the men's bathroom off the lobby when the door swings open and a man enters. I frown. The CLEANING IN PROGRESS sign is just outside and I'm left wondering why anyone would be down here at this time.

"Cleaning," I say loudly.

"Sorry, sorry," the man says, about to back away. He slips a little on the wet floor that I mistakenly mopped first, before cleaning the rest. The man clutches at the sink for balance. I back out of the stall, toilet brush in hand, and our eyes meet in the glass.

Brazuca's jaw drops, mirroring my own astonished expression.

# 3

"DO YOU JUST wait by bathrooms to surprise me?" Brazuca says finally. It's taken a minute for the both of us to get over our shock. He's wearing the same clothes that he had on when we saw each other last, now rumpled almost beyond recognition after a couple days of hard driving. He takes in the hotel uniform worth more than my normal clothes, the neat hair pulled back, and lingers on my face, which is drawn and haggard and irritated by the proximity of so many cleaning solvents. Since I'm standing still, he doesn't yet notice my sprained ankle.

I open my mouth to speak, but no words come out. *Sorry I hit you with a tire iron, interrogated you, threw your car keys into the woods, and left you stranded in the middle of nowhere* doesn't seem to cut it.

"See, no weapons this time," I say instead.

He eyes the toilet brush in my hand. I put it back in the cart and turn to him, palms up.

He's not overwhelmed with gratitude. "What a relief," he replies, rubbing the back of his head. "We have to stop meeting in men's bathrooms, Nora. It's getting a little weird."

"Bridges were better."

"Safer," he agrees. "For me, anyway."

We sigh, almost in unison. I remember the time when we were just silent alcoholics, without weapons and dangerous

bathroom encounters between us. Brazuca is no doubt wishing for the time before he agreed to become my sponsor. Sometimes it takes just one bad decision to derail your life. I know
that better than anyone.

He puts up a hand. "Before you say anything. Just give me
a minute here." I watch as he splashes his face with cold water,
dries it off with a plush hand towel, rolled just so because I'm not
the one who rolled it, and places it in the discreet laundry basket
near the sink. Frowning, I pick up the towel and put it into my
laundry basket. Then I add a clean towel to the stack. Carl was
very particular about numbers. The cleaning cart is remarkably
organized, with compartments for every little detail.

"So I had to wait until morning to find my car keys," Brazuca
says. "In case you were wondering."

Here it comes.

"The gas station attendant couldn't understand how I could
have lost them in the woods. He wanted to call the authorities
to warn them about a 'sketchy woman driving an SUV,' but I
convinced him otherwise. You want to know why?"

"You're a good Christian?" I venture.

"My parents are Buddhist, actually."

Go figure. It's the west coast, after all. And hippie parents
would explain the alcoholism. "That doesn't mean you're not
Christian."

He ignores this. "I didn't let him call the authorities, because
I didn't want you to get in trouble."

"Thanks."

"Oh, don't mention it," he says, his voice like warm honey.
That's how I know it's going to be bad. Brazuca is a charming

man, but he has never turned it up on me before now. He is smiling a smile that doesn't reach his eyes. "I looked into the disappearance you mentioned," he continues. "There was a missing person's report filed, the third one on that same girl. Turns out, she's adopted."

I flinch. I've never had much of a poker face.

"Oh, yeah. I was pretty surprised to hear that one, too. I stopped by to have a chat with the parents. Her father says that he contacted the birth mother but she didn't want to help. He was disappointed because she didn't even seem to care . . . But he just didn't know her very well, did he?"

He waits for a response. I don't give in to the pressure, so he takes my silence as an affirmative.

"The birth mother, what an interesting case, and I've seen a lot. She was in and out of foster care as a kid. Left the Canadian Forces after basic training. And then there was the generally disobedient behavior. Bad attitude. Disappeared off the map for a couple of years after the discharge . . . want to know what happened to her?"

"Fuck off."

"That's exactly what she did—how did you know? And then she was found dumped in a ditch, wrapped in a blanket, raped and beaten to death. Except she wasn't actually dead, despite appearances. Just barely alive. Spent six months in a coma, during which time her attacker was never found. She woke up and discovered she was pregnant, but the province stops funding abortion services after five months, so she couldn't do anything about it. Plus, she wasn't especially talkative back then. She tried to self-abort or commit suicide and was considered a threat to herself and the child. Spent the remainder of the pregnancy recovering in an institution. Once the baby was born, she put it up for adoption and walked away."

I drag the cleaning cart over to the door.

"You see," Brazuca says. "What he didn't understand is that for someone to survive being assaulted and beaten within an inch of her life, bear a child from that assault, battle addiction, and win, that woman is a fighter. Someone like that wouldn't just walk away from the girl if she was in trouble. Especially if she thinks that no one else is going to fight for her. That girl's birth mother already has a problem with authority. Doesn't like them. Doesn't trust them. So she's going to do something, that's almost a given. But she's going to do it on her own terms."

Mercifully, the bathroom door swings open and Carl saunters in, almost bowling me over. He looks at my face, drained of all expression, and then for the first time notices Brazuca, rigid with tension, gripping the sides of the sink.

"Came to see how you were making out," Carl says, much too loud for a nighttime bathroom rendezvous.

"Fine," I mutter.

"That's good," Carl says, hooking his thumbs into his belt loops. He looks from me to Brazuca.

Brazuca scratches at the stubble on his chin and gives Carl a perfunctory nod as he leaves.

After the door swings shut, Carl sighs. "That man wasn't troubling you, was he?"

"Not in the way you're thinking."

He frowns and spends a moment considering what I could

possibly be referring to, then decides it's not worth the effort. "Maybe I should take care of the men's facilities from now on."

I nod. "That might be for the best."

I push my cleaning cart out of the bathroom and move into the dining room, which is next on my to-do list. I wipe down the tables there with a cloth that could be dirty or clean. I'm too rattled to pay attention. Brazuca emptied his sleeve of the cards he'd stashed there, showing himself to be more thorough and vengeful than I'd imagined. Troubling me indeed. He was, and with the only thing that can have any kind of true effect on me.

My past.

# 4

I HAVE A nightmare that goes something like this: I am being suffocated by a pillow and my arms are tied over my head. Eventually, one of my arms breaks free and I find a loose screw from the headboard. Maybe I don't find it loose, maybe I pry at it until it comes off in my hand. Sometimes this detail changes. But what follows never does. My lungs scream for oxygen and my body thrashes about looking for some kind of leverage. I can't feel anything below my waist. No sensation, good or bad. Nothing. As I continue to struggle, I swing the screw down with my free hand and find that there's nothing there but air. I claw and claw with the screw, but it finds no purchase . . . and then it catches an inch of flesh, and tears through it. I fight so hard that my body becomes exhausted and heavy with fear. Then I wake up gasping for breath.

This nightmare used to be a nightly event except when I drank so heavily that sleep would excise it from my mind. It has faded with time, but comes back once or twice a year to remind me what it's like when all of the breath is being cut off from my lungs and no one listens to my screams.

When Carl showed me to my room after my shift with instructions to see HR Lucy first thing, I fell asleep almost immediately in my uniform and woke up two hours later from that dream, which has decided to put in an appearance for the first time this year. I shouldn't be surprised, but I am. I've known it was coming since I met Everett and Lynn at that café but goddamn it, I just wasn't prepared. I pace in my tiny room in the staff quarters, and try to shake off the effects of the nightmare. My body is on auto-pilot and I can't legitimately remember the last time I fed it any-thing other than coffee or granola bars from gas stations.

There's a knock on the door.

"It's me," says Brazuca from the other side.

I stop pacing.

"I know you're in there."

That's not a good enough reason to open the door for anyone.

"I have food."

It takes me two short steps to cross the room. "How did you find me?" I ask, as I let him in.

"I saw the old man lead you into the building, then this light came on."

The staff quarters are tucked away by the west side of the chalet, connected to the main building by a short, narrow hall-way so that it doesn't obstruct the main panoramic views. When you're paying through the roof for this kind of vista, you don't want to see the staff. You just want them to be close by when you need the sheets turned down and your coffee to be hot.

Brazuca holds up a paper bag. "Peace offering from the break-fast buffet."

I look inside the bag and pull out a carton with toast, jam, eggs, and bacon. My stomach twists into a knot at the smell of hot, greasy food. I motion him to have a seat on the bed while I eat at the desk. He stares at me with undisguised interest as I shovel food into my mouth.

"What are you looking at?"

"When was the last time you ate something?"

"Yesterday . . . I think."

He shakes his head. "Let's leave that one alone."

"Like you're any better." I wave my fork toward the vicinity of his rib cage.

"Nora, I just found out that James Whitehall won't be here after all. Problem at their Hong Kong offices. And Lester Nyman is away on business. I'm sorry; the firm is handling the security for the conference and my contacts say Whitehall was supposed to put in a personal appearance. The keynote was by an official of a corporation that's a pretty big fish for the firm. They were WIN's first client when they started up."

"How did they land a big-fish client right off the bat?"

"Nyman is the brains but Whitehall has the military background. Word on the street is that he did some private work—"

"Meaning mercenary."

"Not necessarily, but it happens more often than people think. I heard he worked for old man Zhang when they were based in Hong Kong. But this is a few decades ago, so no one can really trace the connection."

"Old man Zhang?" Zhang sounds familiar, but the carbs, fat, and protein molecules are rushing to my brain, turning it sluggish.

"Ray Zhang. Head of Zhang-Wei Industries. There've been rumors about him for years, mostly that not everything is aboveboard. Some of his associates have triad connections but no one's ever been able to pin anything on him."

We are silent for a moment, immersed in our own thoughts. I remember where I heard the name now. Angus Holland told me Zhang-Wei Industries had dealings with Syntamar in the Congo. Syntamar, the company Starling was looking into before he was murdered.

"Organized crime doesn't get a lot of attention in this country these days," Brazuca says. He hasn't yet noticed my attention is elsewhere.

I nod. "'Terrorism' is the catchword everywhere now. Gangs do what they want."

"Not quite. They would do what they want anyway, but we can't deny that in this current political climate it's easier for them. I don't know if Zhang is triad, or just worked with them sometimes, or if those rumors have no basis in truth. We just don't have that information. Anyway, that's neither here nor there, really. If Whitehall was going to show up, it would be for a Zhang-Wei Industries event. For your missing girl, I would have liked to get you in a room with him to at least ask what kind of stake he's got in this."

"So no talking to the horse's owner."

"With their level of security and their schedules, I doubt it. I guess you were right to go looking into his mouth willy-nilly like that."

He uses these bizarre expressions on occasion, which make me think that even though he has no British accent, perhaps he spent some time overseas in his youth. I've never heard a Canadian under the age of sixty say "willy-nilly." Brazuca leans back on the bed that I've just left, on my crumpled sheets, and closes his eyes. It's surprisingly intimate. One shove will send him toppling to the ground and I'm tempted because I worked all night to earn this bed and he's done nothing but drive.

"Ah," he sighs, rubbing the sore spot behind his head.

And then I remember that it's probably my fault that he can't sit upright, or stand and leave the room now that he has over-stayed his welcome. I'm not exactly a good sport about facing the consequences of my actions, but I read somewhere that it's never too late to start.

I put the empty carton back in the paper bag and toss it in the trash bin by the desk. "What do you know about Syntamar Industries?"

He frowns. "Syntamar? Nothing really, just that there was a roadblock and protest a few years ago about a proposed mine up north and they were one of the investors for the project."

"They had a couple of joint ventures with Zhang-Wei a while back after the two worked the same region in the Congo."

"How do you know that? What's the connection with Syn-tamar and your girl?"

I have a decision to make here. He knows enough of my past to link me with Mike Starling, if he hasn't already, but I'm not quite prepared to tell him that we're not just looking into a dis-appearance now. We might be looking into Bonnie's kidnap-ping. And Starling's murder. "Nothing that I can make sense of, but it came up once and I thought it was interesting."

"I might know someone who could give you some more in-formation on Zhang-Wei," he says slowly. "Possibly Syntamar."

"You do?"

"Maybe," he says, mid-yawn.

I feel drowsy now that my stomach is full so I lay my head on the desk. When I wake up three hours later, Brazuca is gone. All that's left of him is a note on the corner of the desk. "Second floor lounge. 2 P.M."

# 5

BRAZUCA IS WAITING for me when I get off the service elevator just before two. I entered the main floor from the staff quarters, just to avoid passing anyone in the hallway. According to the schedule in Carl's office, there's a meeting taking place in one of the first-floor salons as we speak.

"I have a friend who's here for the conference," Brazuca says, by way of greeting. "He might be able to give us some info on Syntamar."

"Who's the friend?"

"Bernard Lam," he says as we enter the lounge, before I have time to stop and stare in wonder at the man Seb wrote a profile piece on two years ago.

Bernard Lam is the only heir to a billion-dollar fortune. He has been educated at Harvard, Oxford, and even had a brief stint at the Sorbonne. His philanthropy is well known and his face is often splattered about Vancouver's society pages as being one of the city's most generous imports. Vast wealth has not eroded his graciousness and sense of humor, however, or the charisma that radiates from him in waves.

"Bazooka!" he calls affectionately as he spots Brazuca from across the lounge. It's dim and quiet in here so it takes us a moment to pick him out among the plush suedes, leathers, and fur-trimmed throws. The purpose of this room isn't to draw attention to the furnishings; it's to showcase the incredible view of the valley below us. We've interrupted Lam from sniffing a glass of amber liquid like it is a rare and beautiful flower as he contemplates the meaning of life. Or something like that. Lam ignores Brazuca's attempts to sidestep his hug, which does not appear to be an easy task. Lam is tall, but round. His cheeks are full and red with the crisp mountain air. Though he appears to have all his teeth, he still somehow manages to remind me of a large, spoiled baby. He embraces Brazuca, who, in comparison, looks like a sickly weakling drowning in a vat of expensive dough.

Brazuca is released and wheezes in a breath. Lam now turns to me. I've hung out my staff uniform just in case I need to use it tonight and am wearing my best jeans and the only sweater I own with no holes. There's a coffee stain on the back of it and although Lam could not possibly see this from the angle at which we're now facing each other, I get the feeling that this affable-looking man-baby knows that it is there. "This must be your—"

"He's my sponsor," I tell him.

"We're testing her resolve today," Brazuca adds, eyeing the glass of cognac. It seems we're also testing his resolve.

"Ah." Lam puts down the glass. My gaze lingers a good two seconds longer than it should. The bottle that it came from most likely cost more than my monthly salary. "Well, I'm glad you made it. How are things working out for you at—"

"Let's talk about that later," Brazuca says. Their eyes meet over the top of my head.

Lam smiles as though it never happened and turns back to me. "You must be the reason my good friend decided to make the trek. I've been trying to get him out of the city for years. Loosen up a little."

"Yeah, we're here to have a good time. I'm doing some research on rich Asians."

Brazuca sends me a warning glance, which I ignore.

Lam laughs. "Well, you've come to the right place." He takes my elbow. "Come, let's walk."

I stare at his hand until he removes it. He glances at Brazuca over my head. Again. I'm starting to see a pattern with these two. That I'm the odd woman out.

Lam takes a graceful step back. "My apologies if I seem overly familiar. You see, Jon and I go back a long way. Any friend of his, well, I consider that person to be a friend of mine as well. So, please, tell me how I can help you."

"Syntamar Industries," I say, pulling out the newspaper clipping from Starling's storage locker. "Do you know who this man is?" I point to the Asian businessman who refuses to crack a smile among all the other grinning execs.

Lam stares at the photograph for a moment. "No," he says smoothly. "No idea."

There's a flaw in my special skill.

I can tell when someone is lying, yes, but there is nothing I can do to make them tell the truth. I can only look into their eyes and let them know what I see. That they're not fooling me. If it sounds like precious little, that's because it is. But it's all I have. I stare at Bernard Lam, who I want to believe is kind and honest, but wanting it doesn't make it true. Now I'm angry. "Do you always lie to your friends?"

"Pardon me?"

"You just said any friend of Brazuca is a friend of yours. So we're friends now, then. Why are you lying about the man in this photo?"

Lam looks to Brazuca for help, yet again, over my head. I get close to him, close enough to smell his crisp, woodsy after-shave. Now I appear to be drowning in a vat of doughy billion-aire. "Don't look at him. Look at me. A girl is missing, okay? A teenage girl and I'm trying to find her."

All of his attention turns to me. I've invaded his personal space but instead of backing away, feeling threatened, he seems to enjoy it. Or maybe he's just used to women wanting to get close. Curl up next to his piles of spare cash, maybe. "What does Syntamar have to do with it?"

"I don't know yet that it does. This is what I'm trying to find out. And I need to know who that man is."

"Honey," he says, even though I might possibly be older than him, "maybe we should take a walk."

"Sugar lumps, I don't go for strolls with liars."

Lam's face breaks out into a huge smile. "I like you. You don't beat around the bush. All right, if you won't be dissuaded." He glances around, but apart from a bartender at the end of the room, minding his own business, we're alone. "This isn't ex-actly the place for candor, baby, but if you insist. The man in that photograph is Ray Zhang."

I glance at Brazuca. He gives me a small shake of his head. "Of Zhang-Wei Industries?"

"That's the one. He's very old now and, rumor has it, very ill. Also, he doesn't like to be photographed, so I'm very surprised he allowed that one to be taken." He pauses here, and seems to come to a decision. "Ray Zhang is a back-channel man, always has been, and he's built an empire from using subversive methods. Still, I doubt he has anything to do with your missing girl. Not really his style."

"Is there anyone from Zhang-Wei here? Someone I could ask?"

Lam hesitates for a moment. "His daughter-in-law is doing the keynote this weekend. She represents the company now, but they have offices in both Hong Kong and Vancouver and she usually spends most of her time in Hong Kong. They're mostly into resource and mineral extraction and, though I don't recall the specifics, I remember hearing that they used to do business with Syntamar."

"How long is she here for?"

"In the country? I have no idea. We're not exactly friends. I wouldn't advise approaching her unless you absolutely must. Jia Zhang does not care about missing girls. She will eat you alive, as she tried to do with my father's company many times over." He says this all lightly, as if we are on a golf course about to enjoy a few beers and tee off. There's a certain amount of respect in his voice for the Zhangs, even if he doesn't like them.

"It wouldn't hurt to ask," I tell him.

I feel like there is a thread that I'm not seeing. Zhang is connected to WIN, which, for some reason, has been looking for Bonnie. He is also somehow connected to Syntamar Industries, which Mike Starling was looking into just before he was murdered. So maybe Zhang is the horse's owner, not James Whitehall or Lester Nyman.

"It might hurt to ask. With Jia, that's a risk you take. She keeps a private security guard with her at all times when she's in the country. His name is Dao. He is not one to take people who bother her lightly and he has . . . let's just say he's got a bit of a shady past and a reputation for brutality."

I consider this for a moment. "So you're talking triad?" Brazuca had mentioned the same thing when we spoke about Zhang.

Lam takes a sip of his cognac. He closes his eyes in pleasure. I imagine what it must feel like going down his throat and warming his belly, and suddenly it's too hot in here. "There are rumors," he tells me once his eyes are open again. "But I wouldn't go sharing that opinion if I were you."

Brazuca goes to the window and looks out at the snowcapped mountains. Lam notices for the first time the bruise on the back of his neck. "Jon! What happened to you?"

Brazuca's voice is deliberately light. "A run-in with a tire iron, nothing to be concerned about."

"I see." Lam's expression is grave. "So this is serious."

"This is just a bump," Brazuca says, glancing over at me. "I've had worse. Tell us about Ray Zhang. Does he have a thing for little girls?"

"Nobody knows that much about his personal life, but I would be shocked if he did. He just doesn't seem the type."

"But."

"But I don't really know. Almost everything about him is pure speculation. He's a widower with one son and a grandson. I've met his son Kai once or twice. A spoiled brat—and I know a thing or two about that. He's completely westernized but likes the idea of old-school gangsterism. Although I doubt he really has the capacity for it. Him I can see messing with little girls, though I doubt his leash is long enough for that these days."

Lam smirks to himself, enjoying some private joke. Now it's Brazuca and I exchanging glances. "Jia, on the other hand . . . I wouldn't be surprised if she was running a gang or two of her own, but I don't see Ray Zhang giving her, or his son, much leeway in that department. He is ruthless about his company and won't see anybody smear it."

"Any idea where we can find him?"

Lam hesitates and I sense he wants to evade the question somehow, but it is Brazuca who asked. There seems to be a bond between them that I don't understand. "Rumor has it that a subsidiary of his company has permits to do survey work on Vancouver Island for a copper mine. I go fishing there every now and then. About two years ago, I heard from my real estate agent that Jia inquired about a cabin that I put on the market, near Tofino. She never bought it, it wasn't big enough for her, but they were looking in the region. After that, Ray Zhang retired and I haven't seen him since. Nobody has."

"What's the subsidiary for the copper mine? Syntamar?" I remember they had given up a project on Vancouver Island for Zhang-Wei's help in the Congo.

"An operation called Lowell Metals. Small change, but if you're in the mining business, you want as much real estate wrapped up in your name as possible. Lowell changed hands a couple times, from what I remember. Maybe it was owned by Syntamar at one point, but I can't say for sure."

Lam's phone buzzes. He glances over at Brazuca apologetically. "Duty calls."

"You're a playboy," Brazuca says. "You don't have a duty. You don't do real work."

Lam laughs. "I've missed you, Bazooka, I really have. You're absolutely right. I don't have real work but I do have a real fiancée now, which is about the same thing as far as my father's concerned."

Brazuca raises a brow. "Oh really? Didn't get an invitation to the engagement party."

"I don't have many friends in this world and I would never subject one of them to such mind-numbing boredom. Pity I had to be there myself. Like I said," Bernard Lam says with a sigh, "I'm doing my duty."

He downs the last of his cognac and picks up his phone with the energy of a man walking toward a noose. Some, myself included, might say that he is.

# 6

BRAZUCA PAUSES OUTSIDE the lounge. We both need a minute to recover from being exposed to something so close to our personal heaven and hell. Back when I was drinking, it was vodka that I turned to. Brazuca admitted to me once that rum was his weapon of choice. The smoothness of it. But these preferences are only important at the beginning of one's descent into hell. After a while, the kind of liquor ceases to matter, as does the quality.

"If I was drinking that, I couldn't afford to be an alcoholic," Brazuca says. "Maybe my wife wouldn't have divorced me."

"If you were drinking that, your wife would have just had less to take in the settlement."

"That's a little sexist of you. She made more money than I ever did."

Hmm. I never imagined Brazuca with an executive for a wife. "In that case, you should have taken her for more, and then you might have been drinking the good stuff for the rest of your life."

He smiles and I notice that he has no stubble. He has thrown caution to the wind and committed to a beard. The darkness of it makes his teeth look even whiter and I, once again, speculate at his dental care routine. "What do you say we give up this investigating stuff and go get smashed? You know, for old times' sake."

I wonder if he knows how tempting this is for me. How easy

it would be to just throw caution to the wind and just this once, do the one thing that I've wanted so badly every single fucking day since I've been sober. The rub is, it's never just this once. Just this once is not an option for an alcoholic.

Brazuca sees the look on my face and his smile vanishes. "Hey, I was just kidding."

"We've never gotten smashed together."

"How do you know? I don't remember half of what I did or who I met when I was drunk."

"You saying I'm not memorable?"

This time, he's the one put off balance. "No, ah, that's really not what I—what I meant to say is that . . . oh, I see what you're doing. Funny, I've never seen you smile before."

Is that what I am doing? I stop.

"So, look. You're not going to get away with being a night cleaner for very long. They're going to figure it out sooner or later." He hands me a plain white card with a magnetic strip on it. "My room. Just in case."

I stare at the card. Printed on the back is his room number. I hadn't really given a thought to where he was staying. "Bernard Lam got you this room?" He would never have been able to afford it on a cop's salary.

"Nora, give it a rest, would you? I'm here to help you. Not everyone's an asshole that you can't trust."

"A girl is missing, Brazuca. Maybe not everyone is an asshole, but it's not like they're going out of style, either."

A pair of businessmen brush by us on their way to the lounge. One of them looks at me with mild distaste, as though I brushed into him.

"The horse is out of the barn," I say, nodding to his zipper.

He looks down and his face reddens when he discovers that the horse is, in fact, still tucked safely inside the barn, where he put it. The men, both of them, glare at me and then disappear into the lounge.

"That was mature," Brazuca says. But he's smiling. I can feel myself smiling back, even though this kind of camaraderie I reserve only for Whisper. I have to admit, it is nice to share with a human once in a while. Brazuca's smile disappears. "Nora, I have a bad feeling about all this. I think you should go back home and let me look into it from here."

"That's not an option."

"Damn it! Is it because when you went missing, no one looked for you? Is that why you can't let yourself trust anyone?"

And just like that, my good mood fades.

"Jesus," he says. "Don't look at me like that. I've read your story in the papers and I've seen your police reports, okay? I know there were no missing persons alerts out for you. I know you think the system is screwed up, but what you're doing here isn't the answer. You're endangering yourself, can't you see that? These aren't people to play around with. Why would you . . . Is it because you regret giving her up? You want to find her so that you can be a part of her life?"

I refuse to answer this question. Some things can only be faced in the dark of the night, muttered into a pillow while Ray Charles plays in the background to muffle the sounds, and then shaken out again in the morning.

"Forget it," he continues, when the silence has stretched on for so long that we both realize that we're teetering on the edge of something big. "I already know. There's only one reason you would. She's your child. You must, somewhere inside of you, you must love her. Or at least care about her, even just a bit."

Really? This kind of assumption makes me angry. I could have played that card a long time ago, because nothing is stronger than a mother's love. But I'm not this child's mother in any way other than lending out my womb and passing along some dubious genes. Bonnie's mother is back in Vancouver, contemplating the end of her marriage. Surrounded by shirts that smell of perfume that she doesn't wear.

"Maybe it's responsibility," I say. "Maybe no one else will take responsibility for her disappearance, at least not enough to do a damn thing about it."

He looks at me sadly and for the first time I see myself in his eyes. A woman with so many demons she can hardly keep track of them. They have spilled out in every direction and are now out of my grasp. "What is love, if not responsibility?"

He turns away now, as if I have disappointed him greatly. As if I am the one who has opened up a raw, pulsing wound inside him and then stepped on it—and not the other way around. I could get into my complicated parentage. I could point out to him that my dubious genes are at least part indigenous from my father's side and part something I don't even know from my mother's. Because she left when I was a child and I don't know a thing about her, not even where she came from. What I do know is that I look somewhat like my father, and girls who look like me are more likely to go missing, and less likely to have their disappearances investigated.

And what if Bonnie has more of me than is healthy for her?

I could tell him all these things, but I don't. I know he'll understand, stare at me some more with pity in his eyes, and I don't want any of it. After last night, it's far too much, far too soon.

He pauses at the end of the hallway. "I'll see what I can find out about Zhang. I'll text you later."

"My phone isn't on."

"Just check it every couple of hours. I'll be in touch."

He limps around the corner and disappears from sight. I think about the promise I made to Tommy. That I will find Bonnie and, when I do, she will be okay. Because that's all my mind will allow me to consider. That at the end of this she will be safe, like she was supposed to be from the start.

# 7

I HIDE IN my tiny room until it's time to show up at the maintenance office for my shift. When I do, Carl comes in right behind
me, covered in snow. "That drive is killing me," he mutters.

"So why do you do it?"

He shrugs. "The wife."

"Yeah, I hear you."

He looks at me. "You got a wife?"

I've noticed that the other female employees wear skirts with
tights and black kitten heels. But Carl has given me the male
uniform. I think about being offended by this, but I have never
in my life worn heels and teetering about does not seem to be
the best way to get information about Bonnie's disappearance.

"Nope. No wife for me."

"Oh. I didn't mean . . . well, I did, but it was just because—"

"We're good, Carl." I really don't want any more insults to my
lady parts. "I don't have a wife yet. But maybe one day."

In one of my survivor groups, a woman who used to share
every week said that she couldn't go back to men after what
happened to her. She still had the urges, but her body automat-
ically shut down if penetration was involved and mentally she
would grow cold and distant. She turned to one of the other
women in the group for comfort, though that kind of support
was frowned upon in our support group. I'd seen them both at

the grocery store about a year later and they looked happy. The woman who did not do penetration even winked at me at the checkout. Winked. Like we shared a secret. Maybe she and Carl know something I don't.

"You see Lucy?" he says, turning away to take off his heavy snow boots.

I nod, which he catches in the small mirror on the wall.

"Paperwork all good to go?" He frowns, and his voice is oddly wooden.

I nod some more. At this point, I hesitate because I like Carl. We've bonded over cleaning detergents and, sometimes, that's all it takes. Or so I think.

"That's interesting," he says, sounding disappointed. He faces me fully now. "Because I talked to Lucy on my way up and she said she hired a couple more replacements for swing shift and that new girl who didn't make it is gonna be up in the morning. Imagine my surprise."

We stare at each other for a moment. He reads the truth in my eyes. "I can explain."

"Oh?" Carl crosses his arms and waits.

"Okay, I can't really explain."

"Just tell me the truth. You planning to kill one of those rich folks up there?"

"No."

"Steal from them?"

"No."

"You just needed a place to stay, right? And then I thought you were the cleaner from Abbotsford and opened my big mouth." Carl shakes his head. "Can't keep my trap shut. My wife warns me about it all the time . . . Look, I get it. You're having some rough times—it's okay. Been there myself. I hurt my back working the oil fields few years back. It wasn't easy to get back on my feet. The wife . . . well, she really picked up the slack. Wouldn't have made it without her. So, yeah, I understand why you lied. But you can't stay, all right? I have no say in hiring and they'll fire me if they knew I let somebody unauthorized come up here."

"Can I leave in the morning?"

"Yeah, I'll take you back down myself. Just keep to your chambers. I'll clean up after you're gone. And . . . you can keep the uniform. They got lots. They won't miss it."

He rummages through his wallet and pulls out three twenty-dollar bills. "For last night. It ain't much, but it's all I got on me."

I take the money because it would have been suspicious if I didn't. Last thing I need is for Carl to grow more of a conscience than he already has. To him, I'm a drifter. What he doesn't realize is that I'm merely adrift.

At the door, I turn back to him. "Thanks, Carl."

He nods. "You're welcome. Just stay out of sight, will ya? And Nora?"

"Yeah?"

"I'm going to need your access key back."

I reach into my pocket and hand him a white, rectangular swipe card. I still have Brazuca's room key in my pocket, though. Just in case.

# 8

AS MUCH AS I don't want Carl to lose his job, I have other priorities. Instead of heading to the staff quarters out back, I turn toward the service elevator leading up to the second floor. The lounge is filled with men in wool slacks and cashmere sweaters, the real stuff. Two staff work the bar, pouring expensive liquor with smiles and receiving exorbitant tips in return. The light is so dim that almost everyone looks ten years younger and far more attractive than they did going into the meeting rooms this morning.

When the bartender at the far end of the bar turns away, I grab a tray and begin clearing tables on the other side of the room. There's only one other woman here and, thankfully for me, she is sitting alone with a cup of tea, staring out the window. She sets her cup down gently on the table beside her and I pick it up.

"Finished with this, ma'am?"

She glances at me, her dark eyes like two polished marbles. I now understand what it's like for people when they look into my eyes, but hers, somehow I sense that hers are different. They have absolutely no expression in them. "It's only half-empty," she says.

"Depends on how you look at it."

A smooth, professionally shaped brow arches. "I see. But if it was half-full, which is what I assume you're talking about, why would you take it away?"

"My apologies," I say with an exaggerated bow. "I wasn't thinking."

She stares at me with those unholy eyes and then turns back to the spectacular view. The sun is setting, bathing the mountain in front of us in a soft, golden light that is tinged pink at the edges. A bald eagle soars overhead and, with a flap of its wings, disappears from sight.

In the reflection of the glass, I see moisture leaking through the front of her blouse and suddenly the fact that she's the only guest in the room not drinking alcohol makes sense. She's nursing. And I remember what Bernard Lam has said about Ray Zhang. That he has a grandson.

I stand there a moment too long, riveted.

She catches someone's eye in the reflection on the glass. A figure detaches itself from the long shadows at the corner of the room and a tall, muscular man approaches. He reminds me of the not-cops, but there is an ease with which he moves that makes me think he is far out of their league. In the glass, I see the man's face. He is Asian, with a long jaw and full lips and his head completely shaved. It is impossible to tell his age, but I put him anywhere between a hard-lived forty and a soft fifty.

"Dao," Jia Zhang says as the man approaches. "I'd like to show you something in a minute."

They exchange glances over my head. Boy, do I really hate that. "Of course," he replies, his voice quiet. All the hairs on my body bristle and a chill builds up from the soles of my feet, travels through my body, and wraps itself around my heart.

It is the voice of my nightmares, the voice that ordered the disposal of my body, the voice in the hallway of the office on Hastings Street.

Our eyes meet in the reflection of the glass. Against the backdrop of snow-covered mountains in the distance and a pristine, winter valley below us, he looks directly at me.

And he smiles.

# 9

I DON'T KNOW if he recognized me from that night fifteen years ago, but I don't wait around to find out, either. I grab my things from the staff quarters and as I step outside, the cold envelops me like a frigid blanket. The lights from the chalet illuminate the access road, but gusts of snow and ice kicked up by the wind limit visibility. Carl told me that no, these conditions are not because of a storm. That's just how it is up here. I start walking, but a noise from the building makes me look over my shoulder. Backlit from the chalet lights, a figure bundled in a heavy parka approaches, limping badly. I have no weapons on me, nothing but my pack. The ice that has gathered on the ground does neither of us any justice, though he seems to be faring better than me.

"Where the hell are you going in this weather?" Brazuca shouts. The wind carries off most of his words, but I still catch the tail end of them.

I keep walking, even though it's difficult. I've forgotten how to walk in the snow, being that Vancouver hardly ever gets any. And my sprained ankle isn't up to the task. Brazuca, however, seems as adept as an injured man could be in this environment. Big, fluffy flakes fall on the pathway to the access road and though it was salted not too long ago, they stick. Even limping, Brazuca's got an advantage over me in this terrain, his long legs eating up the distance between us. He grabs my arm.

"Get your hand off me."

"Only if you get your ass back inside. You gonna walk back to town? In this?" He gestures wildly at the snow-covered road.

"No, I was going to steal a car."

"You were going to—something happened, right? Just come back inside and we'll talk. Let me help you. Please."

I hesitate. The wind blows the hood off my head and sends my hair flying. I'm so cold that I can't feel my feet. Would I make it down the road in this? Brazuca holds out a mittened hand.

We don't meet anyone on our way back to the building. Inside Brazuca's room, I take a moment to get my bearings. There's a queen-size bed, desk space, and a seating area with two plush armchairs. All the furnishings are done in sleek, lacquered teak and soothing blues.

Brazuca limps over to the tea station and puts some water on to boil. At places like this, you have the option of ordering tea from room service, getting tea from the dining room, or making it your damn self. Brazuca is a man after my own heart. He brews two cups of ginger tea and hands me a mug.

"So," he says. "You going to tell me what happened to make you run out of here like the place was on fire?"

I shake my head and inhale the steam coming from the mug. "How do you know Bernard Lam?"

He closes the drapes and drops himself into an overstuffed armchair. He waves at the chair across from him and waits until I sit down to begin. "Five years ago, there were shots fired outside of a nightclub and a woman died. Bernard was there. He was one of the witnesses we questioned. His car got hit, so we thought he had something to do with it. Nothing came of it when we questioned him, but the next week we followed him to another event and more shots were fired."

"Five years ago?"

"That's what I said."

"Hmm." I glance at his bad leg.

I see a flash of white teeth as he smiles to himself. "You got that, did you? I pushed him to the ground and got shot in the process."

Ah, so that's his big story. Now I understand. Bernard Lam gave him access to this chalet because he owes Brazuca his life. It's as good a reason as any. "Why was someone trying to kill him?"

"We still don't know. He hired a private security firm for personal protection after that but no further attempts were made on his life and we're still not sure about the motivations of the attacks. But I've looked into it every now and then."

We sip our tea quietly.

"So," Brazuca says. "What made you run out of here like that?"

A woman is entitled to her secrets. She should be able to hide them away for as long as she wants, without people constantly prying, trying to take a peek inside her head. But secrets are exhausting and that's the plain truth of the thing. The effort of keeping them locked away, shielding them from view . . . I'm only human, after all. I look away from him, though, because it is the only way I can do this.

"That night . . . the man who ordered me to be dumped in the woods, he's here. It's Dao. Jia Zhang's private security."

Brazuca stills. "Was he the one who—"

"No. But he works for him. I'm sure of it."

Brazuca leans forward. He knows better than to try to touch

me, but by reducing the physical distance between us and lowering his voice to just above a whisper, he has succeeded in creating as intimate a conversation as we could possibly have. "Was it Ray Zhang that night?" he asks, in a surprisingly gentle voice. A detective's voice when questioning someone fragile. He doesn't need to bother. If I was going to break down, it wouldn't be here or now. It would be much later, alone at the side of the road with a bottle of vodka in one fist and whatever blunt weapon happened to be handy in the other.

I shake my head. "No. Not if Ray Zhang is the man in that photo I showed to Lam. But he was Asian. I remember that much. And younger, maybe even younger than me. I had a singing gig at one of the basement bars in the city. A real dive, but the drinks were never watered down, so it saw a lot of action on Saturday night. Still not the kind of place that would attract the likes of Ray Zhang. I sang and then had a few drinks and then didn't wake up for months afterward. I was talking to someone, but he was younger, even then."

"But you don't know who else was there after you blacked out."

I shake my head and sip my tea. The warmth of it spreads down my throat and to my belly. Brazuca is silent for a moment.

He puts down the mug and steeples his fingers. "Nora . . . I'm sorry that happened to you."

"I don't even remember it. Sometimes I get flashes. Voices, faces, but no one that I could identify until tonight."

"So you were assaulted that night by someone connected to Zhang and then fifteen years later the child that you bore as a result goes missing. Why would they take her? Why now?"

There's something that has been bothering me but I can't

quite place my finger on it yet. "A journalist named Mike Starling found me out in the woods. He was hiking with a few buddies and they stumbled on my body. He took me to the hospital and then reported on the story. His editor liked the personal connection and made him dig deeper for a larger series. He knew my story, but never revealed my identity—as far as I know. Several years ago he hooked me up with Seb Crow and then I never heard from him until after Bonnie went missing. He wanted to meet with me, but when I finally agreed he didn't show up . . . but some WIN Security men did. I dodged them but there's only one way they could know about our meeting."

"Okay . . . so they got to Starling. Someone must have connected you to him from the articles."

"Right. And when I went to Starling's apartment, he was dead. Bled out in his bathtub."

"Jesus."

I tell him about the storage locker, the stem cell research, and Syntamar.

Brazuca stands and begins to pace. "What does that have to do with Bonnie?"

"Stem cells harvested from umbilical cords have been used to treat certain diseases since the eighties." I learned that from Starling's research.

"You think they stole your cord blood?"

"I don't know. How would that happen?"

He shakes his head. "No clue. But that blood is what links you two. You're connected to Dao from that night. Dao is connected to Zhang, who works with WIN. WIN just so happens to be looking for Bonnie. And then when you broke into WIN, Dao is the one sent to your office. And someone murders Starling to get to you because they realized that you were the one Starling was writing about and that he knew you. That's why he was targeted. They're looking for you now."

"But Starling made a point of mentioning in his articles that my memory of that night was gone."

"Still, they knew about it. I think that they must have contacted Starling somehow and he traced them back to Zhang. That's why he had a picture of Zhang with the Syntamar board. He must have been looking into this for quite a while."

"But what does any of this have to do with Bonnie?"

"I don't know. She's really the key to all this." Brazuca rubs at his eyes. The hot ginger tea after being outside in the cold has left us both warm and sleepy.

I look at the luxurious bed, which is big enough for three people. And even peons at this chateau get fine sheets worthy of, if not a prince, then certainly one of his advisors. "I'll take the floor."

"No, dammit. I'm the man here." He says this with surprising heat. I look over at him. His brows are knit together and a flush creeps up over his collar. I've never seen him this flustered.

"So? What's that got to do with anything?"

"So, I'll sleep on the damn floor and you, the woman, can sleep on the bed. For fuck's sake, Nora."

"But you're a cripple," I point out. "It wouldn't be fair."

He sighs. "Chivalry is dead. Fine, I'll take the bed." He limps over to the bed, tosses me the comforter and a pillow, and sits on the edge. I don't watch as he removes his shoes and his belt. He stretches out with his eyes closed while I make a bed on the floor.

# 10

WE LIE IN silence for a while, separated mostly by altitude. The light is still on in the room, but neither of us makes a move to turn it off. It's sometime after midnight, but there are no clocks in the room so I can't place the hour exactly. I'm not sure why, but I'm unsettled. Though I'm exhausted and this comforter is the coziest piece of fabric I've ever encountered, I still can't seem to close my eyes. I know Brazuca is awake, too, because of his uneven breathing.

Finally he gives up the pretense of sleep. "Nora, you up?"

"Yeah."

"We've both had a rough couple of days and I just want you to know . . . If you need someone tonight, well, you can have me. Just putting it out there since you're too much of a coward to make the first move."

For a moment, I forget to breathe. "What are you talking about?"

"You know what. You're not comfortable around men for obvious reasons but we both know you're attracted to me. So if you need me, I'm here."

"What makes you think that I'm attracted to you?" When could I have possibly given him that impression? Maybe he thinks assaulting him in a bathroom with a blow to the back of the head is some kind of come-on.

"I don't know," he says. I can hear the smile in his voice. "Could be because you're always staring at me when you think I'm not looking."

"I do that to everyone."

"Do you stare at everyone's mouth, though?"

Have I been doing that? Possibly. Probably. It makes me mad that, first of all, now that I think about it I have paid close attention to his dental hygiene and, second, he noticed. "Fuck you."

He yawns. "If you want. If not, I'm going to sleep. But you should know that I may not be around forever, and the rate you're going, looks like you're in the same boat. Besides, you hit me with a tire iron and we all know what that means." He has remained still throughout the conversation and now turns his face toward me and gives me a beatific smile before closing his eyes again.

For some reason, I don't quite know what to do with my hands. They have shucked off the covers and are wringing themselves nervously. I go into the bathroom before I do anything rash. In the shower, I scrub myself until I'm raw with luxury hotel soap that smells like roses and try to summon those feelings of fear and shame that have kept me celibate for so very long, but either they have subsided over the years or something has shifted inside me. All that's left is a curiosity that I can't suppress.

I stand in the doorway, wrapped in a towel, and stare at Brazuca on the bed. He's now on his back, his hands resting beneath his head. But I can tell from his uneven breathing that he is not asleep. "Why would you do this for me?" I say finally.

"Does it really matter?"

"Yes."

"Because I want to." Even though his eyes are closed and I can't read what's behind them, something in his voice indicates to me that he's telling the truth.

"And do I have to . . ."

"No. Just come here."

I turn off all the lights except for the one in the bathroom and grab his belt and a tie from the curtains. He opens his eyes as I straddle his chest and tie his wrists to the bedposts. He doesn't resist. "Take off the towel or you'll smother me," he says softly.

I pause. I haven't been naked in front of someone in years, more than a decade, but he makes a good point.

As if he's read my mind, he closes his eyes again. I look down at his calm face and think about kissing him. A deep breath and the towel is cast aside. I lean down. My mouth hovers just over his, our breath intermingling for several seconds before it becomes too much to bear. I sit up and position my knees on either side of his face and for a moment he just breathes me in before I feel his tongue.

I want to hate it, but I don't. It feels too good to be real.

It's over almost as soon as it started and the whole thing has taken me by surprise. This time the aftermath of orgasm doesn't come from shame. My body doesn't break out into a cold sweat. I come down and, even with my hands wrapped around the bed frame for support, I'm free falling.

Brazuca doesn't ask for reciprocation and I don't offer. I'm not sure I would be any good at it anyway. I've never claimed to be a decent lover, not even before the red sheet. I lie on my side with my face turned away from him and wait for my heartbeat to slow down. He disengages his own wrists and disappears into the bathroom. I wonder briefly if he has done this out of desire or altruism, but in the end it doesn't matter.

I slip out of the bed and am buried under my comforter on the floor by the time he returns to the room. My clothes are back on and the towel is hanging off the foot of the bed.

We lie in the dark again for some time, both awake. The air between us is awkward but not unpleasant, given what has just transpired. My first partner-assisted orgasm in more than a decade. Well, a partner that's not an inanimate object.

"I bet that cognac was amazing," I say, because it has been on my mind.

"Liquid gold," Brazuca agrees from the bed. He turns to face me.

I don't look at him. "Too bad we don't have any self-control."

"Speak for yourself," he says in a thick voice. "I have lots."

"Says the alcoholic."

"See, now, that's just the pot calling the kettle a kitchen instrument. I'll have you know, my self-control is legendary."

I think about that for a while. Eventually a heavy sleep anchors me to the ground and when I wake up, Brazuca is gone and I'm grateful. Is there any person alive who is good with intimacy?

# 11

SOMETIMES I FEEL a huge weight crushing down on me and at other times I think it's just my imagination. Could be as simple as a bout of depression, but when I really think about it there's nothing in my life to be depressed about. I'm alive, I've laid off the booze far longer than I ever thought I could, I have a dog to walk the streets with at night and to ignore me during the day as if she were a cat, and I'm steadily employed by people who don't ask too many questions and apparently don't mind me camping in their basement. It's a better life than some.

So why then does this crushing feeling come back?

An alcoholic cannot afford to be depressed if sobriety is still a goal. She cannot allow despair to gnaw at her self-control until it consumes her, until she no longer recognizes where she begins and the sickening feelings of doubt and shame end. I know this but, still, I can't help the betrayal that seizes me now. When I learned of Bonnie's disappearance, I went to him first. There's a bond between an alcoholic and her sponsor, an unspoken agreement. The promise of secrecy. Once again, he has proved better at secrecy than I have. And, let's be honest. Last night was about more than release. It was about that trust which, along with the benefit of the doubt, I very rarely extend.

When we were teenagers, Lorelei asked me if I'd ever been in love.

Love?

What do I have to give to love, to feed it so that it grows lush and beautiful like you see in the movies? The happy ones, I mean. Not the sad ones about the downside of love that people walk out of theaters feeling cheated by. I'm talking about the good love that some people get to have, the kind that nourishes the soul, helps it bloom in the springtime no matter how frigid the winter that precedes it. Everything I have is broken or bent somehow, stained so bad that no amount of extra-strength detergent could rub it all out, no matter what the ad says. I have no money to offer to love, no wisdom or kindness. Inside me I have nothing but vast reserves of suspicion and heartache, a current that runs so deep and dark I feel its chill right to my core. And, as it turns out, this current never plays me false.

I stare at the email from Leo. He hasn't been able to get through to my cell phone, so he took a chance and sent his message electronically. No matter how many times I read the words, the results from the plate inquiry are still the same.

Silver sedan.

Registered to WIN Security.

# 12

SOME OF THE headlines from my dark period go like this:

UNIDENTIFIED WOMAN FOUND BEATEN IN THE
WOODS, LEFT FOR DEAD

BEATEN WOMAN SEXUALLY ASSAULTED BEFORE
BEING LEFT FOR DEAD IN WOODS

BEATEN WOMAN STILL IN COMA, AUTHORITIES
SUSPECT SHE IS OF MIXED-NATIVE HERITAGE

BEATEN WOMAN LEFT FOR DEAD WAKES FROM
COMA, DOESN'T REMEMBER HER NAME

WOMAN LEFT FOR DEAD WAKES FROM COMA TO
DISCOVER SHE IS PREGNANT

I especially like the last one because it omits the word *beaten,* but number three is a doozy, too. To "suspect" me makes it sound like being of mixed heritage was the crime. I'd pointed out to Starling that these headlines were idiotic and, also, don't write articles about me, but it's too much to ask a reporter not to report on a story in which he plays an important role—and there is no role more important than "rescuer." Even if the "rescued" just wants to crawl into a hole somewhere and disappear. Starling commiserated that, yes, they were mostly shitty headlines, but that was the nature of the game, and he had little control over them anyway. No matter how much he wanted to move on to other things, his editors wanted him to expand my story and try to find new angles to it. To examine it from as many perspectives as possible and find other women who have experienced similar attacks. I answered his questions as briefly as possible, but I still answered them. He was the only reporter I would talk to. I was his big story, whether either of us wanted it or not.

Things changed when he noticed a TV journalist hanging around the hospital, asking questions about "Mary," my alias in his feature piece on me.

"He tried to kill me," I said to him when I found out about the other reporter. "The man who left me in the woods. He thought I was dead."

Starling dropped heavily on the armchair by my hospital bed. "Yeah, I know."

"I talk to you only and you keep my name out of it. No one would know who I am, you said. That was the deal, remember?" Starling had to work hard to convince me to open up. That it was important that people heard my story. I don't care much about people, then or now, but he had saved my life and I pay my debts, then and now. But this . . . I didn't want another journalist connecting me with what happened.

"It was the most widely read human interest piece this year, Nora. I might even . . . I might even get an award for this story."

"Fuck your award and fuck you." I remember pacing on my swollen feet with my belly so distended that I could barely see the ground in front of me. "You can't come here anymore. I'm serious."

"I know, I'm sorry. You don't think . . . you don't think he'll come after you, do you? The man who did this?" He gestured helplessly at my stomach.

"How the hell should I know?" I snapped. "I don't *remember* anything about him."

"So I'll stay away."

"You better. I did what you asked. I helped you with your story, okay? We're even."

"This was never about us becoming even, Nora."

"Don't say my name! Not here, not anywhere. You got your story, people are reading your stupid articles again, and everything's coming up roses for you. But just take a look at me. Nothing is going to be the same for me ever again."

"Maybe we should go to the police," he says, his voice hesitant.

"Were you even listening to me? I said it when I agreed to talk to you. No cops."

I'd told him what it had been like, living on the streets. How the police were to be avoided at all costs, how they never helped you if you were homeless or busking. How they pushed you around and made you leave public spaces. How they let other people treat you like garbage without intervening. Cops would never believe someone like me. Never. Not even with Starling's support.

After Leo's message comes in, I start going through Brazuca's things. Tossing them out of his duffel bag and then packing them back with absolutely no regard for the order in which I found them. I search for clues that will tell me that I was wrong to trust him . . . look, this giant WIN Security ID card has been here all along and, Nora, you bloody fool, you didn't see it.

But there's nothing there except for a few items of clothing, toiletry bag, and shaving kit. There are no clues because he's too smart to leave them.

But I already knew that, didn't I? I already knew because I searched through his things while he was in the bathroom, before I even got the registration details from Leo. You see, you can't really change who you are. And now, in the cold light of day, with no one's face hovering under me, I'm glad for it.

# 13

I'M SITTING IN the dark with the curtains drawn when Brazuca returns. The morning light will make an appearance soon and I've already overstayed my welcome.

"I made a few calls," he says, shucking off his coat and shoes. "There's a doctor friend of mine, used to work as a medical examiner for the city before retiring."

"Yeah?"

"Turns out, cord blood is chock-full of stem cells that are normally found in bone marrow. They make every kind of blood cell. They're used to treat blood disorders because they're versatile. You were right about that. But here's the thing. It's not enough for a full bone marrow transplant. Not enough for any real treatment for a full-grown adult."

"What about an infirm one?"

He stares at me, perplexed. "What are you thinking?"

"No one has seen Ray Zhang for over a year, right? What if he's sick and needs a transplant? They somehow got a hold of the cord blood and find a match—"

"How?"

"Black market? Private blood banks? Public blood banks? They have resources. Money isn't an obstacle for these people."

"So they track down the source somehow and find Bonnie."

I frown. "It's far-fetched."

"It connects some of the dots. Best theory that we have." He yawns. "Most of the other guests are gone. Some stayed back to do some helicopter skiing but not a lot." Not surprising. The majority of the men at the conference were pushing the far side of fifty. I can't imagine many of them agreeing to jump out of a helicopter on skis. For fun. "Jia Zhang left about an hour ago."

"Lam?"

"Him, too." Brazuca collapses on the bed. I rise from the armchair by the window and go to him. He doesn't protest when I tie his hands to the bedpost, but he does keep his eyes open this time. "Again? Okay . . . but maybe we could try something different."

"Oh, it'll be different. Hey, when you got shot, did they try to put you on a desk?"

Brazuca raises a brow. He sees the strange look in my eyes, my dilated pupils, and becomes concerned. "Yes, but what's that got to do with—ow, is that really necessary?" he says, as I tighten the straps.

"But you had to see a shrink after the shooting, right? To clear you?"

"That's standard procedure." His voice is light, but his eyes are narrowed. This time I don't straddle him and I'm not wearing a towel. He catches a glimpse of the empty bottles on the floor. Whoops. "You've been drinking."

Boy, have I ever. I laugh. "That's quite a minibar you've got here. Fancy. Too bad I didn't get to the cognac first, though. My only regret."

He pulls against his restraints. They don't budge. "Untie me right now."

I don't.

"So, you get shot and the shrink recommends that you ride a desk. Maybe the shrink already knows you're an alcoholic, maybe the shrink doesn't really like you very much, but the point is, that recommendation wasn't your first strike."

He says nothing.

"You're a crippled drunk who's maybe as addicted to pain-killers as you are to liquor. You don't want to be on the force anymore so who do you go to for help when you need a change of career? The man whose life you saved, right? You know he's got private security now, so maybe he'll put in a recommenda-tion to the company he uses, which, coincidentally, is the same company that Ray fucking Zhang uses. WIN Security. You're not a cop anymore, are you? I'm guessing you haven't been one for a while now."

There is a pause as Brazuca assesses his options, but he and I both know the game is up. "How?"

That single word breaks my heart. It's not even an outright acknowledgment. Not a "Yes, you clever girl." Not an apology. Just a measly "How did you find out? Where did I go wrong in my attempt to pull the wool over your eyes?"

"Leo ran the plates from the car you followed me in."

He sighs. "Okay, so now you know. I'm actually glad that you do, because believe what you want, I didn't enjoy keeping that a secret from you, but I knew you'd never trust me otherwise. You can untie me now."

I still don't feel like it. "When I hit you on the bridge, you told me you were a cop."

"Because it was the easiest explanation. You're right about everything else. I went to WIN when I got shot."

"Why are they looking for Bonnie?"

"I don't know! That's what I'm trying to figure out. It doesn't make any sense. It's not even an official case for them. I work for these guys and they're pros, really, they are. Mostly ex-military. Very organized. But there's something not right about this case. Almost like they've gone off the rails, and I think it's because of Zhang. He must be very powerful. Listen, Nora, please. I may not be a cop anymore, but trust me on this. I'm on your side."

Is he lying? I can't tell.

I move toward him. Too late, he sees the bottle in my hand.

"Hey!" he shouts. He bucks off the bed, but I know a thing or two about tying restraints. Rule number one: make a tight knot. Rule number two: make three more. I drive the heel of my hand into his bad leg and he howls in pain.

"You've fucked my sobriety, Brazuca. So I'm going to fuck yours." Alcohol has loosened my tongue and delivered to it dialogue from a terrible movie. Have you ever met an eloquent drunk? There's a good reason for that.

He struggles, but his right leg is now next to useless, which makes his left easier to tie down with his belt. "Don't do this," he whispers as I approach the head of the bed.

I sit on his chest to keep him steady. "You said let's get smashed together," I tell him, grabbing his jaw and holding his mouth open with one hand. "I'm only taking you up on your offer." I pour with the other. He sputters but I keep pouring until I know that he's swallowed some. "Hey, maybe you and your pal Lam can go drink some of that cognac now. It's never too late." And then I do the next bottle. After that one I stuff a pair of his shorts into his mouth. It's a clean pair. I'm not a monster. He shouts in protest, but no one can hear him.

"There, there. Go to sleep," I say before I leave, with the rest of those little bottles tucked into my pack. I've managed to dissolve a handful of the extra-strength painkillers I snatched from the animal hospital into the tiny bottles of rum, so I know Brazuca will be out of my way long enough for me to get him off my trail.

I walk to the access road, where Carl is waiting, and feel the self-loathing rise up in me. Loneliness makes me do awful things. Like place my trust in people who don't deserve it.

"Where ya off to, lady?" Carl asks as he starts the engine.

The morning is crisp but clear. I can see that the snow kicked up from the night before has covered the landscape in its cold, beautiful embrace. Everything but the access road, which is freshly salted. "Let's not go there, Carl."

"Fair enough," he says. "We've all got our secrets."

No shit. I've had a nice steady buzz since I found out about Brazuca but now it's starting to fade. Good thing I stuffed the remaining contents of the minibar into my pack. When we make it down the mountain, I'll crack open one of those little bottles to get me through. Not now, though. Not in front of Carl. He's a decent sort, but he wouldn't understand.

# 14

IN HER DREAMS she is wrapped in a blanket and carried through the woods. The man carrying her smells like sweat and pine needles. It is not unpleasant and the girl knows she probably smells a lot worse than he does. She has been out here for . . . days? Weeks? She doesn't know. Bonnie asks the man where they're going but he doesn't respond. Her lids are too heavy to open, but she can hear the forest sounds and smell the damp earth.

Cradled in his arms like that, Bonnie thinks of her father. Who used to muss her hair and laugh at her stupid jokes. Who used to play sports with her and drive her to school when she woke up too late to take the bus. Her father who had changed so much in the past year, who became like Lynn. Unable to look her in the eyes. Last Christmas they opened their presents wordlessly and then went to the movies to see something about how a superhero came to be a superhero and found some superhero friends. Both her parents thought it would be something that she would enjoy, but they all had ended up loving it because it had been funny. They left the theater still giggling about something or other and then went back to their quiet home where nobody laughed anymore.

But that's so far away from her now. Now she is being carried through her island like a child. By a stranger. Through the forest they go, until there's a new scent that fills her nostrils. The fresh, salty smell of the ocean.

# FOUR

# 1

I CAME DOWN from the interior through a combination of hitching and using public transportation. It was difficult but not impossible, and the steady supply of miniature bottles from Brazuca's hotel room helped ease my way. I drank to take the edge off and became as soft and devoid of sharp angles as the snow-covered landscape, where thick, damp flurries met frozen ground. The edges returned the closer the city loomed until the snow turned into slush and then disappeared altogether.

I show up to my old alcoholics support group after three beers and two shots of vodka in the space of two hours. I'm loaded, but not so loaded that I can't follow the conversation and stand up at break time without falling on my face.

"Hey, you," says my ex-sponsor at the coffee station. The one I thought worked for the intelligence service. "We haven't seen you in a while. How are things going?"

Nosy bitch. "Great!" I say, a little too loudly for the basement of a community center.

Her eyes are wide with concern. False? I can never suss out kindness when I'm drunk. "You seem a little off today, hon, that's all. Anything you want to talk about?"

"Why you all up in my grille, Sierra?" This is something that I've heard on television but have never had the opportunity to use. Sierra obviously isn't her real name, but she has a flare for the dramatic.

"Okay, okay, that's enough." Simone, who has been watching me from the back of the room ever since I came in, inserts herself between us. She grabs my elbow. "Come with me." I don't protest as Simone drags me from the room, up the stairs, and out into the parking lot. She's a lot stronger than me, even in the ridiculous platform heels she insists on wearing to these meetings.

For once, it's not raining. Simone pulls me under a streetlight and examines me. "You asshole," she says finally. Even though the instant coffee from the meeting has masked the smell of alcohol on my breath, Simone knows the signs. She's been there enough times to.

"That's not very nice."

"Tough, we're at an AA meeting, we're not supposed to be nice."

"Uh . . . you sure about that?"

Because I'm not. I thought the point of a support group was to be nice to people that you'd normally cross the street to avoid at 3 A.M. on a Tuesday because they'd be as faded as you and you don't want to see the shame in them, and recognize it in yourself. I thought that was the whole point of support groups for alcoholics.

"Come back when you get your head straight. You don't belong here tonight."

She's right. I don't belong here. But I don't belong anywhere else, either. I think about my father, who also didn't belong. And then he put a gun to his head and pulled the trigger. I don't think about my mother, though, because whoever she was, when she abandoned us she lost my sympathy.

And then it hits me. That Bonnie may feel the same way about me.

I walk away. Simone follows and then steps in front of me to block my path. "I'm sorry, I don't mean that but hell, Nora. What about Whisper, eh? You think she deserves a person who's too drunk or hungover to take care of her?"

It's a cheap shot, but Simone has never been one to mince words. "I gave her away."

Simone's jaw hangs open just a little bit. She shuts it and I can almost hear the snap. "I see. So you've given up on the one being that loves you more than anything in the world. The one who chose you."

What I love about Simone is that she's never reduced Whisper's presence in my life to simply one of a pet. She's recognized her for what she has always been to me: a lifeline.

"She deserves better," I say.

"Yeah, and if everyone got what they deserved this world would be pretty damn unrecognizable. But that's not life. We stick with what we know and Whisper isn't going to be happy anywhere else. Did you drop her off at a shelter?"

"What?" I reply, offended. "Don't be ridiculous. She's with people I trust."

"Well, that's a relief, anyway. But you should have come to me before it got this far."

At least I've done something right here. It was talk of Whisper and her ratty little terrier, Benedict, that initially brought the two of us together. Simone knows how important Whisper was in my path to sobriety and is using her as leverage in this guilt trip. Damn it to hell. It's working. Even though I'm wasted, I feel the edges again. So we sit in her car and I tell her about Bonnie and what I discovered at the luxurious ski chalet up in the mountains, on the road there and in the city when this all started. Bonnie, Starling, the not-cops . . . Ray Zhang. Jia and Dao. Dao.

Simone is the first to speak after that information overload. "I'm glad I was sitting down for all this."

"I'm glad I didn't have to hit you with a tire iron first."

"What?"

"Nothing." Just the way I share information, apparently.

"But what I don't get is how they found her in the first place. And how did they get their hands on your cord blood? Fifteen years ago, this research was brand-new. We didn't have the private facilities that we do now where families could pay a premium and bank the blood for later. We didn't even have a public bank. I'd imagine that there were research facilities that needed the blood, but you'd have to consent to that, Nora."

"I didn't."

"I don't see how that's possible."

"Don't you?"

Simone sighs. "Yeah, you're right. I guess I do." When you're on the fringes, like us, people do what they want and assume you don't know what your rights are. With Simone, they'd be wrong. "Okay, so they somehow get their hands on her cord blood, red market style—"

"What?"

"The red market. That's what they call the black market for blood and organs. Body parts."

"Oh."

"So," she continues. "It means that she was a match for some-one important because they had to use subterfuge to get it. They'd have to if it wasn't a legal donation scenario. And now they want more because the sample is too small to do much and they need a close match. Increases the chances of the body accepting the transplant. They trace the sample back to her."

"Somehow."

"Somehow," she agrees. "They figure she's the child that was born from that night all those years ago and find her. Could be the adoption records? I don't know. Maybe they watch her for a while. Maybe they've found out that she's prone to running off whenever the going gets rough. This time it's about the boy-friend and they grab her as she's on the way to meet him. They figure they have some time before anyone comes looking for her, but she was already gone a couple of weeks before the par-ents approached you, right? And you found those security guys watching her house."

"Right."

"So, if they have her, why watch the house?"

"They lost her."

"Or she ran away from them."

"Because that's what she does."

She nods and for a moment seems lost in thought. When she speaks next, her words are slow and measured, as if she herself is trying to grapple with their meaning. "She knows they're look-ing for her, she knows she's important and maybe she can iden-tify them, so it becomes about more than the blood for them, it becomes about managing the situation. Finding her and tying up the loose ends. That's why they've pulled out all the stops. Going after you. Killing the journalist, shooting at a kid in the woods . . . that's just crazy." She looks at me, her liner-enhanced eyes dark and wet. "The stakes are high for them, Nora. This whole situation has gotten completely out of hand—and this is coming from me. You know I'm usually the one to appreciate the drama in life. I hate to say this, but—"

I see where she's going with this. "No cops. They won't believe me. You know how this sounds."

"Not even—"

"Not a chance."

I haven't told her about Brazuca and I never will. Whether he is still tied to a fancy bed with one hell of a hangover or back at the WIN offices is a mystery to me. I refuse to think about him, though, because liars don't deserve my pity.

"So," Simone says, after a while, "what are you going to do?"

I remain silent. I don't know what I can do.

"This is so fucked up."

"You're telling me."

"Hey." Simone puts her hand over mine. I flinch, a habitual, unconscious shrugging away. "Sorry," she says, removing the hand. "Didn't mean to upset you. Nora, this isn't your fault. What happened to you all those years ago, what happened to Bonnie. None of it is on you. I want to hear you say it."

I shake my head. There's no telling what would happen if I open up that door. "I need you to help me find out where Zhang lives in Vancouver." I get out of the car then and walk away. I know she's disappointed in me, or else she would have followed.

The basement feels empty without Whisper. It's as if when

she moved in with me, she brought a kind of fullness and peace to my life, and without her here, I don't know how I was able to stand it before. I'm coming off a buzz now and I'm so very tired. I push Whisper from my head because it hurts too damn much and I bury myself under the covers. I put my secondhand MP3 player on shuffle and the first song that comes on is "Ain't No Sunshine." At first this makes me think of Whisper again, but then I start to wonder. Has it stopped raining since Bonnie went missing? Maybe I'm just too drunk to remember it clearly, but I don't think so. Nimbus clouds have hung overhead like a protective shield, diffusing light and spewing precipitation. It might just be my imagination, but I don't think the sunshine has broken through since she disappeared. Not once.

When I wake up I check my email and see that Simone has sent me some reports with the subject line: *This happens.* Two reports are of private cord blood clinics, one in Hong Kong and the other in San Francisco, that have had donor information stolen through employee breaches, and one leads to a chat site about brokers and rogue operators in medical communities around the world that hawk pilfered organs and blood on the red market.

This happens?

No shit.

# 2

WHEN I SURFACED from a deep sleep all those years ago, it was with a head that felt as though it had been bludgeoned like a seal pup and a swollen belly that protruded so far out from my emaciated frame that it announced its arrival into a room a full second before the rest of me followed. My broken bones had been reset, my motor functions were slowly being restored, but my mental state was cause for concern and the doctors refused to release me. They thought I would hurt the child, and I can't blame them. Also, my silence on the matter didn't help clarify things. After I tried to escape twice, one of these instances bizarrely chalked up to a suicide attempt, they transferred me to a small psychiatric hospital to be closely monitored.

Starling visited me often, but he was the only one. We spent the time sitting on opposite sides of the room while he tried to convince me to get in touch with my sister. It would make for a touching feature, siblings reunited in the face of tragedy. I told him to shove it, but his professional commitment to my health, and my story, was unwavering.

In my tiny room, I would stand at the window overlooking the back entrance and watch as the doctors and nurses snuck out for a smoke. Only the tops of their heads were visible from my vantage point, but I could always identify my doctor because his hairpiece would wave at me in the security light over the

back entrance. Once a day he came to my room smelling of cigarette fumes and Old Spice to check my chart and ask me how
I was doing. I'd say, "Would be better with some vodka," and
he would smile his bland smile in response. This was our little
dance and it never wavered in the three months that I was held
hostage.

Fifteen years have passed since I last saw him. The day that
Bonnie was born. They put me to sleep while they cut her out
of me and I woke once again to find my body changed. Emptied of the life that it carried, the vessel now bloody and hollow.
The baby was born sometime in the early hours of the morning and after I woke, I lay there stunned and exhausted while
the day crept on. It was dark when he led me outside, dressed
in street clothes from the lost-and-found box, and told me that
there would be a bus at the stop across the street in the next ten
minutes. He handed me bus fare and an extra ten dollars for
good measure. He also told me that I needed to make different
choices in life, and this was the time to start.

"You want to go, right?" he said, in the brief second that I
hesitated.

The pause wasn't about having second thoughts of staying at
that place; it was because I thought that I was dreaming and it
was time to wake up. I wanted to give myself a minute to let my
conscious mind take over, but his impatience unnerved me. We
stood there for a moment that could have spanned a lifetime for
all I could grasp of it. And then I was across the hospital's parking lot and at the bus stop. We stared at each other from either
side of the dark, slick street and then he went back inside. A few
minutes later, the bus showed up and I went to a shelter I knew.

It's astonishing to me how much of this I remember.

Now I look at him and the memories blow right past until one of them sticks to him. At first he doesn't remember me from that day but he is forced to take a closer look because there's something familiar about me. Something he can't quite put his finger on. And I am, after all, leaning against his car. The parking lot is small and shaded by trees. There is no one else around and Eric Zakarian is clearly uncomfortable by this unexpected development in his day. His eyes dart from me to the building's entrance. It's too far for him to run. The years of being a smoker and thirty extra pounds have done nothing for his cardio.

"My God," he says, when he finally recognizes me. He can't hide the sudden fear in his eyes. Good. Welcome to the club.

He looks at the entrance again.

"You'll never make it," I tell him.

"What?"

I nod to the door. "You'll never make it back inside before I catch up."

"Wha-what are you doing here? Look, if you want to talk, we should go somewhere else." He's trying to hide his fear, but not doing a very good job of it. He has forgotten that I know what calm looks like on him. That I saw him every day for months and, though it was a long time ago, I can still read his moods.

"No," I say, patting the hood of his BMW. I lean against it casually, mostly to take the pressure off my ankle. But he doesn't have to know that. "I think we should talk right here."

"What do you want?"

"I want to know where the blood from my umbilical cord went after you chased me out of this place."

He turns pale and sweaty, all at once. "I don't know what you're talking about. You should go before . . . before I call the cops!"

"Sure, let's call the cops. I'll tell them that while I was under anesthesia, you harvested my cord blood without permission and sold it to some broker."

His jaw trembles, which only happens with men like him when they're confronted with the truth, and then, predictably, he denies it. "I've never done any such thing! Besides, they'll never believe you. A pregnant hooker who gets herself into trouble doesn't exactly know what she's talking about, now does she? Now get away from my car."

I don't move. Hooker?

He seems to be gaining confidence the more he speaks. "Get lost! I told you, nobody's going to believe you. Look at you," he says, squinting over at me. "Haven't changed a bit. Go clean yourself up and leave me alone."

I sigh. Drinking vodka mixed with lemonade from a glass bottle has not improved my mood. I'm feeling abnormally violent tonight. I smash the empty glass bottle against his car and hold up the jagged remainder of it. His denial was all the confirmation I needed that my cord blood was harvested, but for some reason, at this moment, confirmation just doesn't seem good enough. The jagged edges of the bottle make a loud screech along the driver's side door of his BMW.

Zakarian stands there and watches me defile his car. He has been frozen into place, eyes wide with fear, ever since I smashed the bottle. "You're next if you don't tell me exactly what I need to know. I know you're lying because my cord blood was used."

He licks his lips. "What do you want?"

"Why would someone need it?"

"Stem cells," he says quickly, confirming what I already knew from Starling's research. "Leukemia, sickle cell disease, immunodeficiency, lymphoma, a host of diseases, really . . . The research is still progressing, but stem cells from the umbilical cord are more malleable than those from an adult. Problem is, there's not a lot of it so it's not the Hail Mary some people make it out to be. When the research was starting, samples were hard to come by."

"Could it treat an elderly man?"

"I don't know . . . depends on the man and the disease. Look, this isn't exactly my specialty, okay?"

I take a step closer. "Why did you take it?" Even if Zhang and his people had read the article and connected me to Mary, the woman found in a ditch, who turned out to be pregnant, it wouldn't make sense that Zhang had anticipated an illness and then waited fifteen years to snatch Bonnie. There had to be another motive for him.

"My wife at the time was involved in some research and there was this source that contacted her, a broker of sorts . . . They needed donations but people weren't giving them up easily, not when private clinics were just starting to offer parents the opportunity to store the blood for their children's health down the road. The source was paying, but not a lot—not as much as you'd think—" He licks his lips and stares at me. "Please don't hurt me."

Another step. "Go on."

"She knew about you, that I was treating you, and she said

her source would be interested in the sample—for research! But the research didn't get funded and, I think, the blood stores they had ended up changing hands. I don't know where it went."

I feel sick to my stomach, which, thank God, is empty. If there was anything in it, the contents would be spewed onto his hundred-dollar wing tips. I would make sure of it. I take another step closer. "You stole from me."

He remains silent. I take another step. Now there's just a foot of space between us. "The child that you helped deliver all those years ago, she's been kidnapped because of what you did."

He blanches at the smell of alcohol on my breath. There's nothing more terrifying than being attacked by an unhinged drunk, unless it's an unhinged junkie. "It was for research! To help save lives."

Okay, now he's full-out lying. Even he can't actually believe that. I press the bottle to his face and a bead of blood blossoms at his cheek. He whimpers, stumbles back against the car. "Save lives? You endangered a child."

"No, I swear, I never wanted anything bad to happen! I just . . . it was exciting research and the broker, he was paying."

I laugh. It's not a pleasant sound. "And you thought I'd never find out." I draw a thin line from his cheekbone to the top of his jaw.

He gasps and tears roll down his cheeks. They are not tears of guilt or shame or sorrow. There is no apology in them. No, these are tears of fear. "Please," he whimpers. "Please just leave me alone."

The blood doesn't gush, it trickles.

"Sorry isn't good enough," I say, my voice barely a whisper.

"I'm leaving now, but don't get too comfortable because I'll be back and you'll pay for what you did."

I won't, but he doesn't have to know that.

"It wasn't just me!" he shouts at my back as I walk away. "My ex-wife, her name is Amanda Notting. Why don't you make her pay!"

Amanda Notting has no idea that her ex would give her up to a deranged drunk. Marriage. What's the point?

I continue to walk away. I feel reckless, unhinged. Alive. If only there was an available face around . . . but no, I have crossed lines there, too.

# 3

THE DINER ON Hastings isn't much to look at from the outside, but the coffee is only a dollar and they'll microwave a breakfast sandwich for you at any time of the day. Whether or not this is a good idea is debatable, but it allows them to keep the lights on and the doors open. It's now just after 9 P.M. and the grease of the eggs and cheese is dangerously close to turning my stomach. It's the only solid food I've had all day, though, so I force myself to keep it down. The effort I have to put into this simple activity almost makes me miss the beginning of the crawl on the twenty-four-hour news channel on a screen mounted just above the counter.

*Body found in Stanley Park. No identity has been confirmed by the police yet, but witness reports allege that it is possibly a child or a small woman.*

And that does it. The grease wins out.

I barely make it to the alley just off the diner before the bile comes spewing out. An older couple, out for a night stroll, glance my way in disgust as they walk past me heaving my guts out. "Goddamn drunks," says the man, just before he's out of earshot.

I lean against the wall, harsh breaths seizing my throat. The dampness in the air almost suffocates me. The man is not wrong, but alcohol is not the sole reason that I'm in an alley bringing up my only meal of the day. From a wealth of past experience with this kind of thing, take it from me, it's always better to upchuck out in the street rather than a toilet that isn't in your own home. Nobody wants to clutch a porcelain bowl that the public has had access to. Outside there will be no other patrons banging on the door, no disgusted employees giving you the stink-eye when you exit because they have to clean up after you. Out on the streets, the rain will wash away what it can and whatever remains is no worse than what was already there to begin with.

I could take a bus to Stanley Park, but from where I am the easiest way to get there is to just follow the seawall. I walk as quickly as I can and then throw all caution into the wind and start running. There are usually plenty of joggers along this route; sometimes running the seawall resembles something closer to a stampede, but people normally don't do it this late at night wearing boots and a rain jacket. I get a few stares, but I can't be bothered. The memory of the man I'd found in the park all those years ago lingers, along with Starling's face as he sat in a tub full of blood. And now I can't help but imagine the teenager in the photos sprawled on the ground, her eyes looking sightlessly up at the night sky.

The police are near Second Beach, by a dense copse of trees. Locating them was as easy as listening for the sound of human voices carried over the tops of the trees and then finding the lights that the police have set up around their barricade. There is a crowd gathered because, despite the drizzle, the weather is quite mild tonight and the discovery of a body in one of the biggest tourist haunts in the city is a big deal.

A bystander, a young woman in her twenties, stands apart

from the rest and it's to her I go first. I don't much like being in crowds, or near them, and this seems to be a woman after my own heart. She's wearing hiking boots and a raincoat, dressed for the terrain and the weather. Her sensibility appeals to me, and her clothing is dark so that none of it catches the light and hurts my eyes. I'm feeling faint after the run on an empty stomach. She could still be batshit crazy, but I'll take my chances. If it's Bonnie's body on the ground, protected by a privacy screen and further shielded by a cluster of cops, I might as well know now.

"Did you see the body?" I ask the woman.

She is too focused on the scene to spare me more than a sideways glance. I keep a few feet between us as a buffer so she doesn't smell the vomit on my breath, so she won't turn away before I get my answer. "No, just got here about ten minutes ago. Nobody seems to know much of anything, except for that guy over there." She points to a man in hiking boots, holding on to a dog on a leash. He's speaking with a police officer by a patrol car some distance away. "He found the body."

I hang about at the edges of the crowd, waiting to see what will happen next, waiting to see if someone will say something about the body behind the protective shield. Whenever the man with the dog is finished talking to the police officer, I'll try to find a way to get to him, but they're chatting comfortably and there's no sense that he'll finish up there anytime soon. There's no Brazuca here to give me an inside tip . . . but, then again, he wouldn't be here, would he? He would be hanging out with his buddies at WIN Security.

Just as the crowd thins and people start trickling away, there's a commotion on the far side of the copse. I see a man pushing through the crowd.

What I loved about singing the blues is that it cuts straight to the heart of a thing. You come naked with your soul lying carved open and exposed on the slab or you don't come at all. Give it real or keep it to yourself.

That kind of raw, that kind of honest you don't often find in life. I see it now as Everett barrels through the bystanders, Lynn trailing behind him like a pale, confused toddler who has just woken from a bad dream and can only focus on putting one foot in front of the other. Her luxurious hair is swept off her face and into a bun that is sagging at the side and coming apart. Everett has gained about ten pounds since I last saw him, but the weight doesn't suit him. It sits mostly near his neck and his gut, but everything else is thinner than I remember. These two have been falling apart for a long time, but now they can't hide it anymore.

"Is that my daughter?" Everett shouts at the first cop he sees. "Bronwyn Walsh. I filed a missing person's report—"

The cop flinches and holds a warding hand out to keep Everett from coming closer. A few other officers stir, coming to the first cop's side. "Sir—"

"Is it her? Please . . . please help m-me," and here Everett's voice breaks. Everyone stares at the father whose child this could possibly be because they can't help themselves, because it's part of the reason they came here. To witness a human tragedy. It's not something you can look away from.

The officer sees Lynn behind him for the first time. She has her hand to her throat and is gazing at him with frightened eyes. A tiny, birdlike gasp emerges from her mouth, attempting to sound like a word, but failing miserably. There is so much despair writ plainly on their faces. I move closer to them while the other bystanders edge away. There is too much emotion there; they're afraid it will spill on them and mess up their shoes.

"Sir, we're not in any position to identify the body right now—"

"I'll take over from here, Ray." A plainclothes detective pats the cop's shoulder. He looks at both Everett and Lynn. "I'm Detective Lee. You say your daughter's missing?"

Lynn can only nod, while Everett gathers his courage.

"Yes," says Everett. "Bronwyn Walsh. She's fifteen years old, about this tall." Everett gestures at roughly chest height. "Dark hair, dark eyes. Please, please just tell us. Is it her?"

Lee's voice lowers so that it's almost a whisper. I have to step in to hear. He puts a hand on Everett's shoulder and squeezes. "I answer and you'll go straight home? Let us do our work here?"

"Y-yes." It's Lynn who speaks now. She has found her voice, and it is stronger than I expected. "We won't bother you anymore."

The detective nods. "From what you described, it doesn't sound like a match. I can't say any more, okay?"

All the air goes out of Everett's lungs and he staggers. "Thank God. Oh, thank God." He reaches out blindly for Lynn's hand, but she doesn't even notice. He is left to flounder with nothing to hold on to. No anchor. Adrift in his own emotional turmoil while his wife stands next to him, lost in her own thoughts. I watch a change come over her. Whoever died here tonight, it wasn't her daughter. And for the first time, I glimpse what her love for Bonnie is. Complicated by circumstances, but no less real.

The detective is watching them as closely as I am. "You said you filed a report?"

Lynn nods. "Bronwyn Walsh."

"How long has she been missing?"

"Going on three weeks."

Lee hesitates for a moment so brief that I think I'm the only one that notices. He takes down their info, scribbling on a little notepad that he pulled from his back pocket. "I'll look into it. All right then, off you go." He waits for them to leave, the expression in his eyes shuttered.

Lee eyes the crowd, skipping past me like cops always do. He's looking for anyone or anything that stands out and, on that front, I'm safe. At some point in the next several hours, the body will be identified—it usually always is—and Lee will have to break the news to some relative or friend that there's been a death. In that moment, as the detective looks right at me and then past, not really seeing me at all, I feel a sudden, blinding terror.

How many people looked past Bonnie like that? What if she is invisible, like me? And what if I'm her last hope?

What a terrible thought.

# 4

I RAN AWAY from foster care just after I turned fifteen, after Lorelei and I had been long separated. I always knew where she was, and knew that she was doing a hell of a lot better than me. I lived mostly on the street until I applied for the Forces. They wanted a GED, and that wasn't so hard to get. But after my disastrous attempt at military life, I was back on the streets. Back busking, singing. Lorelei had laughed, when I had the bad judgment to tell her on one visit up to her dorm room in college, and I never mentioned it after that. She was right, in a way. What was someone like me doing singing music that held its roots so far away, singing on the streets for money?

This is how powerful culture is.

A music born out of the dregs of slavery in the Mississippi Delta, a sound that echoes the pain of disenfranchisement, institutionalized racism, and abject poverty of an oppressed people, can travel past Confederate borders, beyond national borders, to the continental western coast to be played on a scratchy record after choir one day to a roomful of children, to a girl for whom life had given nothing good but a strong, clear singing voice. Most American music has its roots in the blues. I know that now. Usually twelve bars. Usually rhythmic lyrics. Gospel, rock, jazz, country, folk—all pull from it. But all I heard back then was John Lee Hooker's magical voice coming through the record player. I didn't understand much of what he sang about, but I didn't need to. The choir was the only thing then that kept me going because every now and then Pastor Franklin would feel generous and put on a blues record for us after practice and we would hear what it was like to connect with someone else's soul. I didn't have the same capacity for hope that the spirituals required, so the blues suited me just fine.

And I wasn't bad at it, either. I went up north to plant trees, and with some of that money, and the busking, I was making enough to rent a space in a room and get by. I didn't mind it all that much because singing was all I liked to do anyway. Back in that first foster home, the only thing that made that place bearable was they used to take us to church and I sang with the choir. It stuck with me.

After I moved out west I started to go to open mikes. What can I say? I was stupid.

When I did these gigs, I usually wore a bright color just in case someone wanted to find me afterward and give me money or buy me a drink. Lighting was not the strong suit in these establishments. Sometimes a T-shirt or sweater, sometimes a hat or a scarf. The night that ended all that for me, it was a yellow baseball cap. I got up, strummed the guitar I had stolen from another busker the week before while he took a nap, and sang "Hound Dog," the Big Mama Thornton version (not that swiveling Elvis stuff), just to get the crowd singing along, and then I transitioned immediately into "I Just Wanna Make Love to You." I used to enjoy that kind of thing, and those songs worked well in a crowd. Nobody does it like Etta James, but I know that it worked for my voice. I also managed to get off a few bars of

"Baby Please Don't Go" before they kicked me off the stage, but I'm no Big Joe Williams . . . even though I've got a fair hand at the guitar.

Now, looking back, I know that I should have been more careful, that I should have never worn that yellow cap that was like a spotlight, that I should have left right after the set. I shouldn't have been a drunk, even back then, and I shouldn't have dared to dream anyway. There were about a million should-haves and could-haves that raced through my mind over and over again in the years afterward and, for the most part, they all led back to me singing these flirty songs in a basement dive in the wrong part of town.

Like I said, the lighting wasn't good.

I remember thick black hair and almond-shaped eyes so dark that they rivaled my own, and that he was handsome. Or maybe that's just how he seemed after a couple of beers. What we talked about that night remains a mystery to me. I can't imagine it was all that interesting, or else he wouldn't have had to drug me. Or maybe he was going to do it anyway. I do recall thinking that with his fancy shoes and expensive watch, maybe he knew some people who could help me. It wasn't anything other than my voice that brought him to the stool beside me and maybe, just this once, my voice would be enough for someone to reach out a hand.

Like I said, I was stupid.

I do remember a hand, though, but it wasn't outstretched in friendship or to initiate any kind of professional relationship. No, it was on my shoulder, caressing the inch of skin just under the sleeve of my T-shirt. Did I mind it, then? I can't really say.

I just don't remember. All I know now is I despise the color yellow and I rue the day I ever took that hat off a bubbly coed who shared my dorm in a hostel that one time, back when I was still naive enough to sleep in a room full of other people without keeping one eye open.

# 5

MY MOTHER IS a mystery to me.

I was too young to remember her when she left, and Lorelei was just a baby, but I knew that she didn't die like our father used to say, because he could never tell us what she died from. After our father was gone, our aunt would refuse to respond to any questions about our parents. I overheard her once on the phone with one of her friends, calling our mother a foreigner, her lips pinched with hatred. But she never said from where and I never caught her talking on the phone like that again. I just knew that she was alive, because you don't hate the dead. Not like that. Then when our aunt got sick and gave us up, I just had Lorelei.

After I woke up and shared my story, Starling wouldn't let up with the reconciliation line. "You need support," he persisted. He sensed my reluctance to reach out to my sister, which I was too hormonal to hide. "She can't refuse you. She wouldn't refuse you, Nora, not after what you've been through."

I don't blame him for thinking that way and pestering me with his amateur bullshit psychology. Everyone and their cousin think they know something about the human condition and I blame the self-styled gurus on television. In a perfect world Lorelei would fall into my arms and whisper platitudes of sisterly love in my ear, but a perfect world this one ain't. Starling just didn't know her. He didn't know how cruel beauty like hers can be. How it can make someone think that she is better than everyone else, better than you, who have always taken the licks for her and love her all the same.

I sit at her kitchen table with my stomach in knots and wait for her to wake up.

David comes down the stairs first and pauses in his slippered feet when he sees me. I've only met him once, on the porch when I stopped by to see Lorelei when I got my first chip. They got married when I was in the coma, and she still doesn't know where I'd been all that time. She was too embarrassed by me to check and it must have been a relief to her that I never popped back into her life for the wedding.

David stares at me now like I'm a specter from a horror story brought to life. Worn as I look, I don't blame him for taking a cautious step back. "You ruined my car," he says, after a while. He turns on the coffeemaker and busies himself with making breakfast while he gets his bearings.

"You had insurance, right?"

He frowns. "Let me get your sister." He goes, leaving the breakfast fixings, padding down the hall and up the stairs. I can see the appeal of David. At first, I'd wondered because Lorelei could do so much better than a blandly handsome environmental lawyer, but now it is obvious. David is good, hardworking, and utterly predictable in his devotion to her. He goes grocery shopping on the weekends, fishes on Vancouver Island in his spare time, and drinks Bud Lights. I hear he has Nuu-chah-nulth ancestry. That some of his distant relatives still live on the island and that was what attracted her to him in the first place, but what has kept her at his side is likely the same unruffled nature that, within a matter of seconds, went from being shocked at an unwanted family member breaking into his house to starting breakfast because people have to eat and he likes to cook.

A few minutes later I hear her small feet fly down the stairs. She stops at the doorway barefoot and wearing only one of David's T-shirts, her hair in a disheveled halo framing her heart-shaped face, her eyes blazing with an unholy fire. David trails behind like he's attached by a string, but all of my attention is on her.

She stares at me, furious.

Something inside me dies.

There are resident orcas that live off the west coast and have some of the highest toxicity levels of marine mammals in the world, with pollutants swimming about under layers of blubber, keeping them warm and hazardous. Sometimes they wash up on the beach but their carcasses are so poisonous that people have to stay far back from the toxic PCBs they release. Why they stay somewhere so bad for them is a matter of pure speculation, but perhaps these waters are like family to them. It's the orca equivalent of home. Familiar, even if it is killing them slowly. I understand that because I moved west, from Manitoba, where we grew up, to be closer to the sole familiar person that I have in this world. No matter where she goes, I have followed her because should something happen, I'd like to be close. Or maybe I need to make sure I'm here if she needs me. Not that she ever would, and not that it would ever be the other way around. Whatever it is, I understand these orcas and why they'd choose a hazardous ocean over cleaner waters somewhere else. It's what they know.

I see now that this visit was a mistake, that whatever I'd hoped to accomplish here—reconciliation, understanding, a word of kindness—it was never going to happen.

"You're drinking again."

I'm not surprised she noticed. The boozing hasn't improved my appearance. There are bags under my eyes and my skin is sallow and drawn. I've been living off candy bars and pizza for too long and my clothes are still so old and worn that even I have become aware of their shabby state.

"I want to explain," I say, careful to keep my voice neutral and calm, like when you're talking to a bear. Hands up and back away slowly. I should have done it when I saw her come down the stairs. Her defensive nature makes it impossible to deal with her in any other way.

"Oh, now you want to explain," she snaps. "Now. After our SUV is at the bottom of a fucking ravine!"

I decide to give her some backstory, to prepare the both of us. "After I enlisted—"

She laughs. "You want to go there? That was ages ago. And then you got kicked out. Just like you get kicked out of everything. You used to be the smart one . . . what the hell happened to you?" She leans against the doorjamb and narrows her eyes at me. "I could have told you it was a mistake, you know. You. In the fucking army. Trying to live up to that bullshit Dad went off about before he killed himself. Honor my ass. They were never gonna accept him for who he was and so he made up these stories to tell us and *you bought it*. You couldn't even finish high school and you think you could have made it in the Forces."

"Lorrie—" I begin softly, trying for a fresh start. She is right about why I enlisted and why I failed. So was Brazuca. A problem with authority is ingrained in me. But our father was the only parent we remembered and even though we sometimes saw through his lies, they were so sweet. He spoke of belonging, of the camaraderie that he felt in a few, fleeting moments. I was old enough to remember those stories and I used to tell them to her. It was his sister we lived with before we were shipped off to foster care and separated who told us the truth. That he was as unhappy as everyone else, and made up stories to make himself feel better.

Lorelei's nostrils flare and I realize my mistake of using her pet name from our youth. She hates it even more now than she did then. She holds up a hand, as if to ward me away, as if I'm some kind of curse that has been brought down on her head. "No. Just don't. After what you did you have no right to come here, to call me that. Who do you think you are, showing your face here?"

"I'm sorry."

"You should be ashamed of yourself."

"I am."

"I shoulda known when you showed up at my door that you were still up to no good . . ." She pauses and then something ugly in her breaks through her pretty façade. "Mary."

I go still. "What did you say?"

Her smile is bitter. "You think I didn't know? You told that journalist, that goddamn parasite, everything about our family!

About Dad being adopted into the States, how he came back here and found nothing but a sister who was as fucked up as he was, how he killed himself. Us being in foster care and you being on the streets. Mary? Yeah, what a choice of a name. No saintly virgin you were. What, you think I don't read the newspaper, Nora? Jesus. You told him all your shameful little secrets about what a dirty slut you've been—"

It couldn't have been worse if she'd hit me. My knees go weak and I'm thankful for the small mercy of being seated. I'll admit our visits were infrequent but she never mentioned once that she'd connected me with Starling's story. And, if she knew about Mary, she knew that there was a child. She had a niece, and she didn't care.

"I was drugged."

"Please, you were a drunk. Always were, always will be. That's what got you in trouble, Nora. You can't deny it. Isn't that how you got the drugs in you? Couldn't have been that hard."

The chair scrapes against the kitchen floor as I push away from the table. I'm angry now, too. "Someone had to be a fuckup, just to show how perfect you were in comparison. How else would they know that the sun shines out of your ass?"

"Get. Out." There are no words for the amount of scorn and bitterness she can level in just two syllables. It's an art, really. She snatches David's phone off the counter. "Or I'll call the cops. I swear to God I will."

Does she even believe in God? It seems like something you should know about your sister. I go to the door and watch my hand as it hovers over the doorknob. I want to say something so penetrating and hateful to her that she'll remember it for the rest of her life. I want my words to have the power that her words have over me. But in the end I can't and they don't because they never have. She's always been better than me in all the ways that matter and I've always been okay with that. So I settle on the only thing that comes to mind.

"You'll never really know," I say to her, hating how shaky my voice is. "What it was like to find him." Lying in a pool of blood, a gun in his hand, his skull blown wide open. I was a child, but she was even younger. I never allowed her to see him like that. Even at that age, I knew that something like that could break her. Like it did with me.

Her eyes narrow into little slits. "Spare me your sob story. I've heard a million of them. Dad was weak and so are you."

See, this is what happens when you try to explain yourself.

I release the breath I've been holding. "You should change your alarm code." As last words to the only family I have left, they're more than a little anticlimactic, but all I can muster. She has always had this effect on me. It feels like the end of something, but that's her intention. The end of a bad relationship that soured just after I turned thirteen and she caught me behind the school surrounded by empty beer bottles, a group of stoners and a joint being passed around us like a hot potato.

She watches me go, expressionless.

"Is that my tire iron?" David says, before I'm out the door. It is sticking out of the waistband of my sweatpants.

"No," I say and then I walk out. Really, who can tell one tire iron from another? I would have given it back if my reception by them had gone otherwise, but I'm not above pettiness.

Also, what's another lie between family?

A few minutes later David pulls up to the bus shelter in a rental sedan. Probably a perk of his purchasing insurance on his SUV. I'm alone at the stop for the moment and there's no bus on the horizon. He gets out of the car with an envelope and holds it out to me. "Here," he says. "Take this."

Inside the envelope is eight hundred dollars in cash.

"We want you to have that, to help you out since you seem to be going through such a rough time." He pauses and tries to broach his next topic delicately. "And, it's probably a good idea if you don't come back anytime soon. Your sister is . . . well, it would just be better to stay away for now. Okay?"

After Howlin' Wolf had made his mark on the blues, after he'd played show after show, growled song after song, after he'd strummed and howled and made the kind of money a blues man never even knew that he could back in those days, he tried to reconcile with his mother, who had cast him away because he played the devil's music. She threw the money he tried to give her in his face.

I'm no upstanding woman of God, but enough is enough. I toss the envelope back through the open car window. "You can't get rid of family, Dave," I tell him, before turning away.

I know, because I've tried.

# 6

THERE IS A working pay phone at the train station. Simone answers on the third ring in a cool, masculine voice. "Simon here."

"It's me."

There's a pause and then her voice takes on a sultry note. Whether or not this is a deliberate move or an unconscious one, simply because this is how she's used to speaking to me, I'll never ask. After what I've just been through with Lorelei, I'm glad for the familiarity of it. "Where are you?" Her voice is full of concern. I hear her clicking away at a keyboard and become acutely aware of how traceable phone calls are.

"Don't worry about that."

"You sound shaky."

Dammit, I do. I stare as a transit official walks right by me with a steaming cup of coffee and then turn my back to him. "Have you found where Zhang lives?"

She pauses for so long that I think she's going to refuse. "His assets are spread around, but I've managed to locate a few property records. Call back in twenty minutes."

"Can you make it fifteen?"

"Don't push me," she says, and hangs up.

I duck into the public washroom, where I spend eighteen minutes trapped in a stall or at the sink, scrubbing my face and hands and finger combing my hair. Almost twenty minutes later, I call back. She reads out three addresses. A house in Richmond, a condo overlooking English Bay, and a mansion in West Vancouver. "You have a map up on your screen?" I ask her.

"Right here. What do you need?"

"If I was going to hide someone, it wouldn't be in a condo. Too public. Elevators, neighbors, that sort of thing."

"I see where you're going with this," she says slowly, her fingers still tapping away. "Okay, the house in Richmond was once part of an exclusive neighborhood, but it's become quite dense."

"Too many prying eyes. You can't exactly control the situation there and if there was an escape—"

"Someone would have seen something. Which leaves the mansion as your only real option . . . Look, if they haven't found her yet, do you really think she'd be in the same area that they kept her captive?"

"She hasn't gone home, been to see her best friend or her boyfriend. Where else would she be?"

"Nora, I hate to say this, but maybe she's gone. Maybe she's dea—"

"Thanks, Simone," I say, placing the receiver gently back on its hook before she can continue that thought. If she's right, then it was all for nothing and I can't accept that. I take the SkyTrain into the city and try some positive visualization. The other passengers are giving me dirty looks and I realize, quite suddenly, that despite my efforts in the bathroom back at the station I must smell completely awful. I've been on the road too long, have spent too much time in my own company to notice, but others are not so forgiving. I think about stopping by the basement, but with Whisper gone it won't be the same and I don't want to be in our home without her.

I take the bus from Granville Station to the north shore. A sudden cold front turns the rain into pellet-sized hail that clatters against the window at the rear of the bus where I'm seated. I watch as the pedestrians and drivers, united in their astonishment, scramble for safety. The bus, however, has a schedule to keep. About thirty minutes later I get off at Marine Drive and the Dale. It's a short walk to Water Lane, where a dozen cars are parked at the side of the road.

The address that Simone gave me belongs to a massive mansion, secured from view by tall hedges and a stone wall. A real estate open-house sign points to the driveway. A well-dressed older couple emerges from a Porsche and walks onto the property without sparing a glance in my direction.

"Thank God you're finally here!" a voice behind me exclaims. I turn to see a brunette in her fifties, wearing a pencil skirt and sharp blazer, emerging from a BMW. She's glaring at me as if I'm the source of all that is wrong in her world. From her dress and attitude, I take her to be the real estate agent. She stubs out her cigarette and looks me up and down. "Well, I suppose you'll do. Come on. I hope you know a thing or two about pruning."

People mistake me for the help all the time. I guess I have that kind of face. At least she hasn't cast aspersions on my tits or my hair. Yet.

"What are you waiting for? Let's get a move on," the woman says, striding past the huge mansion and manicured lawn, and down a path that leads to the back of what I can only call an estate. She stops in front of an overgrown rosebush and frowns.

"I don't know how your people missed this the last time, but a couple of our prospective buyers have commented today. Take care of it."

She turns on her heel and walks away.

"Hey!" I call to her retreating back.

She looks back at me, tapping her foot impatiently. "What? I'm assuming you have your own tools somewhere in your vehicle, right? Because I'm not prepared to teach you how to do your job."

"I'm just doing them a favor today, but I'm a cash operation."

"Oh, for fuck's sake. Here." She digs around in her purse and hands me a fifty-dollar bill. "Anything more you'll have to invoice. Just get it done."

I pocket the fifty and give her my most obsequious smile. "So the people who live here, they're selling the house? How come? These are pretty sweet digs."

She's not used to answering questions from the help but apparently decides to put me in my place. "The people who own this house haven't lived here for over a year and, not that it's any of your business, yes. They are selling. That's why you're here pruning the rosebushes that some anal retentive millionaires have been muttering about."

I nod and walk up the path, back the way we came, my steps eating up the distance between us. "You're getting your tools, right?" she says as I pull closer.

"Nope," I say, quickly passing her.

"But what . . . ? You're going to come back with them, aren't you?"

"We'll see."

"Who . . . who are you?" She's now concerned that she's given away too much to someone who has no business being on the property.

I throw a look at her over my shoulder. "Me? I'm nobody."

"Hey, you thief! You owe me fifty bucks!" she shouts at my back. But she can't do anything about it. Her high heels prevent her from moving at a pace faster than a constipated dog and she has no chance of catching up to me.

Women.

# 7

THE HASTINGS OFFICE boasts three tiny windows that look out into the dank alleyway. One in each of the offices and one in the reception area. It's not much of a view so Seb and Leo don't pay it any attention. Whisper, however, is not used to such luxuries and has planted herself right by the reception window to monitor the situation. I stand in the rain and watch as Seb scratches her head on his way out of his office and Leo kisses her snout on his way into his own.

I look at her for a long time, but I have no desire to go inside. Things are clearer to me out here. I'm lying and I'm drinking, two things I swore to myself and Whisper that I'd never do. I'm also stealing, and while I never had a vow about that, it's just another shitty thing that marks the bottom rung I'm clinging to. I'm a thieving, drinking liar, but I haven't hit rock bottom yet and there's no sense trying to fix what's right until I have.

Leo goes to my desk and rifles through it. He finds an old sticky note and punches a number into the office phone. Seb wanders over and, while Leo's attention is on whoever is on the other end of the line, he slips a strip of jerky to Whisper. It is gone within seconds.

Since Bonnie disappeared, my internal axis has tilted. I wonder now if my place is inside that office or out here on the street. I'm scared of the answer, but there's nothing I can do about it. I know it's not her fault. I can see the pieces of the puzzle falling together now and whether or not she ran away from home, she would have been caught up in this mess in some way. But I can't deny that it's because of her that, after all these years of trying to straighten myself out, I'm still on the outside looking in.

My homeless friend is asleep near the dumpster. His feet poke out of the holes in his socks. I pull out the extra pair from my pack, stuff them into a plastic bag, and put them near him, careful to keep near his feet and not his face. You don't want to startle a sleeping body on the street; they are as likely to wake up angry or scared as not.

He stirs just as I'm about to turn away and blinks up at me. "I'm still here," he says, his voice hoarse and scratchy. I don't know if he's recognized my face from before or if he's just talking because he sees that I'm no threat. "They try to take me away—"

A harsh cough racks his body and it takes him a full minute to recover.

"Who? Who tried to take you away?"

He closes his eyes and turns his face away. "Still here . . ."

When Leo disappears into his office, Whisper turns to the window. She stares at me through the rain-splattered glass pane for several long seconds, then she starts to howl. By the time Leo comes crashing in from his office to see what's wrong, I'm already gone. I've done what I needed to do. She looks as happy as she ever has, which is not saying a lot given her feline disposition, but at least she doesn't look abandoned. She has graduated from one person to love her and now has two. That is not a bad life and I haven't done wrong by her.

As far as tying up loose ends goes, this is the best I can do.

# 8

BONNIE WAKES TO flashing lights and the incessant beeping of an ECG machine. There are tubes going into her arms. She thrashes and screams, but her reflection in the mirror tells a different story. It tells a story of a girl lying in bed without sound or motion, her dark eyes red-rimmed and wide open with fear. She knows what the tubes mean. She knows that they are monitoring her, that they have taken her back because they want her blood. She doesn't cry, though. It will be over soon.

How long will it take to drain her completely? She hopes it's quick this time.

# FIVE

# 1

WHEN YOU FEEL like having an enema without all that pesky shitting, try using the provincial ferry system. It is not the only way to get from the mainland to Vancouver Island, but it is a fraction cheaper than taking a seaplane—and that's not much of an endorsement. I've spent more money in the past few weeks than I have in a year and am not much in the mood to watch my bank account balance sink even lower, so I open my wallet and bend over.

We sail past little islands, lush protrusions of land thrusting from the depths of the ocean. Without all the tankers blocking the view, it's easy to imagine that we're in an earlier time, that we're perhaps the first Europeans to come sailing through these waters, gaping at the cool beauty of it. Everything is shrouded in mist, like the setting of a fable. Only the foghorn dispels this notion and reminds us that we exist in the present day and all romance is dead.

I spend most of the ninety-minute journey in a bathroom stall with my bottle of vodka, which is as good as any way to take a ferry. It is a harrowing journey, even when ferry operators are not busy mooning at each other on the bridge, missing important turns and crashing ships into small islands. This has happened only once in the province's history, that I know of, but it's one time too many for my comfort. I take solace in the knowledge that the island I'm headed toward is at least large enough to be seen from a distance.

Two women enter the bathroom while I'm closeted in my stall, laughing about something or the other. I watch through the narrow space between the door and its frame as they take colored pencils to their eyes and lips, and brush their lashes with an inky wand. They don't seem concerned about the possibilities of disaster and for a moment I wish I was with them, laughing it up while the engines could be failing at this very moment. But then I take a swig from my bottle and my calm is restored. When the man's voice announces over the loudspeaker that we're nearing our destination, I pull on my hood and head for the deck.

It's as bad as I thought.

The wind and rain beat at my exposed skin as I wait around the offloading area. Others line up, pressing their bodies closer and closer in hopes to be among the first to leave, but, as always, I prefer to keep my distance. As the ferry pulls into the terminal, I breathe a sigh of relief. Vancouver Island is famous for its landscapes, especially the wild, rugged beauty of the rain forest and coastline. It's understandable; people from all around the world come here to surf, whale watch, and hike during the summer and storm watch in the winter. They should come while they can. It might not be here for long. Once every few hundred years or so, a large earthquake grips the western coast with tremors massive enough to rend through the earth here and cause a tsunami. No one knows when the next one is going to happen, but some scientists say it's going to be soon. Real estate agents say we've got some time.

Whatever it is, for now the island is still intact and open for business. There is tourism to be promoted and mining to be done.

I've been thinking a lot about mining. Because something Bernard Lam said has been bothering me.

# 2

PEOPLE TAKE MORE than they give; that's just the nature of the human beast. On the island, they've been taking since the first ships sailed over from Europe. Along with entire cultural heritages, languages, and childhood innocence, on Vancouver Island they have also diversified their portfolios and grabbed up what they could in coal and copper. On the northeastern tip of the island there's a copper mine that was excavated so deeply that it was once the lowest point on earth. When I first read that fact it gave me pause. The irony was not lost on me. The lowest point on earth, created by man.

It would be funny . . . except it's not. It's true.

There's limited bus service through the Island Highway but I manage to catch one when I leave the ferry terminal. Only a handful of people are taking the bus today, so I have plenty of room to stretch out in the back. I sleep for about an hour but it's a restless sleep because I keep hearing Dao's voice in my ear. *Get rid of her,* he says, over and over. But this time, in this dream, he's not talking about me. He's talking about Bonnie. And I wonder if Everett or Lynn can sense whether or not she's alive, if they can feel her out there somewhere. Because I can't. I've never been able to sense her. I've never wanted to until now.

When the bus pulls over at my stop, I feel like I've been run over by it instead of riding in it for several hours. I get off just outside the Comox Valley and start to walk. It will be dark soon, but I want to see this before the light goes. It occurs to me that I might be wasting my time, that I should just continue straight on to where I will inevitably be heading, but something is missing here, other than the girl, and I just can't figure out what it is.

A narrow private road leads to the proposed Lowell Metals site. Though no mine has been built here so far, evidence of survey work is apparent, with notices posted along the road. As I walk, I wonder what I'm hoping to find here but find myself unable to turn away. A light drizzle falls, but it's not unpleasant. I continue down the road for about thirty minutes, the forest pushing in on me from both sides, and cross over a ridge where the road opens up to a large, cleared lot. There's a pickup truck parked to one end of it with Neil Young playing softly through the cracked windows. The lot is empty but for me and the truck. The door opens and a woman steps out. She's wearing jeans and a rain jacket unzipped over a plaid shirt. Her long black hair has streaks of gray in it and her eyes are as deep set as my own.

"Can I help you?" she asks.

"Do you work for the mining company that's doing survey work here?"

She laughs. "Where you been, girl? There ain't no more work being done out here. The company withdrew their application last year." It takes me a moment to understand what she's said and she takes pity on me in my state of confusion. "What exactly are you looking for? If you just tell me what it is, maybe I can help you. "

I shake my head. "I don't know. I thought . . . I'm looking into a man whose company wants to mine here. I just wanted to see the place."

"You with Greenpeace or something? Coal Watch?"

"No," I say. "I'm just looking for information."

"Information about what?"

And something about her face, which is kind and open, unlocks the floodgates inside me. It's no longer about trust or lack thereof. It's about finding Bonnie. I've taken so many chances in this search that what's another? "Information about a girl that's gone missing," I say. "I'm following . . . a trail. Leads to the man that owns this company and I can't find anything on him anywhere else."

Her expression softens. "Oh, honey. My nephew went missing two years ago. My brother, well, he hasn't been the same since. Hurts, don't it?"

I nod. More than she knows. My right ankle may never be the same.

"How long ago was this?"

"A few weeks."

"I can tell you're not from around here and neither is your girl, else I would have heard something about it. I work with the community, we organize to keep special interests in the region in check, but we hear things."

"What can you tell me about Lowell Metals?"

She shrugs. "Nothing. No one mining operation is much different from the other, honey, that I *can* say. They send their people with the trucks and the equipment to look at the land and then they send their reps to talk to us. Can't think of anything that stands out with Lowell, not with what you're looking for." She pauses for a moment. "I don't know how it would be related, but there is something about this situation that don't make sense here. This project failed two assessments. Lowell never managed to get any community engagement. People weren't willing to sell out on this one. But they were going to try a third time. Rep came through here to drum up some meetings on how they were going to do better. Then . . . it just disappeared. Notice was given that they were dropping it and that's that. All that time and money, and not one word of explanation."

"Somebody had a change of heart."

She looks at me, considering. "Must have been somebody powerful to get them to give up out of the blue like that. After two tries and committing to a third?"

"Did any of the . . . mining officials, the money people, ever buy property in the area?"

"No, why would they? No one wants to live near a mine."

I turn away from her and peer over the ridge to the valley below. This is what I had to know before moving on. To cover my bases.

"Beautiful, ain't it?" she says, coming up behind me. "I've lived here my whole life and it still takes my breath away. See that river over there?" She points to a stream of water running over a bed of rocks, edged in by the forest around it. "Salmon spawn there and flow downstream. Our ecosystem is dependent on these spawning beds. It feeds the region around it, in more ways than one. The nutrients from those fish fertilize the forest. You ever been down Ukie–Tofino way?"

I shake my head. Ucluelet and Tofino are on the west coast of the island, famous for its scenery.

"Well, you should go. The Pacific Rim National Park is down there. They got lakes and the ocean. The trails, too, keep everyone busy. People not from around the island always end up there one way or the other. If you're looking for somebody, but you don't know where to start . . . well, I'd go there."

I've been thinking the same thing. "Thanks," I say, turning to go.

"Well, hang on a minute," she says with a frown creasing her forehead. "You can't tell me a story like that and expect me to let you walk back. I can give you a ride to the highway, then you'll be able to hitch your way down. Don't worry, people do it all the time and besides"—she pauses, looking me up and down—"I got a feeling you can take care of yourself."

It's late afternoon. The days are still short and even though the weather is mild, there's no denying that we are still in the midst of a coastal winter. So I take the ride because I know that it will be dark soon and there's nothing more to do here. No more stalling. Bernard Lam talked about a property on the island, and if the Zhangs were looking back then, maybe they found a house that Lam didn't know about.

She pulls over the pickup and holds out her hand. "I'm Trish," she says, shaking mine firmly in her grasp.

"Nora."

She hesitates and seems to go through some sort of internal battle. It takes me a minute, but I see what's happening. What's in front of me right now. A private woman's struggle to open herself up to someone else. "Look," she says finally. "It's going to be dark soon. You've got a long ride ahead of you, and that's if you find somebody going your way this time of day. The roads are good, but they ain't that good. Come stay with me. I won't take no for an answer."

I reach for the door handle. A single woman's personal space is a sacred thing. "No."

She laughs and pulls the truck back onto the road while I stare at her, astounded. "You think you're stubborn? You should try me sometime . . . but, hey, you just did, didn't you?"

My initial sense of panic subsides as she drives along, playing her folk music, with no idea how close she is to a tire iron to the back of the head. I don't quite know what to say, so the drive is mostly quiet. We go into the town proper and pass a few cars along the way, but not many. Soon enough, she turns onto a residential street and pulls into a gravel driveway, which leads to a small bungalow and neat yard. Dusk has fallen.

"It's not much," she says as she turns off the ignition, "but it's home. You hungry?"

"Yes." I can't remember the last time I ate a meal that didn't come out of a candy wrapper, but now that she's mentioned it, my stomach starts to rumble.

I follow her inside as she flips on the lights and leads me through a narrow hallway and into the kitchen. The room is small but clean. There is not much counter space, but she's the only one here so there's no clutter. She turns on the oven and pulls out a pan from the fridge with marinated salmon in it. I sit at her table and watch as she bakes the salmon and fixes a salad to go along with it.

She takes out two plates and sets the table. "Bathroom is the first door on your right over there, if you want to wash up before dinner."

Though it's phrased otherwise, this is not an option. In the bathroom, I scrub my hands clean, wash my face, and tie back my hair. The timer goes off in the kitchen and when I get back out, Trish is sitting at the table with the salmon and salad at the center of it and two glasses of water at our place settings. I know she keeps liquor around, because I glimpsed a few bottles when she opened her cupboard, but either she's not interested in sharing or she suspects that I'll drink more than I should.

She spreads a napkin over her lap. "We can just dig in, Nora, since I can tell you're about as religious as me."

We eat in silence. Every now and then I meet someone I just can't figure out. Trish is a prime example. Honest, but not forthcoming. She offers nothing but hospitality, not even conversation. I begin to wonder if she's regretting inviting a stranger into her home when she sets down her fork and stares at me over steepled fingers. I hope she's not going to offer any advice and soon enough, I realize that my energy is wasted. Some people don't give advice and, thankfully, she's one of them. She nods to a photograph on the wall. A man and a woman stand beside a tractor, beaming at the camera. The woman is obviously Trish and I can tell from the man's features and bone structure that he is related to her. "That was taken about ten years ago," she tells me. "Me and my brother, before my nephew ran away."

"You said he went missing."

She shrugs. "Same difference, ain't it? He's gone and I know in my heart that he's never coming back."

All of a sudden she looks old and tired. "I hope you find what you're looking for, Nora. God help me, I know what it's like to go through something like that and most people never recover."

"What did your brother do?"

"You mean when he found out? He looked for him for about a year, then he gave up. Last I heard, he moved to Victoria. He hasn't been the same since. That boy was his pride and joy, just sixteen years old when he left us. It ain't right, but that's life." She shakes the thought away and looks at me with bright eyes. "A lot of people who joined our fight against big companies, they don't believe in development. They don't think that we can move forward, but not me."

I'm taken aback at this abrupt change in conversation.

A smile appears at the corner of her mouth. "Nothing is constant," she tells me. The smile disappears. "Nothing stays the same. You think I don't know that this entire region will be unrecognizable in a hundred years? If there's one thing I've learned from the scientists that have come here and looked at our land and the projects that have been proposed here, it's that when you introduce something new into the environment, there's a ripple effect. It changes everything around it. And when you introduce something radical like a human being and his desire to take what's under the surface, then you've got no chance. These changes have already begun and we can't go back."

"So then why bother fighting them if you think they're just going to win in the end?"

"You mean the mining companies? I don't think they're gonna win. I think there's got to be a better way. If we're going to move forward, then we *move forward*. Find something different than just digging for coal or copper. If we're so smart, we can learn from our mistakes and figure something else out. Development doesn't have to mean extraction or big industry." She stares at the photo on the wall. "My brother used to work up in Port Hardy, the copper mine up there. He hated that damn place, but he supported the mining efforts going on over here because they make it about jobs and jobs are what feed families. But he didn't see the bigger picture."

"Not many people do."

She laughs and rises from the table, gathering our dishes. "You got that right." I move to help her clean up but she waves me away. "Go get settled in the living room and I'll be right in with some clean sheets for you. Hope the sofa's okay."

It is. Far better than my usual basement cot. I thank her as she makes up my bed. "Oh, it's no trouble at all. I don't mind the company. Good night, Nora." She looks at me for a long moment before disappearing down the hall. Moments later, I hear a door open and shut.

I turn off the lights and wait a couple of hours on clean sheets, with a flat pillow that has seen better days tucked underneath my head. I should sleep, but I can't. When the house is quiet and settled, I fold up the sheets, place the pillow on top of them, and grab her keys from the hook beside the door.

I would feel bad about this if it were anyone else, but Trish is a smart lady and smart ladies are well familiar with the consequences of making bad decisions, or else they would never have gotten that smart in the first place. She should have known better than to introduce a radical element to her home because radical elements like me are inherently unstable and can't help but do what we do best: fuck over everything good that wanders into our path.

# 3

NEVER, UNDER ANY circumstances, travel by car on the long road from Port Alberni to Tofino by night, especially in a pickup you've stolen and don't completely trust. Narrow mountainous roads will threaten to send you careening over the edge into the forests or waterways below. By day, it is an incredibly scenic journey, but by night you feel as though the trees have come alive and are closing in around you, threatening to smother you in a cedar-scented nightmare. You don't have to imagine the wolves and bears in these forests; you know that they are there and that you've just entered their territory. At least it rains here more than it snows, so there is that . . . but still.

I make it down in one piece and sit in a parking lot at the intersection at the bottom of the Pacific Rim Highway as the morning light filters over the tops of the trees. Turn right and about thirty minutes later, just past the national park, will be the tourist town of Tofino. There are some residents there, but they mostly come out during the summer to make a living off of the tourists. Turn left and about ten minutes down the road are the beginnings of Ucluelet, which is less well known but just as beautiful. I put a little vodka in the coffee I bought from the resort welcome center that sits at the junction and wonder, if I were a wealthy businessman who wanted to live here but valued my privacy, where would I choose? I know where Kai

Zhang would probably go, but he's not footing the bill. It's Ray Zhang that I have to consider here.

I leave Trish's pickup in the parking lot with the keys in the ignition and turn left.

After I've been walking for about fifteen minutes, a woman pulls over in her tiny Volvo with an ocean kayak on her roof rack and shouts, "Get in!" through the passenger window. I'm not stupid, I know that her being a woman doesn't make it any more safe to be near her, but she's clearly from around these parts and I need some guidance. I climb inside the car, which is strewn with takeout containers. The woman is somewhere shy of forty, so my age, but she is in far better shape, dresses nicer than you'd expect from the disreputable state of her car, and seems, on the whole, to be a blond, shaggy-haired west coast girl with a sunny smile.

"Hiya," she says. "Going into town?"

"Yup. I'm looking for a very rich man."

She laughs, which almost sends the car into the trees. Are there no straight roads in this place? "You don't seem the type," she says, after wrangling the car back onto the road.

"Is it my clothes?"

"Something like that. But good luck anyway, sweetie. If the big game is what you're after you should try back in the summer. Right now all we have is us townsfolk, the local First Nations community, and the resident hippies. There are a couple of mansions up this way, though."

"Really? I'd like to see them."

"Just follow the coastline. Just like they do everywhere, the rich folk live up in them big houses with floor-to-ceiling windows, facing out onto the water. Just take your pick and you'll find some loaded guys, if they're here for the winter. Some of them actually do come down to watch the storms."

"Storm watching." I feel a secret thrill at the idea. Storm watching seems right up my alley. I wonder what Whisper would think of it, but banish the thought. When you give someone away, you can't do it in half measures. That's not fair.

"Oh, they love that kind of thing. They might be too old for you, though," she says, glancing over at me. With my hood up, it's almost impossible to tell my age. "I mean, those rich guys."

"I don't mind." This comes out much too glib, like I do this all the time, hitchhike in loose-fitting secondhand clothing to exotic locales searching for rich men to seduce. We both know that despite my indeterminable age I'm far too old for that game. We spend the next five minutes without speaking and then she drops me off in the co-op grocery store parking lot, just past the main commercial center of the town. The town is composed of a few streets with coffee shops and tourist traps, on a hill overlooking the harbor.

"You'll be all right?" she says absently, her mind already somewhere far away from me.

"Sure. Just point me to the mansions."

She laughs, not realizing that this is a legitimate request on my part. "Good luck with your search. Hope you find what you're looking for . . . and hey, if you've got two rich dudes and you want to pass one along my way, just let me know."

At the store I pick up a dark green tarp, a few extra pairs of socks, heavy galoshes, and several of the free community newsletters on my way out. Outside, I hunch into myself and stare across the street at the dock. It is pretty, painted in red and yellow, but seems too busy a place for wealthy people who want a luxury west coast view.

I try to think like a rich asshole who kidnaps young girls for their blood. It's not as hard as you might imagine.

What would I want from a place like this? If it was a city, I'd want to be right in the center of the mix, where all the people are, so I could show them how much better I am and how much more I have. But we're not in a city; we're in a town situated by ancestral lands. A town where tourists come and go. And nobody wants to mix with tourists unless it's to take their money. So privacy is what I'd be after, privacy and a view that is mine and no one else's.

If I was rich and wanted to buy property in this place, that would be my number one criterion.

# 4

NOTHING COULD BE more indifferent to the caprices of human endeavor than the tides. Don't get me wrong—we can do a lot. We can move mountains if we really want to, or just blow them up, frack them, dislodge their innards, and ship their lifeblood down to the coast to open up new markets like the good little capitalists we have become, but no matter what we do, we don't have anything on the moon.

What do you mean you need to get somewhere at a certain time, traveling by boat? I don't think so. You would like to take a walk along the coast without waves crashing against the rocks and whipping you off your feet? Maybe not. Sometimes, just sometimes, the indifference works in your favor.

I have spent the past several hours in a heavy rain jacket and galoshes, hiking the coastline, looking up at the glassed-in enclaves of the wealthy that crop up every now and then. I imagine what it must be like to come from a place like Hong Kong to here, where the silence itself is so complete that the sound of the waves at high tide seems like an intrusion. What it would be like to move from a place where seven million people are stuffed every which way into just over four hundred square miles to here, where you can walk for hours and not meet a single soul. To be Ray Zhang.

The rain has been falling throughout the day, but I've been

lucky that the tide has been out for most of my walk. It's just starting to come in when I arrive at the southern tip of the peninsula. On a narrow stretch of beach strewn with driftwood and the bulbous remnants of bullwhip kelp, I look up to see a house that is all glass facing outward to the ocean. Dusk is about to fall and there is a single light on in one of the upstairs bedrooms. Through a gap in the billowing white curtain, I see two naked people locked in an embrace. I stare, as I usually do when confronted by people having sex, but this time it is not out of a perverse interest.

I have finally found the house I've been searching for.

The room is dimly lit, but the sun is setting so quickly that the single lamp in the far corner might as well be a spotlight. I would know Dao's shaved head anywhere. Jia has let her heavy dark hair down and it cascades over one shoulder. He towers over her and for a brief, breathless moment it looks as though she is in pain, but then she smiles. Both of their faces are visible to me, but they are lit and I am not so they don't see me crouched near the edges of the rocks.

It's only after I've been watching for a good minute that I notice that along the covered walkway leading to the house from the beach, there is an old man in a wheelchair facing out toward the ocean. He is wrapped in a blanket. Looking at me. Then his look skips past me to the direction that I just came from and at first I think it's his way of telling me to get lost. But no, he is staring from me to that place intensely. His eyes go back and forth, back and forth, like the movement of a typewriter. I'm missing something here. Jia and Dao disappear from view. Somewhere behind the curtain they have taken each other to bed. I wonder where Jia's husband is. Because how else to explain Dao's presence? Where the hell is he while his wife is fucking the help?

The figure in the wheelchair is still staring at me. There's something unnerving about his watchfulness. I sense that there is little out here that he doesn't see. The tide reaches my feet and I can no longer crouch here waiting for something more to happen. I either take the path that leads from the private beach and into the mansion's grounds, or I go back the way I came.

After a brief hesitation, I retreat over the rocks and hike for several minutes before I get to the closest property to the Zhangs'. It is not nearly as big, but the view is still spectacular and there is a narrow dock jutting out into the water. This house is done in refurbished driftwood and is somewhat larger than a cottage. Outside is a shed with a window. Through the dirty glass pane I see two sea kayaks stored in a space large enough for three. I imagine a teenage girl slipping through this window.

There's only one way to know for certain and, after my first attempt to wedge myself through, it turns out that the small window is not so small after all, but it can be managed. The sun sets completely and rain batters the shed. I am so tired that, now that I have a roof over my head, it's impossible to move any farther today. I recline across one of the sea kayaks and discover that there is a compartment inside that is filled with bottled water and an emergency food supply of dehydrated snacks. I pull a blanket from my pack and mull over this discovery.

And wonder if the old man in the wheelchair wanted me to find this shed.

Just before I fall asleep, I chase the water with a shot of vodka. Just a little bit. Just enough to keep me going. Out of morbid curiosity, I turn on my phone. There are messages from Seb and Leo and one from Brazuca. He doesn't say anything in the message, but I can feel the weight of his silence. I think about the brief moments that I'd felt like he was a friend, back at the luxury resort in the mountains, and I feel the shame build up inside.

As tired as I am, I don't sleep for very long. The ocean is too near for me to relax. There is no sticky railing protecting me from it here. No barrier to keep the cold surf away and no way to tell if the dark current from Japan is doing its job. I dream about a tree the size of a building with many glass windows set into its trunk, windows roughly the size and shape of the one that looks into the kayak shed. A breeze rustles the branches of the tree, setting the open windows banging against the bark. The door to the tree hangs open and as I stand in front of it, I try to peer in without having to enter. From what I can tell, there is nothing inside. A great wind blows, setting the windows swinging again, this time so hard that they all shatter and the glass rains down on me. I wake then and feel the cuts of many shards of glass all over my body before I remember where I am and what has brought me here.

Just before dawn, when the sea is so quiet that hardly a wave can be seen, I push one of the tiny, lightweight sea kayaks out of the shed and launch it from the docks. As I paddle away, using a technique that I once witnessed on a nightly news program, I hope that Bonnie was as terrified and addled as I think she must have been. An idea has taken hold of me, and it has been a difficult one to banish. I have spent most of the night thinking of what she would do in this situation. Would she stay near the house, would she try to find some reprieve on land? I know that I wouldn't. Even my discomfort with the ocean would urge me to take the route that would be the last option they'd think of. If I would choose the sea, then there is a chance that she might have also. Maybe there's some of me in her after all. If they, with all of their money and muscle-bound security operatives, could not find her on land, then there is a good chance she's not there to be found. Because she is my daughter.

Between you, me, and the two huge boulders I pass through on my way to the dock, I am also avoiding something that I have been dreading since I got off the goddamn ferry. Going back to the sea has become inevitable. This region is home to many tiny refuges, small islands that provide shelter to the wildlife on this coast. I hold on to the hope that Bonnie has found one.

# 5

THE MIST ROLLS over the sea, obscuring everything in sight. It moved in so quickly that I haven't had time to turn back. I can barely see beyond the front of the kayak, never mind the little islands that dot the coast. In winter, which we are at the tail end of, the storms rise and these islands are completely battered by giant swells, eroded by heavy slashing rain.

I paddle in the direction of the island that I spotted before the fog creeping over the water snuck up on me. The nearest one to the docks I left behind. As I get closer, I see the entrance to a tiny cove. And I can't help but wonder at this feeling inside, telling me that Bonnie might have seen this, too. That she might have pulled her stolen canoe up to this rocky shore and then pushed it out to sea again. That she might have felt some measure of safety here in the wilderness. I imagine that no wolves or bears live on this isolated patch of land, since it's much too small to support their food sources, but there is always the risk that they will swim across to take a sniff.

I search the island for signs of a struggle, indications of violence. I find none of these things, but I do see a big tree and my dream comes back to me.

In old growth forests you can find red cedars that are as thick as a cluster of people and high as buildings. An old tree sometimes loses its guts . . . literally. Life hollows it out so that even the smallest opening on the outside leads into a wood-paneled cavern. There are three hollowed-out trees on this island. I search all of them and in the last one I find a strip of bloody fabric, a few food wrappers, and a single trail of adult-size foot-prints outside, leading away from the tree and back toward the shore. Left here in haste.

I'm too late. And now there is only one thing left to do. One place left to go.

# 6

FOR THE MOST part, the deer that live in the forest around the Zhang property are benign. They are used to the prevalence of humans in this town and though a few of them startle at my continued presence in the bushes, they eventually remember that they're herbivores and get over it. I huddle along the tree line, wrapped in my tarp, with balled-up pages from the community newsletters stuffed into my clothes for insulation, and try to ignore their stares. It's a true rain forest here, and the temperature is milder than it is on the mainland. Even though it's winter and even though the storms are fierce, it hardly ever dips below zero. And it smells like trees, which I'm beginning to get accustomed to.

The rear of the house, facing out to the beach, can't be watched during the day because of the floor-to-ceiling windows, but the property is a good deal more private from the front, where trees close in from both sides. There is a small gap where I can keep an eye on the driveway. I see no sign of Bonnie but that doesn't mean she's not in there.

I've been watching for several hours now, but there has been precious little to see. A midnight blue SUV pulled into the drive earlier this morning, but hasn't emerged since. Only Dao and Jia seem to come and go as they please. Dao appears to be the only security they have here, but that could be because he's a multifunctional security operative. Security, sex, and who knows what else. There's a cleaner who comes around midmorning and doesn't leave until early afternoon. Just before dinnertime, Dao and Jia get into a shiny gunmetal 4x4, washed and detailed to gleaming sheen, presumably with the tears of teenage girls, and leave.

I don't know how long I have, but I enter the property by circling around the surrounding trees. They didn't fence their property line, they can't fence off the beach, after all, so it's not difficult to get closer. The side door is locked but the back door off the porch isn't and I take a moment here because I know what this means. Someone is inside with the old man. I don't dwell on who the someone is because, who am I kidding, I already know.

It all seems far too easy, but maybe I'm finally cashing in the lottery ticket that I've been waiting for my whole life. Maybe, just maybe, the universe has come around and decided to be in my favor this time. But just in case it isn't, I pull out the tire iron from my pack. I've kept it because there's comfort in this weapon, a reminder that my first instinct is usually the best and, besides, it's useful. Should I happen across a stranded motorist or something.

The mansion is quiet as I step inside. The back door closes behind me without a sound, gliding on oiled hinges. I take a moment to listen carefully anyway. Maybe the old man and his keeper are taking a nap.

I play what-if again, and why not? Speculation has gotten me this far. If I intended to kidnap and trap a girl, where would I put her? Not somewhere that a glass wall could look into, certainly.

I go deeper into the house, toward the front. Everything here, all the furnishings, all of the art, is simple and elegant; purely west coast, lovingly added as an homage to the region. I can't shake the thought that this home isn't for someone who'd want to mine it. There's nothing extravagant here, nothing showy. This is the home of someone who loves this part of the world. I force myself to focus. I'm not here to examine their interior decor. I'm here to find the girl.

*Or whatever is left of her,* says a nasty little voice in my head.

There are still far too many windows in this place, so I try doors, opening and closing them as quietly as I can until I find the one leading down a set of driftwood stairs, fashioned into smooth planks, and into the basement. Along a dark hallway I find more doors. This begins to feel like a nightmare. The rooms down here are mostly empty but for cleaning supplies and an assortment of medical equipment that I couldn't name for the life of me.

I can hear nothing but the drumming of my own heartbeat and my footsteps on the floor. I think about removing my shoes to remain quiet, but decide to keep them on in case I need to make a quick exit. I reach the last room at the end of the hallway. The first thing I notice is that it locks from the outside. There's only one reason for that. Inside the room I find a small cot, a blood pressure and heart rate monitor, and an IV stand. The room is more sterile than the others and nothing here seems discarded or simply for storage. No, the contents of this room were put here for a specific purpose. There is a dark stain on the hardwood floor by the cot.

I put my pack down to keep the door from swinging shut

behind me and squat next to it. The rust color confirms my suspicions. It's blood—and I would bet the few dollars remaining
in my bank account that this blood belongs to Bonnie. I touch
my hand to it and hope that she didn't suffer to give it, but that's
stupid because of course she suffered. We wouldn't be in this
mess otherwise.

From my position on the ground I see a slim book shoved
under the bed. When I pull it out, I find that it's the diary of
a teenage girl. Until now it has been pure conjecture that she
would be here and now my suspicions are confirmed. Years of
ingrained snooping encourage me to open it and skim the first
page.

> So, Mandy is a bitch. She borrowed my purple hoodie.
> She's probably never gonna return in, but if she does, it'll
> be so stretched that I'll just have to give it away, anyway.
> God.

Angst-filled teenager musings fill about half the pages in the
journal. How old-fashioned. Why didn't she share all of this on
social media like the rest of kids her age? I stop at an entry right
before one of her runaway attempts—but not the final one.

> Called Dad today to say bye, but only got his voice
> mail. He's working a lot lately. Won't be home until late
> and I just know if he sees me he'll know. There's no way
> in HELL I'm gonna say bye to Lynn. She's not my mother.
> I **saw** those texts on her phone. How could she do that to
> Dad? To us? She tells me I'm supposed to wait until I'm

older to have sex and she's boning some guy at her office?
**FUCK HER.**

When you're a child, the stakes are very high. Everything matters; every look, every word has some kind of greater implication to your placement in the world. Bonnie's primary instinct is for flight—it's not a bad one. She probably gets that from me. She ran away when she found out she was adopted. She ran away when she found out about Lynn's affair. And then she ran away one last time to be with her boyfriend.

The diary contains some breathless entries about Tommy and how she felt so alive when she met him, blah, blah, et cetera. Young love and all that. There are two pages devoted to their first time in Bonnie's room on that eyesore of a bedspread and how much it hurt. From my reading, the second, third, and fourth times were no better but things started to be a little more tolerable by the fifth and sixth and she started to feel more comfortable with it by the seventh and eighth. There was no ninth because Tommy was sent back to live with his mother. The final entry was dated three days before she ran away from home for the last time.

> Called Dad again and some woman answered his
> phone by accident. When he came on, he acted like
> nothing was wrong but he sounded weird. I asked him
> who it was and he said it was no one but I know he's
> lying. I just know it. The bitch called him babe.

Lynn and Everett. Those bastards. Not one decent, upstanding role model among them. I think about the happy lies in the adoption letters that they submitted. Their drama is what caused her to run away in the first place and this is something that I can't ever forgive them for. Because she wouldn't have been on the streets for these people to snatch up if they had done their job properly.

Near the end of the book, after about twenty blank pages, I find a half a page of cursive writing in Bonnie's hand. The writing here is different from the rest; a hurried, unconscious spewing of thoughts.

> I got a reply from that website I signed up for. Not from my real mom. I still don't know who she is, just that she's not even looking for me. It's from this man who says he's my dad. He wants to meet.

Too late, I hear the soft rustle of clothing behind me and become aware of movement in my periphery. I don't have time to raise my tire iron before I feel a sharp blow to the back of my head. Everything goes fuzzy. Was this what Brazuca felt when I hit him? I fall forward.

My face presses against the stain on the floor. The blood from my nose mixes in with it, the fresh with the old, and my last thought before everything goes black is that here on this floor is blood spilled from two generations.

# 7

I WAKE TO the sound of dripping.

*Drip.*

Like Tommy's blood on the snow . . .

It's starting to come back to me. The woods. The snow. The cold.

*Driiip.*

Like Bonnie's blood being siphoned out of her . . .

Right. I saw some of it on the floor.

*Drrrip.*

Like my blood as it falls from my nose to the ground in front of me . . .

Oh, yeah. I fell face-first. This is starting to make sense.

*Drippp.*

Like rainwater falling from the gutters.

Now I hear the sound of rain on the windows. How could I have missed it? It's like the mansion is under siege. But the sound of water on windowpanes is good. It means I'm out of the basement. Out of the room that locks from the outside.

I listen carefully and, besides the drops splattering the window, I notice two things. The first is the crackle of a fire. I'm indoors so there must be a fireplace in this room. The second is someone else's breathing. It's not close, but it's not too far away, either.

Someone is in the room with me.

My tire iron is gone and I have a stinging ache at the back of my neck. My limbs feel weighted down, but when I open my eyes I see that there is nothing pressing on me—nothing physical, anyway. No, this weight is strictly psychological, and I'm suffering from acute regret that at the tender age of . . . I can't remember right now, but it's too fucking old not to have learned from my past mistakes and let someone sneak up on me.

I'm on a hardwood floor next to a roaring fire. I do a quick check and my pants are still on and my stomach is still flat. I let out the breath that I've been holding. So this isn't a repeat of an earlier nightmare, it's a brand-new one. There's a man standing at the window across the room. And what a room. You could have teleported it straight from the chalet in the mountains and into this house and no one would have blinked an eye. It's that lush. The view is that spectacular. I feel like I should have paid admission for this view, but the pain in my body is telling me that I already have.

"There was this slut," the man says, staring out at the ocean. Dusk hangs in the sky like a magenta cloak with darkness tugging down at the edges. Though I must not have been out for very long, the landscape has completely changed. Waves rise up and hurl themselves against the rocks and rain slashes at the windows, seeming to move sideways. The weather has taken a violent turn and lying there, trying to ignore the pain throbbing just behind my temples, I don't take this as a good omen. Something is wrong with me, but I can't figure out if it's simply a result of being hit on the back of the head, my psychological weight finally taking over, or something else.

The man at the window doesn't turn around. All I can see is the back of his head. Thick black hair, like a schoolgirl's dream, and a haircut that cost more than your average schoolgirl would dare charge to her daddy's credit card. "But God, she had the voice of an angel. A butch, ugly angel. Couldn't get it out of my head." Somehow he has sensed that I'm awake. I'm used to slights about my looks, so his words don't bother me. He hasn't told me anything that I don't already know. "Turns out she wasn't an angel after all. Dropped in the woods like the garbage she was. Rolled up in a purple sheet."

I blink once, twice, and on the third my head clears just a little more. Just enough to inject some survival instinct back into my body. I glance around the room for weapons. A vase nearby looks like a good choice, but it is too heavy to be hidden behind my back. I push myself to my knees and palm at the wall, hoping for balance. The change of plane blurs my vision and my legs tremble. I squeeze my eyes shut and when I open them again I realize that he's watching me through the reflection in the glass, like Dao did up in the mountains.

"She was a whore and got what whores deserve. She was supposed to die that night."

"What did you do to me?" In my mind, these words are shouted from my mouth in righteous indignation. In reality, they are squeezed from my tender throat like rusty water from a damp rag. I taste blood in my mouth and spit it out onto the floor in front of me. Somewhere in there is a tooth. I remember falling on my face, but not losing a tooth . . . in any case, it must have happened. The evidence is in front of me.

Kai Zhang laughs and faces me for the first time. The first

thing I notice about him is the scar on his cheek. From what I did that had prompted the beating all those years ago. A loose nail, grasped between my knuckles. In addition to that, there is a healing cut on his forehead, not courtesy of me. And despite these two marks on his face, he is still handsome. "You asked me the same thing back then, do you know?" He reaches into a pocket and pulls out a Baggie with a handful of tiny pills.

I grow still as I realize what has happened. There are no words for the dread that I feel. So the weight isn't just psychological.

His eyes dance in the firelight. "Yup," he says, smiling. "You stupid cunt. Coming to my house. Don't you know what I can do to you? Don't you remember what I did to you?" He crosses to me and hits me with the back of his hand. I fall back on the ground.

"Try to kill me and fail?" I say through the fresh blood in my mouth.

Some of it falls on the ground at his feet. He puts a finger to a drop and then licks it off. My stomach turns. Thank God there's nothing in it but vodka and a granola bar.

"Yeah, we'll see about that." He pulls me up by the arm. I rake my nails from my free hand across his face and he flings me across the room. My body hits the window and slumps to the ground. My head is pounding. I look down and see that the ankle I'd sprained jumping from the balcony at the library is now twisted completely. He sees this too and grins. "Oooh, my bad. Let me kiss it better for you."

I kick out with my other leg as he reaches me, but there's nothing to brace against and my foot just taps his thigh, no stronger than a butterfly kiss. He pushes it out of the way, grabs my bad ankle, and twists it even more. The pain is unbelievable, but I don't cry out because I know that's what he wants. I don't remember much from that night fifteen years ago, but I know that you can't beat someone to within an inch of her life without enjoying it. The one good thing the pain does is focus me.

"Where's Daddy?" I say, through gritted teeth.

He shrugs. "Asleep. Dead. Who cares?"

"You go to all this trouble to take the girl, to get her blood for him, and you don't care?"

He stares at me for a long moment . . . and then laughs. He looks down at my foot. "I wonder if I snap it from both directions, if it'll just come right off."

"You have too much time on your hands."

"You sound like my father. Well, until the stroke, and then he didn't really sound like much of anything at all. He used to be so strong, but now . . . He can't walk. He can't talk. He just sits there like a baby."

"Where is she?"

"Who knows? Who cares? None of this was my idea in the first place."

I blink up at him and try to clear my vision.

He's not lying.

"I'm sick and tired of this whole damn thing," he continues, with a grimace. "My own wife made me get her. How messed up is that? And it was *so* easy to get her to come with me—just like it was with you."

"You drugged me."

"You're a drunk. I almost didn't even have to."

I flinch. It's too close to Lorelei's point of view for me to not react.

But he doesn't notice. "What were we talking about? Oh, yeah. That little bitch. She was looking for *me*—can you believe that? Found her on one of those underground chat sites for adoptees. She said she was going away for a few days to see her boyfriend anyway so she'd come meet me before. And then you know what she did?"

He twists the ankle a little harder.

There is so much pain I think I'm going to faint. "What?"

"She hugged me." He laughs. "Just got right in the car after that. Didn't have to give her anything. Just said I want her to meet her mom, too, and she couldn't wait to go with me. Oh, man." Now he's laughing so hard that he wipes a tear from the corner of his eye. "I think I need a drink."

He goes to the liquor cabinet. There's not a lot about the time I was enlisted that I value; my stay was far too short for it to have made a lasting impression. The one thing that sticks with me is that there is so much a body can still accomplish under stress. The body is far more resilient than you'd think. My ankle is shot and my limbs feel heavy, but I'm conscious, so I must have some time until the drugs take full effect. I run my hands over my ankle, but I can barely touch it without feeling like I'm being stabbed by an ice pick. The lace on my boot has come undone. I pull it free while his back is still turned. "What happened to her?"

He pours two snifters of brandy. "After I told her we were going to meet you, I bought her some hot chocolate, put a little something in it, and bam. She was out like a light while we got her over here to do the tests. Did you know the results take a couple weeks?" I did not know that. Huh. You learn something new every day. "Found that out the hard way. Kept her sedated while we sent her blood off but the little bitch got away before all the results came back. They blame me but, like I said, it wasn't my idea." He takes a gulp of his brandy and moves toward me with the other glass.

I stare at the cut on his forehead and smile. "So she kicked your ass." And then I say, just to piss him off, "From what I remember, it's not that hard to do."

His expression darkens and he flings the glass into the wall. It doesn't shatter, though, just bounces off it and onto the floor. The most he has accomplished with this move is to wash the floor with very expensive brandy. I laugh. "Do you always fuck everything up?"

He pulls me up by the collar so I'm face-to-face with him and kisses me, forcing his tongue into my mouth. His hot, brandy-sweetened breath clouds my face. I can feel his adrenaline, his excitement. It's now or never. The lace is still bunched in my hand, so I knee him in the crotch. Not very hard, but enough to get him to take a step back to protect himself. I go with him, though, and use the weight of my body to drive him to the floor. I don't care how I land, just that he is now off balance and I'm no longer standing on a broken ankle. His hands are around my throat and my lace is around his neck, crossed in front. He squeezes while I pull on either ends of the lace. It's a weak attempt, but it's all I have. The desire to release the lace and claw away his hands is strong, but he has the strength advantage and is not drugged so if I meet him on those terms, I might as well just give up. His face turns red to match mine as blood flow and oxygen are restricted. He gives me a little shake, upsetting the delicate balance, and my hands falter. There is a dark spot in my right eye that's growing darker by the second and I can feel my consciousness going. I pull my hands from his throat and do the thing that feels right, pressing my thumbs into his eyeballs. He screams and slaps me away, but at least now my airway is free. We lie there on the floor, gasping.

"I-I can't see! You fucking cunt!"

My hands grope the floor, looking for balance, and brush the glass he threw against the wall, the one that refused to shatter. And then I feel something inside me open up and take flight. With all the strength left in my body, I smash the snifter against the floor. A single shard breaks off into my right hand, piercing the skin. The shard is slippery with blood, but that doesn't matter much as I crawl to where he is on his hands and knees, feeling for the wall. My foot drags behind me and my breath comes in harsh gasps. I'm making too much noise, but he's beyond caring. His eyes are a bloody mess.

"Where is she?"

He screams in pain. "I don't know!"

I grasp the shard, even though I can feel it slicing through my hand, and let the pain focus me. I take a handful of his beautiful hair in my hand and wrench his head up to face me. His hands reach for my throat again but I'm ready for him this time and use the force of my weight as I press into him to drive the shard into his jugular.

"The sheet was red," I say to him now, because this is the kind of thing that one shouldn't forget. I want it to be the last thing he remembers. The woman that he wrapped up and left for dead, her shroud was a red sheet ripped from his bed. The blood from her body, my body, darkened it in spots to a crimson so deep it was almost black. I don't want him to leave this world without knowing the color of that sheet. His blood spurts out, mixing with mine from the cut on my hand, as he opens his mouth to scream. No sound comes out and I watch with heavy-lidded eyes as the life seeps out of him, his mouth forming a grotesque O, shaped around a sound that never comes. I fall heavily on top of his body and black out for a moment.

And then the sound returns to my ears. I crawl to the wall, using it to get to my feet. All I think about now is the girl. I have slain one of her dragons, but the job isn't finished. And he knew where she is; I heard it in his lie. Using the wall for balance, leaving behind smears of bloody handprints, I focus on reaching the door. Lightheaded and dizzy, I see the sideboard with the brandy nearby, and I can't resist taking a swig, washing the taste of his brutal kiss from my mouth.

Hands on the wall again.

The door looms just ahead.

And then something jolts me awake. Something that makes no sense. A high-pitched cry coming from the floor, from a small plastic radio lying there. I blink at it for seconds, minutes, who knows how long. The cry becomes more insistent. In here, in this room spattered with blood on the floor and smeared on the walls, where a dead man lies, this sound is incongruous.

Down the hall I go, peering into doorways, flipping light switches and leaving behind bloodstains on every surface I touch because what does it matter, I'm running against the clock. Against chemistry, biology, and my own damaged anatomy.

I hear the sound again.

The last door at the end of the hallway leads to a large bedroom where the old man sits in his wheelchair next to a bassinet. And then all of a sudden it makes sense. All of this, it wasn't for the old man who loves this place, who built this house and put in it all the things that reflected his passion. The old man who put in motion plans to divest from mining in the region. The old man who was shut in this house that he loved so much after he'd had a stroke.

It was for Bonnie's little brother.

That's who she's a match for. Not her grandfather. Not Ray Zhang. And in a sudden moment of clarity, Kai's words come back to me. His own wife made him do this. For their baby.

I slump against the wall, feeling dizzy, and stare at the old man. He stares right back. Both of us are completely helpless in the face of the baby's cries. The photograph that Mike Starling had clipped showed a strong man, a proud one, too. But time has taken its toll. In his eyes there is only pity, but I have no idea who it's for. His face blurs in front of me and no matter how much I blink, all I see is red.

# 8

BONNIE DREAMS OF the voice, the voice that has haunted her for days now. She can't open her eyes, so she knows she must be dreaming, but it's terrifying still. That cold voice, so brusque, is now tenderly whispering to her. The dream is so real that she can feel the breath on her forehead, a hand tucking a tendril of hair behind her ear, a long fingernail simultaneously scratching a line down the side of her neck where her jaw begins. She cannot put a face to the voice, but she would know it anywhere. So she screams and screams and screams until there's the sound of pounding feet on the ground, rushing to her side. It is her dream, so why shouldn't she be rescued?

She hears the voice protesting, saying that Bonnie must be delirious. The voice is accusing somebody at the hospital of hurting her. She's dreaming of being in a hospital? Bonnie knows, though she can't say how or why, but the voice is lying. That woman always lies.

"Ma'am, please give us the room," says someone else, a man whose voice Bonnie doesn't recognize. Though this person speaks with authority, there is an underlying concern here.

"Please step outside. We'll call you when she's settled."

"Of course," says the woman who haunts Bonnie's dreams.

"Take good care of her or you'll be hearing from my attorney. I'll be back."

Bonnie's breath quickens. She is safe for now, but that awful woman will come back for her. She said it herself, and this time she isn't lying.

# 9

A FRIGID GUST of wind jolts me awake.

Something hard presses into my stomach. The ground is near my head and I don't know where my legs are because I can't feel them. For a brief, terrifying moment I think that I'm in the nightmare again, but there is a fleeting memory of Kai Zhang's face smeared with blood. Gradually my senses return to me. I am outdoors, hanging upside down, slung over a muscular shoulder. By the uneven, sinking steps that I feel the man holding me take, I sense that he is walking on sand. Then his pace evens out and we are on solid ground again. A wooden dock. There is a sliver of moonlight out tonight and the rain seems to have given us some respite. I twist my head around and see a woman's form trailing the man who carries me.

"She's awake," the woman says.

I recognize that voice. I last heard it in a dimly lit lounge overlooking a spectacular winter vista. A second later, my world turns right side up as I'm dropped. My vision blurs for a moment, a residual effect of whatever drug her husband had given me, and then clears. I'm now in a boat, sprawled on the deck. I watch as Dao helps Jia inside and goes about preparing the boat for launch. He tosses in a box of garbage bags and some weights.

"I told you that it was her up at the chalet," she tells him.

He frowns. "I thought she was dead. Saw her car go over a railing."

Jia sits gracefully on the bench and regards me from her perch. "You killed my husband," she says, as conversationally as if she's talking about the weather.

"Did you a favor," I say, my voice thick. "So that you and lover boy over there could finally be together. You're welcome."

Dao turns from where he is untying the ropes anchoring the boat to the dock. There is a pause, then Jia shrugs. "So what if she knows," she says to him. "She's going to die soon anyway. She can't hurt us and now we have that girl, too."

I can't hide my shock.

She laughs. "Oh yes, she was brought in with severe dehydration by some guy on a research trip. Documenting erosion or some bloody thing that these environmentalists bother decent businesspeople about. Took us a lot longer than it should have to find out where she is," she says, with an annoyed glance at Dao. "Whoever was monitoring the hospitals has displeased me."

"I'll deal with them later."

"You better. When we pick her up tomorrow, make sure it's quiet and make sure you get rid of her for good. We're far too exposed on this already. It was a mistake for me to go to the hospital today."

Dao gets behind the steering wheel. "I thought it would have been easier for a woman to convince them to release her to us."

"Well, it wasn't, was it?"

"No," he agrees, like the excellent employee that he is. "I'll take care of it tomorrow."

He launches the boat while I try to get my bearings. It's the way he said "take care of it" that I can't get out of my head. If they're willing to kill her, it can only mean one thing. "So she isn't a match for the little spawn."

With a surprising burst of fury, Jia backhands me and, oh, there it is. Another tooth comes loose. I spit that one out, too. "The cord blood worked but you used it all up for the first transplant. You needed more. And then her bone marrow was rejected, wasn't it?" It's the only reason that they'd get rid of her. If Jia's sickly child was a match for Bonnie, they would keep her alive just for that. For parts. "What is it, leukemia?"

A pained expression softens her face. "Such a nasty word to give to a baby. He's just a child. My little angel. I would do anything . . ." Her voice falters, but she can't seem to stop herself from continuing. "You're right, of course. We found the initial cord blood match from a transplant registry. But my son . . . when he relapsed . . ." Tears stream down her face. "There were no other matches. Neither of us, Kai or me, was a potential donor. Dao had always suspected that Kai had another child out there, read about some woman in the paper who turned out to be you. When we tracked down the girl, we thought she would be the answer. But it was for nothing, all this trouble. She's only a half sibling, you see."

She falls silent, turning inward and away from me. And I see the desperation in her now. It is the same desperation I had sensed in Everett when he first called me. For the life of her child. "So he's going to die."

All the softness in her face disappears and a flush of color stains her high cheekbones. "Shut up."

"You're out of options now that Bonnie's blood won't work. He doesn't have that much time left."

"Shut up!"

"A baby with cancer." I shake my head. "With your kind of money, you'd think you could find another match on the red market, but you can't, can you?"

She stares at me. "I wonder . . . Kai was an idiot—no one, not even his father would deny that—but what did he ever see in you? I wouldn't touch you if you paid me."

For some godawful reason, this strikes me as hilarious. I smile, but it hurts. "Word on the street is that there isn't a hell of a lot you wouldn't do for money." I never heard that, on the street or anywhere else. I just assumed.

She slaps me again, this time harder. My brain rattles around in my skull for a brief, stinging moment then steadies itself. No teeth come loose this time. "That's why you keep the old man shut away, isn't it? He wanted to divest but you're a greedy bitch and when he had that stroke and couldn't keep control of the company, you were glad, weren't you?"

With a swift movement, she grabs my face as Dao launches the boat. "How dare you? Family is the most important thing in the world to me. He hadn't been in his right mind even before the stroke. He wanted to halt production on our projects, even managed to get the island mine shut down before I found out."

"Jia . . ." Dao says, his voice barely audible over the sound of the engine. I'd almost forgotten about him.

"Oh, she dies tonight anyway, Dao. What does it matter? Just

SHEENA KAMAL

focus on getting us as far away from our property as you can. Do your job."

I feel my guts twist into a knot. Dao turns back to the wheel, chastised, but I feel no pity for him. Once the help, always the help. He should know that.

"He got old and thinks he's in love with the damn forest," Jia says.

Something in my head rings a bell, so loud it almost splits my temples. Whatever Kai had given me is pretty damn effective. "The mine. Mineral extraction."

Her eyes narrow. "You're not as stupid as you look. We've been in rare earth mining for decades in sub-Saharan Africa and he didn't give a flying fuck. He comes here after the Congo deal and, after we try to get the mine up and running a couple of times, he decides it's not the right direction for the company."

"But you already bought the rights."

"Just before he had the stroke, he pulled the plug on our application. He wanted to make it into some kind of godforsaken sanctuary. But we mine. That's what we do. We don't create sanctuaries."

"This land is unceded anyway," I tell her, just in case she didn't already know.

"Oh, fuck those tree huggers," she says, in response to that. "We could push it through if we wanted. This isn't my first rodeo, you know. I have people on the boards."

I frown and struggle to hold on to a thought. It's hard, but I manage. "It makes you look weak."

"You're damn right!" A gust of wind loosens her hair and the dark strands whip about her face. She looks like a madwoman and the change in her temperament throws me. The woman I spoke to in the lounge days ago . . . or was it weeks? I can't remember. I'd never imagined her raising her voice or cursing. I'd never imagined her tears. But then again, last week, she wasn't in a boat headed toward my demise, either. "We have mining interests everywhere . . . do you understand? We turn soft on one project, we turn soft on them all. Canada is one of the greatest mining nations in the world, and so is China. Zhang-Wei Industries is positioned to bridge the gap, so to speak. And my son *will* live to see it happen. I will find a way to save his life."

Her mouth moves, but I barely hear the words. She has become banal to me. There is nothing more boring than greed. It is where east meets west and north meets south. At the center of everything is money. How very ordinary. Whatever I might have felt for her because of her cancer-stricken child evaporates. I close my eyes for a brief moment and when I open them she has a gun in her hand. Out of all the ways I see myself going, shot on a boat isn't one of them. Perversely, I feel myself begin to smile. If that's what's about to happen, so be it. I'm feeling reckless again.

I meet her eyes, open my mouth, and let my voice soar.

After singing for the IT crew at WIN, this has been something that I've been itching to do. For too long I've denied myself this pleasure. If it's going to be my last song, let it be the one that I've always wanted to be my mantra, though I've never had the courage to sing this one, until now. I've hummed it all my life, ever since I heard it for the first time in Pastor Franklin's choir. If it's going to be Nina Simone, it has to be the one that I never dared. It has to be "I'm Feeling Good." And I am. Any minute now I'm going to be free of these people forever. An image nags at the back of my mind, a picture of someone with dark eyes like mine, but what more can I do for the girl?

My voice is strong now and I let the rawness in my throat bathe every note with a rasp that would make Louis Armstrong proud. The wind threatens to snatch the notes from my lips but it can't, not tonight. Tonight belongs to me. I sing my song and it does, it truly does. Feel good.

Jia stares. I think she shoots me more out of surprise than anything else.

I feel the bullet tear into my left shoulder and the blast sends me sprawling back on the deck. Dao cuts the engine at the sound of the shot. I feel something sharp pierce my thigh, but that is a momentary distraction from the surge of pain in my shoulder, crashing over me like a tidal wave. I pull myself up onto the seat nearest to me and resume singing. I don't want to look up at her for another second.

Jia raises her gun again, but something catches her attention behind me. I see a movement out of the corner of my eye and turn to it. A dark current rises up from the depths of the ocean and bursts from the water.

For a moment it's as if time itself ceases to exist.

I have never seen anything more beautiful in my life. The clouds part, the moon shines overhead, casting its glow on the water. The dark current (because what else could it be?) sent me a savior. A great, forked tail slams the surface of the water in front of us. A tremor rocks through the boat and Jia loses her grip on the gun. Dao stumbles. He, too, has seen it. If I am Jonah and this is my whale, then it is an opportunity that I won't squander.

I pull out the fishhook protruding from my thigh with a gasp and stumble toward my rapist's wife. She screams for Dao, but I'm already upon her and pound the fishhook, slippery with my own blood, into her neck. Her arms grasp at my throat, my shoulder that her bullet ripped through. Just like her husband did when he twisted my ankle, she presses into the wound that she has created. The pain sends me reeling, but I see the gun she dropped just two paces away and I grab for it. The gun slips from my grip just as Dao comes for me, his own gun in hand. At the steering wheel, he was far enough away to have concern for Jia, but now, right in front of me, his shot cannot miss. The boat lurches again and he slips in my blood. I'm already on the ground so it is easier for me to find purchase. I grab the gun again and this time I don't falter. The shot hits his abdomen and he goes flying backward. The force of the recoil slams into my upper body and my arm goes numb. The gun slips again and goes clattering to the deck.

I hear a step behind me and turn to see Jia, fishhook still lodged in her neck, hair spilling out behind her, almost upon me. Both arms useless now, I can't even maintain a grip on the weapon so I stand on my twisted ankle, angle my wounded shoulder away from her and when her hands are upon me, I twist to the side, pushing her toward the low railing. She loses her balance, the force of deflection sending her careening over. What is a surprise is that she's managed to grab on to the front of my jacket and, in a final show of strength, she takes me with her.

The freezing water slams into me, the shock of it sending me reeling, flailing my arms, looking for something solid. There's nothing but Jia, still holding on. It's so dark down here that the moonlight is lost. I can feel us sinking, feel her grip slacken. I have one good leg left so I press it into her stomach and kick out . . . and I am free.

My head breaks the water and I gasp in lungfuls of fresh air. The water is so cold and sharp that I'm once again able to focus. I know this will not last long. I'm losing too much blood. The waves will pull me under or I will get hypothermia and seize up. So I force myself to swim until my arms and legs give way and then I let the darkness consume me. Before I lose consciousness, I think I see a sliver of light on the horizon, but my mind is too exhausted to be trusted. I go to sleep.

Is it my imagination, or is that a warm current taking hold of me?

# 10

THE MAN AND the dog have been searching all day long.

The light is fading now and the trail that they've been following, winding along the coastline, has not been easy for him. His
bad leg aches something fierce. He knows that they should have
turned back by now, but feels a strange premonition urging him
forward. They're running out of time. He watches the dog stop
to feel the salty air on her muzzle, then trots ahead and out of
sight. He can do nothing to stop her. His limp has gotten worse
from trekking through the rough terrain these past hours and it
is all he can do to stay on his feet.

When Simone had called, Brazuca felt that the inevitable had
snuck up on him. It hadn't struck him with a blunt metal object,
but it might as well have. He had betrayed a fragile trust and
now owes a debt.

"I'm too late, Jon," Simone had said. He had never known her
to sound frantic before. "It took me a while to find this property—I wasn't thinking clearly. I was looking in mainland Vancouver, not the island. I should have found it earlier. Something's
happened to her. I can feel it. I'll stay put in case she reaches out
from this end, but I need you to go over there."

"Simone—"

"Just find her. Please."

It was the *please* that did it for him.

Neither Crow nor Krushnik could tell him whether Nora had gone over to the island. They, too, were worried. They wanted to go with him, but he refused. He'd been halfway down the hall when he heard the soft steps behind him, the click of nails on bare floors.

"You better take her with you, then," said Crow, watching him and the dog from the doorway of their shabby offices.

"Hang on," said Krushnik. "I'm not sure that's a good idea."

But the mangy mutt refused to leave Brazuca's side. She stayed with him during the ferry over and the long drive down to the address Simone gave him. When they arrived that morning to find the house still, a looming, silent presence, he felt a cold fear take hold of him. Then he saw the blood inside . . . God help him, all that blood, and Nora nowhere in sight.

He rounds a corner to find Whisper standing over a steep ravine, looking down at the rocks below. He's about to move on ahead of her, but her ears are up, as though she's caught a faint trace of a scent lingering there in the air. She takes off down the steep slope, picking her way down the easiest path. When she reaches about halfway, the rocks slide out from under her and she goes tumbling the rest of the way. Her nails grate against the ground, looking for purchase, but she finds none. One of her rear legs buckles beneath her. She hits the bottom.

"Hey!" Brazuca shouts as she limps over the rocks. "Come back here, you ugly mutt!"

She ignores him.

"Dammit," he says, before he follows her, using the same path that she had. It takes him a lot longer. Now that he is on the ground, level with the rocks, he sees what she had sensed.

There, near the ocean, hidden by a large boulder, is a huddled form of some sort. The dog approaches it cautiously, sniffs it. Then she grasps an arm in her mouth and pulls until the figure turns over.

"Jesus," says Brazuca.

Suddenly, the dog lifts her head, her hackles up.

A sleek movement at the edge of the forest just above draws his eye and a cat, larger than Brazuca has ever seen, steps from the trees and looks down on them, baring its teeth.

Whisper growls, standing over Nora's body, and bares her own teeth in response. The cat is larger than she is, Brazuca can see that even from below it, but Whisper doesn't back down. Her growl turns into a loud bark and froth flies from her mouth. The cat prowls closer to the edge. Just as it crouches, preparing to pounce, Brazuca breaks his inertia. He steps forward and screams at the top of his lungs, waving his arms above his head.

The big cat hesitates. Its lips folds back over its sharp teeth and, with a great, bounding leap, it returns to the forest.

Brazuca stands frozen, his eyes trained on the trees, for a long moment. Then he turns to Nora. Whisper backs up a few steps and drops down so that her belly is on the rocks but her muzzle hangs off Nora's shoulder.

"A cougar," he mutters as he presses his fingers to Nora's neck, feeling for a pulse. "A goddamn cougar . . ."

Then he fishes for his phone in his pocket and dials. "I need emergency services."

# 11

I EMERGE FROM a deep sleep in a dimly lit hospital room to an image of myself as a teenage girl. Same dark eyes, but shaped differently. Heavy dark hair cut short. Skin that is somewhere between gold and bronze, even though there's nothing vaguely metallic about it. My features are different from what I recall, but who can accurately remember herself as a child? It feels like an image that has been stretched to distortion and then snapped back into place, but doesn't quite sit right. The expression on my face is cautious, and that feels true, but there is something curious and hopeful as well, which doesn't. I close my eyes and wish the picture would go away, but it sneaks its way beneath my eyelids.

"Mom," says the image.

"You don't have a mother," I tell this reflection of my younger self. "She abandoned you. She hates you. You're better off without her."

"That's not true."

"Yes, it is. Nobody loves you, not even your sister, but who cares? She's kind of a bitch." The vision of an SUV comes to mind but I have no idea why.

"You're wrong," the irritating younger me insists. "I have two."

"Only one sister."

"Two mothers. And they both love me. They both looked for me."

THE LOST ONES

I laugh, though my throat is so dry the laugh turns into a mirthless, hacking cough. Everything in my body hurts, everything. Even my eyeballs are sore, like they've seen too much and ache with the pain of it. The thing is, I don't remember what it is they could have seen that makes them hurt so much.

"Nobody loves you," I remind the little me when the coughing subsides. "Nobody loves you . . . nobody . . ."

"Mom," says the voice, as I shrink from it, try to block it from my head. What is she saying? I'm not her mother, she is me. I am her. My mouth can't seem to form a response, so thick on my tongue. "Please don't go . . ." pleads the little me. God, what I drag I was at that age. Please don't go. Please love me. Ugh. I've already told her that nobody does, so what more does she want from me?

"Don't leave me, Mom . . ."

I retreat so far away from myself at these words. This younger me thinks she has a mother; in fact, she's so delusional she thinks she has two. How ridiculous. How absurd. How wrong. Little Nora Watts has nothing but her voice, but all that will bring her is trouble.

"Come on, sweetie," says another voice, this one male. It's vaguely familiar, but I can't quite place it. "She needs her rest now. Maybe you can see her later."

I'm probably never going to see this child-me again because my nightmares are very specific, but I don't say it. I want to tell her to leave and never come back as she puts her muzzle to my limp hand that hangs off the side of the narrow hospital bed. Her nose is cold and wet to the touch. I fall asleep feeling her tongue lick my fingers.

What a strange dream.

# 12

I OPEN MY eyes and wonder what time it is. Dim gray light filters through the single basement window, but that means nothing. It could be morning or evening, or anything in between. But my phone tells me it's just after four in the afternoon. I've slept most of the day away and would have slept for much longer if not for the hair prickling at the back of my neck.

I hear footsteps on the stairs.

Whisper is drugged up on pain relievers from tearing a ligament so she hasn't noticed yet. Plus, she's exhausted from eating at her leg brace. Ignoring the pain in my wounded shoulder, I grab the steel pipe from by the door and stand to the side of it. I open the door just a crack, enough for me to glimpse an auburn-haired woman descend the staircase. It takes me a moment to recognize Lynn. Her hair is darker now than the first time I saw her. More subdued, though she on the whole looks better. She's put on some weight and it suits her.

She sneezes from the accumulated dust and pauses when she sees me staring at her from the doorway. "Hi," she says after a moment of us standing there, sizing each other up.

"Yeah?" I put the steel pipe down. If there's one thing I don't need in my life, it's drop-by visits.

"Your friend the investigator, Leo I think his name is, he said I might find you here, um, in the basement. I came to thank you for . . . for looking for Bonnie. We don't really know what happened, no one seems to, but you found out where she was being kept and when she was in the hospital, before we even knew she'd been found, the hospital said she had a visit from a woman who wanted to take her away. We think it was Jia Zhang. And then . . . she never came back. We think that's because of you. You saved her life." This all comes out rapidly, like she's been planning it for a while and now that the moment is upon her, she just wants to get it over with.

"Where's Everett?"

She seems at a loss for words. "Oh, he moved out. It's . . . it's for the best, really."

"With jasmine woman?"

"What—oh. Yes, jasmine." She smiles sadly. "That's what it was. Her name is actually Adele and she's his boss. Can you imagine? My husband, the slut, screwing his boss on her desk as soon as everyone's gone home for the night."

I shake my head. I cannot imagine this, but I try. Everett Walsh, bent over a desk, between the legs of an elderly floral-scented woman. We stand there for a few moments, Lynn trying to erase a pernicious mental image, and me unable to stop myself from creating one.

She does not seem to know what to do with her hands and, after smoothing her hair and clothes, she sticks them into her pockets. "Can I come in?" she says finally.

I hesitate. No one but me and Whisper have been in here while we've taken up residence, but Lynn clearly is on a mission. I open the door wider and she follows me inside and to the couch from Leo's old apartment that I was supposed to put up for sale four years ago. She looks at the exposed piping along the ceilings. "It's very industrial. That's back in style now, you know."

I nod and wait for her to continue. There is nothing stylish about this basement. Even I know that.

"The man I was seeing, he was also a coworker. Isn't that cliché? Both workaholics. We only had time to have affairs with people at work, really."

"That's where you were the day Bonnie went missing. With him."

"How did you know?"

"Because you were lying."

She stares at me. "You're a surprising woman. Maybe another time, in different circumstances . . ."

I laugh. We would never be friends in any other circumstances.

She smiles. "Okay, maybe you're right. Neither of us seems particularly friendly. And what you know of my family . . . We seem pretty messed up to you—no, don't deny it," she says, even though I had no intention of doing so. "Everett and I were never perfect, but there's one thing you have to know. We love Bonnie. Our marriage died a long time ago and she's what kept us together."

Lynn does not cry and I am glad for it. I never know what to do with weeping women. In a survivors' group once I had become one of those weeping, wretched things and walked out. I never went back after my "share." Lynn pulls a stack of photographs from her purse. "I want you to have these. You don't have to look at them now. Just . . . whenever you're ready. You can throw them out if you want."

She places the photographs on the couch between us. I say nothing; there is nothing to say, really. Whisper, awake now, comes trotting over for a perfunctory sniff of Lynn's crotch. Satisfied with what she has considered her duty, she lies at my feet and puts her head down. For all intents and purposes, she seems to be fast asleep again but I know she's listening.

Lynn looks tenderly at Whisper for a moment, lost in her own thoughts. A question pops into my mind, a question that I've never allowed myself to think about, far less put into words.

"Can I . . ." My throat closes up. I feel invisible fingers squeezing it shut, pressing against my neck, trying to keep the words in. But maybe it's time. "Can I meet her?"

Lynn stills and looks away. "She doesn't . . . She saw you in the hospital. Do you remember?"

"No."

"You said some things . . . Look, this is hard because I know what you went through to find her, but it really shook her to see you. After all that. It's been too much for her. I think she needs some space from all this. From . . . from you."

"No, you don't," I say, just at the point when the silence between us becomes unbearable.

"Excuse me?"

"You don't know what I went through." How could she? I don't even know. Can't remember. Being drugged and losing a few quarts of blood will do that to you.

She sighs. "Fair enough. What I'm trying to say is that Bonnie had this image of you in her mind for a long time and seeing you . . . You became real and she couldn't take it. She needs some time. Can you understand that?"

I don't know what else to say, so I just nod.

Lynn clears her throat. Opens her mouth to speak, and then closes it again. I wait. "She did want to know who her real mother is before this all happened," she says, finally. "Maybe one day she'll want that again."

"She knows who her mother is."

Lynn meets my eyes and holds them. Then she stands and goes to the door. There she hesitates. "Look, I've got a job offer in Toronto and I'm going to take it. Bonnie wants a fresh start, so she's coming with me. Everett is pretty broken up about it, but he knows we need a change. Bonnie and I . . . we're leaving. But I think she'll be in touch, Nora. I really do. She knows that both me and Everett are okay with her seeing you now, so there'll be no more sneaking away," she says, before disappearing into the hallway.

I turn away from the stack of photographs and wait for the footsteps to go away, for the upstairs door to slam shut. When it does, I scratch behind Whisper's ears. "Come on, you faker. Let's go for a walk."

The streets are particularly filthy today and it feels good to breathe in the odors of human refuse once again. Yet another condominium complex is going up nearby and the construction will drive people mad for the foreseeable future. Whisper and I head toward the ocean, hobbling along together, until we come to our usual railing overlooking the Pacific. The sea is even more mysterious now than it had been before I got Everett's call that fateful morning, but I'm okay with that, because it's on my side. I lean over the railing, but no longer imagine a dark current.

A whimper builds in the back of Whisper's throat. I look over to see Brazuca sitting on a bench several feet away. "So you're alive," he says, looking me up and down. I'm not offended by the assessment. It's more a catalog of injuries than anything else. I turn back to the railing. Somehow I knew he'd show up, sooner or later. I feel confident that Whisper will be keeping a close eye on him now that she's realized he's here.

"You know, you're lucky the police have no fucking clue how to deal with the mess you made back there. I talked to some people and . . . you might be in the clear on this, Nora."

That, Seb's intervention, and the drugs in my system when they finally pumped my stomach are what prevented me from being immediately arrested when I woke in the hospital. I'm told I killed a man and that my blood was found at his house. That I'd been shot. That I was found washed up on the rocks of a beach with no idea how I got there. They said that Jia Zhang washed up a couple of miles away with a fishhook sticking out of her neck, but she was dead, drowned. My blood was all over Ray Zhang's house, but he and his grandson were missing. Have been since before I washed up on the coast. That there was a bloodstain in their basement that matched a runaway from Vancouver. Bonnie.

All of these things people have informed me, questioned me about, shouted and argued over. But the truth remains: I don't remember. It occurs to me now that maybe Brazuca had something to do with it, too, but after what I put him through, I'd be shocked that he'd lift another finger for me.

"How did you get in the water, Nora?" Brazuca asks now. "How?"

How did I get from the house to a distant beach? I have no idea. I shrug. "I don't remember."

"What happened to Jia Zhang's man? Dao."

I shake my head. "You'd know more about that than I would."

"I looked for him. Nothing. No one has seen him since that night. Or Ray Zhang. Or his grandson. I take it you don't remember anything about that, either."

"No." But it's not a comforting thought. That he might still be out there somewhere. "I don't know where he is."

That's my story and I'm sticking to it. It helps that my toxicology reports back me up. "I was only trying to help, you know," he says softly, after a minute of silence. "I just wanted you to know that. I worked for WIN, yes, but I had no idea about the Zhang connection when you brought that plate number for me to check. I wanted to figure it all out just as much as you, but it wasn't one of those things I could just up and ask them."

I don't respond. Maybe he's telling the truth, but you can't change the past and I can't for the life of me forgive the only man whose lies I can't recognize.

We stay there like that for a while, each refusing to budge. Finally I hear the rustle of his coat as he rises from the bench. "I should let you know I'm back on the program, Nora. What you did to me up in the mountains . . . you know, rape victims often reenact their assaults but with them in control. I get why you tied me to the bed and drugged me. It was a way for you to feel in control of a situation that you didn't like, that upset and hurt you. Doesn't justify it, but I understand."

"Survivor," I say as he turns to go.

"What?"

"You said 'victim.'"

Once a cop, always a cop. That's how they think and if I've learned one thing from those groups I used to go to, it's that phrasing is important.

He pauses for a moment. "A survivor. Yeah, silly me. You're right." He laughs quietly to himself for a good minute. "I think 'survivor' is the best word to describe you, actually. Take care of yourself, Nora. For what it's worth, I'm sorry I misled you."

I listen to his steps as he walks away, his limp more pronounced than ever, and slump against the railing. I think about what he's just revealed to me. He is back on the program. My body eases a little with the knowledge that I haven't turned him back into a raging alcoholic. Aches a little less. Whisper feels the tension in me release and relaxes, too.

I lied to Brazuca. I do remember something about that night.

There is a channel way down deep beneath the surface of the ocean that carries sound incredible distances. It allows the various navies of the world to communicate with each other underwater, over vast stretches. But it was discovered by whales. Like a radio station that exists just for them, they only have to dive deep enough to get at it. Being that a whale's skull is like an acoustic antenna, transmitting and amplifying sound, they can hear things we can't even dream of. There is a faint memory of me singing for my life on the deck of a boat and a silky fin rising up from the depths of the ocean, slipping up and out of the water in a graceful arc, giving me a distraction and saving my life. I remember singing, although that's absurd in and of itself. But maybe I did. Maybe I sang and my song traveled down to that sound channel and brought forth my savior. All these years I spent looking over the seawall, wishing for the dark current to show me a little love . . . and all I had to do was sing for it.

I stand at the railing for a long time after Brazuca has left.

There is a peculiar quality to the mist when it is about to clear and let the sun shine through it, like the atoms are heating up and getting ready to dissipate. I want a drink, like I always do, but I press the point of a little switchblade into the crook between my index finger and my thumb and allow the sharp stab of pain to quell the urge. It's a place where the scars aren't too noticeable and the cut can't do much damage on its own. I'll stop when I can manage it better; I always have. But for now, I do what I need to.

Whisper nuzzles my knee and licks the soreness away from my hand. She stares out at the horizon. I follow her gaze to where a ray of sunshine breaks through the clouds, brightening the evening ever so slightly.

# ABOUT THE AUTHOR

Sheena Kamal holds an HBA in political science from the University of Toronto, and was awarded a TD Canada Trust scholarship for community leadership and activism around the issue of homelessness. Kamal has also worked as a crime and investigative journalism researcher for the film and television industry—academic knowledge and experience that inspired this debut novel. She lives in Vancouver, Canada.

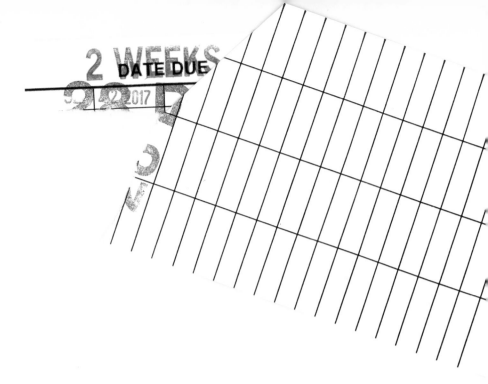